Our Now
and Forever

Our Now and Forever

AN ARDENT
SPRINGS NOVEL

TERRI OSBURN

Montlake
Romance

Published by Montlake Romance, Seattle
www.apub.com

Amazon, the Amazon logo, and Montlake Romance are trademarks of Amazon.com, Inc., or its affiliates.

ISBN-13: 9781503949515
ISBN-10: 1503949516

Cover design by Mumtaz Mustafa

Printed in the United States of America

For my Moxie Sisters.
Thank you for understanding that the whining and
freak-outs are part of my process.

Chapter 1

"You're a hard woman to find," Caleb McGraw said with the soft drawl of a Louisiana native.

Snow Cameron looked up into the face she'd been avoiding for nearly eighteen months and swallowed hard. The moment of reckoning had come.

Glancing around to gauge their audience, Snow was relieved to see few customers present, and none of those even seemed to notice the handsome stranger in their midst. At least not yet. She evoked every ounce of control she had to remain calm, hoping the panic shooting up her spine didn't show on her face.

Caleb McGraw, his jawline made for marble, and his eyes the shade of a clear blue sky, was the perfect combination of Greek god and good ol' boy. She'd like to say his eyes were the first thing she'd noticed when she'd almost tripped over him at a New Year's Eve party nearly two years ago, but his shoulders had been the first draw. Perfect for holding onto during . . .

Sex is what got you into this mess, young lady. Do not go there.

"Well," she said, "my name *is* over the door. What are you doing here?" she asked, which may have been the most idiotic question ever, but Snow couldn't think of anything else to say.

Except maybe, *How did you find me?* Or, *Why didn't you love me?*

Though Snow had spent endless hours contemplating exactly what she'd do were this unwelcome reunion to occur, she hadn't expected both fear and joy to light through her system like lightning slicing through an ancient oak. The fear was no surprise, but the joy was so unexpected she was forced to grip the edges of the cash register on the counter in front of her to keep her balance. Thankful to have the counter between them, she waited for his answer with growing dread.

Crossing his arms, Caleb smirked. "I'd think that was obvious."

Snow studied his face, struggling to read his thoughts. Neither anger nor pleasure showed in his features. Though he loomed above her—six feet three inches of solid muscle, as she knew all too well—his stance didn't feel threatening. If she'd spent as much time learning his mind as she'd devoted to studying his body, maybe interpreting his expression wouldn't be so difficult.

With shaking fingers, Snow swiped a wayward curl off her forehead and was reminded that she was wearing a hat. A very pointy hat, along with a tight black dress, red and white striped knee socks, and platform Mary Janes.

Why did he have to find me on Halloween? she thought.

The downtown vendors of Ardent Springs held a trick-or-treating event for area children every year, which would start in less than an hour. Snow had donned the witch costume to show her town spirit, as there were still several locals who never let her forget that she was a newcomer, regardless of being a resident for more than a year now.

From her left, Snow spotted Lorelei Pratchett hustling toward them from the back of the store, looking intent on learning the identity of the man staring at Snow with unblinking blue eyes.

"I'm really busy right now," she said, hoping Caleb would agree to continue this conversation at a later time, preferably in private. Not that she wanted to be alone with him, but if anyone learned exactly who he was . . .

"Who do we have here?" Lorelei asked once she reached the end of the counter.

"Nobody," Snow said, at the same time Caleb introduced himself.

"Caleb McGraw," he offered, repeating his name for a second time, as Snow had spoken over him the first. "I'm here to see Snow."

Giving her friend a you-lucky-girl look, Lorelei said, "You two know each other?"

"It's been a while," Snow answered, determined to keep the details slight.

"Seventeen months, three weeks, and four days," Caleb said, shocking Snow into silence.

He'd kept track down to the day. Had he been looking for her all that time? She knew he'd eventually seek her out, as they had business that would someday need to be resolved, but since she'd mattered so little to him, Snow assumed there'd be no rush.

Unless . . .

"If you don't mind," she said to Lorelei as she rounded the counter, "Caleb and I need to discuss something. Could you watch the register for a few minutes?"

Lorelei's brows shot up, but she didn't ask any more questions. "Happy to." Making a shooing motion, she added, "You two take all the time you need."

"Follow me," Snow said to Caleb, then hurried through the store to the back room. Once inside, she spun and asked, "What do you want?"

"You know the answer to that," he said, pinning her to the spot with an unrelenting glare.

"No, actually, I don't." She had a guess, and the thought made her nauseated. Another unexpected reaction.

Instead of pulling out the divorce papers she assumed he'd want her to sign, he said, "You left." Two words that felt like a one-two punch.

"Yes," she said, her voice weak. There was no reason to deny the truth.

"Why?"

Tapping into unknown depths of bravado, Snow answered. "Mistakes were made. I didn't see any reason to keep making them."

"After all this time, you think that's a good enough answer?" He straightened up off the wall with his words.

What did he want from her? Some tearful explanation of how he'd hurt her? A philosophical discussion about the negative effects of making spontaneous, emotional decisions and why there's a reason the brain should have more sway than the libido?

Snow had *some* pride left. Even if she was having this conversation looking like she belonged behind a cauldron, minus the green skin. There was only so far she was willing to go for town acceptance, and goopy green makeup went beyond that.

"I have a business to run here, and trick-or-treating kids will be arriving soon." He didn't need to know the fun didn't start for another forty minutes. "If you have more to say, you'll have to come back at closing time when I'm free."

"When is that?" he asked.

She'd hoped her lack of cooperation would result in him storming out and never coming back. The idea of having a second round set up a pounding in her temples.

She considered lying, but something told her to stick with the truth. "Seven."

"I'll be here at six forty-five." With a nod, he strolled back into the store as if they'd done little more than chat about the weather. Caleb should have been fighting mad. He should have been making demands and refusing to be tossed into the street after eighteen months of nothing.

If he had ever loved her, he'd be doing all of those things. His lack of feeling wasn't a revelation, but having the reality confirmed so clearly felt as if the betrayal had happened all over again.

Worried that Lorelei might stop him on his way through the store, Snow hastened to catch up and intercept any further interrogation. Though she'd been back in her small Tennessee hometown for less than six months, Lorelei Pratchett had regained the local tendency to grill strangers who dared step inside the Ardent Springs city limits.

As Caleb approached the exit, Lorelei paused her straightening of a perfectly organized china display to ask, "So how long will you be with us?"

Cutting his blue eyes toward Snow, he said, "That depends on my wife."

Another subtle nod and Caleb exited the store, leaving bells jingling in his wake and a gaping Lorelei shocked speechless for what Snow guessed to be the first time in her life.

"Did he say—"

Snow held up her palm to cut off the question, and dropped into the yellow brocade chair behind her.

Stepping up beside her, Lorelei leaned down and whispered, "Vegas?"

Snow's head jerked up. "How do you know about Vegas?"

"You pretty much gave yourself away earlier this month, at the Ruby festival," said Lorelei. "Spencer and I were talking about setting a wedding date, and you vehemently preached against the evils of getting married in Las Vegas."

Pulling off her hat and twisting the wire-trimmed brim in her hands, Snow asked, "Was I that obvious?" At Lorelei's nod of affirmation, she sighed. "Then, yes. That's Vegas."

⤴

Caleb watched the entrance to Snow's Curiosity Shop from the driver's seat of his Jeep parked less than half a block away just in case she tried to make a run for it. Again. Her unexpected departure eighteen months before had been a blow to his ego, and he'd be damned if he'd take that hit a second time. Not after it had taken him so long to find her.

Tapping the steering wheel, he recalled restoring the '85 Wrangler with Uncle Frazier, the man who'd been more of a father to Caleb than his own had ever been. Rebuilding a drive shaft might be easier than saving his marriage. At least cars came with manuals. He didn't even know why his wife had run, let alone what needed fixing.

The morning he'd woken to find her gone, only two months into what he thought would be a long and happy marriage, he'd looked all over the house, interrogated the cook and gardeners, even Snow's parents, who'd arrived the day before for a meet-the-family weekend, but no one knew where she'd gone.

Later in the morning, his mother-in-law had found a note written in Snow's fluid handwriting and left on the older woman's suitcase. It read, *Don't worry. I'll be in touch.*

At the time, Caleb couldn't decide what had angered him more—that she'd left a note for her mother and not him, or that Snow had included so little information. Where the hell had she gone? Or better yet, why had she felt the need to go anywhere at all?

His parents had been quick to point out how another impetuous decision had blown up in their son's face. One more thing, per Jackson McGraw, Caleb had failed to stick with, as if his wife's leaving had been his own doing.

Vivien McGraw had patted Caleb's arm, tittering that this was all for the best and now he could go about finding the right girl, making the sudden abandonment by his wife sound like little more than losing a button off his shirt.

Caleb didn't want a *new* girl. He'd found the *right* girl, and now he had to freaking find her again.

Dammit.

The fact that there was merit in his parents' reactions only heightened his anger and embarrassment. Yes, Caleb had a history of diving into endeavors like college majors and careers with little forethought. But marrying Snow had not been a rebellious whim, and finding himself divorced at twenty-eight was not the same as changing his major from communications to economics.

This was his life, and if it took every penny in his sizable trust fund, Caleb was going to save his marriage and prove his parents wrong.

Before leaving for the airport the morning of her disappearance, Snow's parents, Mr. and Mrs. Cameron, had seemed embarrassed and repeatedly apologized for their daughter's behavior. They'd answered all his questions about where she might have gone, but in the end, they didn't know any more than he did. They'd agreed that Nashville was the best place to look. That's where he and Snow had met, and the only place she'd ever lived other than where she'd grown up in Alabama.

The fact that Caleb didn't know enough about his new bride to know her geographic history served as one more nick in his already battered ego.

Since that day, Caleb had made six trips to the Tennessee capital and nothing had turned up until today, when he'd stumbled across a flier posted to a music store bulletin board. The event advertised had been held in early October, which meant if the little store on Twelfth Avenue had been more diligent about clearing their board, Caleb might never have found Snow at all.

The slip of paper listed several festival sponsors, including Snow's Curiosity Shop. The odds were slim, but Caleb had been chasing shadows for so long that any lead had felt worth exploring at that point.

And here she was. The moment his watch clicked to 6:44 p.m., Caleb crossed the street with added determination. This time, he wasn't leaving without answers. And better ones than, *Mistakes were made.* What did that even mean?

So they hadn't known each other long before getting hitched in Vegas. They had plenty of time to get to know each other after the wedding. They had 'til death did they part, for crying out loud. All married couples went through a kind of transition period. Not that he'd been married before, but he'd seen enough to know that two months wasn't nearly enough time to settle into a lifetime commitment.

Chimes sounded overhead as Caleb once again crossed the threshold of Snow's shop. He hadn't taken two steps in when a skeleton wearing nothing but a purple top hat warned him to beware of the enchanting witch. The motion-activated doorman was more accurate than he knew, but Caleb wasn't about to be warned off now.

Not only was he not leaving this town without answers, he was also not leaving without his wife.

Chapter 2

Snow had never wanted to lock a door as much as she did at 6:44 that Halloween night. The only thing that prevented it, other than the fact the store was technically still open, was the knowledge that Caleb would not give up so easily. She had no illusions that he loved her or had come to take her home, but he wanted answers.

And Caleb was used to getting what he wanted. In fact, there was a good chance that Snow's removing herself from his life had been the first time anyone had dared take away something that, in his mind, belonged to him. Unfortunately, this was an aspect of her husband's personality Snow hadn't uncovered until *after* they were married.

By the time she'd met Caleb that fateful New Year's Eve nearly two years ago, Snow had eaten enough cup-of-soup dinners to send her sodium levels soaring, and she hadn't been anywhere beyond Alabama and Tennessee in her whole life. So when her doting boyfriend of two months offered an all-expenses-paid weekend at the Bellagio, she'd jumped at the chance to have a true adventure.

Snow knew the nuptials had not been premeditated, as no one could fake that kind of shock when they'd both opened their eyes that bright January morning sprawled naked across a heart-shaped bed, sporting matching ten-dollar wedding bands. But that didn't mean she couldn't blame him for fogging her brain with incredible sex and an endless supply of smooth Southern charm.

The tinkle of bells over the front door brought Snow back to the present. She stepped away from the counter, pressing her body against the craggy brick wall behind her. The only other person in the store was Lorelei, who was taking longer than usual to sweep up, something she'd never bothered to do before. Snow was grateful for her friend's delay tactics. If she'd had to wait for Caleb by herself, she might have snuck out the back door and made a run for it.

Except she would never abandon the business she'd built from nothing. Not after working so hard to make something for herself. Growing up in a family in which money was tight and ambition nearly nonexistent, owning her own business had never entered Snow's mind as a real possibility. If she hadn't been mostly cut off from her naysaying parents for the last year and a half, she'd likely never even have given the store a shot.

Though she missed her family desperately, and made occasional trips to Nashville to ship birthday and holiday presents from a random post office, Snow didn't miss their negativity. She'd found the freedom to become her own person a heady experience. In truth, her defiant move to Nashville to chase the dream of becoming a singing sensation had been little more than a ruse to avoid being stuck in a meaningless life.

Snow had grown up singing in church, and loved performing, but she didn't crave the spotlight or carry any deep desire to be a star. She'd simply used her gift to keep from telling her parents that she didn't want a life like theirs, working her knuckles to the bone for little money and even less respect. When she met Caleb, she'd been earning a few dollars here and there with her voice, but she preferred her day job of working in a Western-wear store engaging with everyday people. To now be selling pieces with history and meaning, and doing it on her own terms, suited Snow perfectly.

As for her pretentious in-laws, who'd made it clear that she would never be good enough for their boy, Snow's little shop may not be on par with the McGraw Media empire, but she was her own boss, successful and happy without their stinking money.

Before her husband reached the middle of the store, Lorelei breezed by the counter saying, "All done. Time to go." Doing a quick spin, she mouthed the words *full report tomorrow*, then proceeded toward the exit as if it wasn't completely obvious why she was leaving in such a hurry.

Panic sent Snow hopping around the counter to beg her friend to stay, but Lorelei was already waving from the other side of the glass. Around Caleb's fast-approaching form, Snow saw the open sign swinging back and forth in the door's window, revealing that Lorelei had essentially closed the store on her way out.

Snow made a mental note to thank her resident baker the next day.

Once Caleb reached her, she expected an immediate flurry of unanswerable questions. Instead he said, "Do you need me to wait somewhere while you close up?"

Patience. Huh.

"You can sit anywhere you'd like," she said, thankful for the reprieve, however short it might be. "I need to count the drawer."

Caleb nodded, looked around, and dropped his solid frame into a periwinkle-blue chair. The feminine curves of the piece threw his own more masculine form into sharp relief. Yet the white polka-dots propelled the image into comical territory. To her surprise, Snow had to cough to hide the giggle.

How could she be giggling at a time like this? Her estranged husband—could she call him estranged when he'd had no say in their separation?—sat in her store as if waiting for her to serve tea and crumpets.

This was no laughing matter. And yet, she couldn't wipe the smile from her face.

"I didn't expect you to be so happy to see me," Caleb said, resting an ankle on the opposing knee.

Snow stuttered as she answered. "I . . . I'm not. I mean . . . You . . . In that chair . . ." Abandoning the effort to explain, she resorted to waving a hand in his general direction.

Caleb examined the chair beneath him. Looking her way with a twinkle in his eye, he said, "I don't see any comfortable brown leather, so blue with polka-dots will have to do."

His words conjured memories of the first night they'd spent together, when they'd made love in a worn leather chair at his apartment. Heat pooled in Snow's belly and slowly spread to her extremities. She didn't need a mirror to know her thoughts were revealed in the redness of her skin. All the moisture seemed to leave her mouth and relocate to her palms.

Opening the cash drawer with a loud ding, Snow said, "You'll need to be quiet while I count." As if she could possibly count money now that her libido was fully awake for the first time in more than a year. She had to fight not to cross the short distance between them.

Memories of flexing muscles, talented hands, and sapphire eyes assaulted her.

Ten, twenty, thirty, forty . . . Had Lorelei turned up the heat before she left?

Snow shook her head, pulled a number out of thin air, and wrote it on her cash sheet.

Twenty, forty, sixty, eighty . . . Why did he have to wear that same cologne? The scent of pine and man and sex danced in the air, which made no sense at all. No one here was having sex. Nor would they be.

Snatching the black hat from her head, Snow slammed it onto the counter and wiped her brow on her sleeve.

"You okay over there?" Caleb asked. His voice even. Unaffected.

"I'm fine," she snapped. Taking a deep breath, Snow rolled her shoulders and said, "It's been a long day is all. I'm tired."

"The sooner you get that money counted, the sooner we can get out of here."

Right. Wait. Did he say *we*?

"I'm finished," she said, closing the drawer and turning toward the back room.

Caleb lifted out of the chair. "Where are you going?"

"My purse is in the back," Snow answered. He didn't need to know there was also a back door.

Once inside the storeroom, Snow pulled the backpack she used as a purse from the bottom drawer of an ancient metal desk, then reached for a trench coat draped over the back of the chair. She was five feet from the rear exit when Caleb caught her.

"Going somewhere?"

Freezing in place, Snow managed not to curse aloud. She jammed an arm into the sleeve of her coat as she spun. "I told you. I had to get my purse."

"And now you have it," he said, nodding toward the bag in her hand. "Don't you think you should lock the front door before you hightail it out the back? Or were you expecting me to lock up before chasing you down? Again."

Dropping her bag back on the desk, Snow said, "Let's get this over with, then." She only hoped she sounded confident and annoyed rather than scared out of her mind. "Ask your questions."

One perfect brow cocked up. "I want to know why you left," he said as he crossed his arms. "And I want to know when you're coming home."

Caleb almost faltered as the color drained from Snow's face. The need to pull her close and tell her everything would be okay warred with his determination that she answer for her actions. Vows meant something, even when they'd been spoken in front of a bad Elvis impersonator. At least they did to him. His wife didn't seem to possess the same conviction.

With her trench coat hanging off one arm, Snow pulled a chair away from the small table to his right and sat down. "I couldn't stay," she said, dropping her head into her hands.

"Why?" he asked. "Why couldn't you stay?"

Shaking her head, she lifted her face, revealing the moisture in her hazel eyes. "We made a mistake, Caleb. The marriage was a mistake."

"I disagree." Caleb leaned his hands on the table. "You never gave it a chance."

"When something is that obvious, there's no reason to drag it out."

"So you left," he said, anger intensified by the hurt that had been prickling his skin like a cactus for eighteen months. "Even if you were right, and we made a mistake, you don't walk away without a word, Snow. Leaving didn't solve anything."

She threw her hands in the air. "You think I don't know that? I panicked, okay? I got in the car and I drove and . . . I don't know." Snow sighed. "I couldn't make myself turn around."

The resignation and regret in her voice created the thread of hope he needed. Caleb dropped into the empty chair next to her. "This didn't happen last week. You've had a year and a half to make it right. To call or at least tell me where you were."

"How?" she asked, her brows drawn together. "How would that phone call have gone? 'Hey, Caleb, it's your wife. Remember me?'"

"That's a start." He tried to take her hand, but she pulled away. Caleb dug deep for patience. "Was there someone else?" he asked.

"What?" Snow jerked back. "You think I left you for another man?"

"I don't know," he said, irritated that she hadn't given a clear answer. "Did you?"

Leaning forward, Snow held his gaze. "The last thing I wanted to deal with was another man. I'd made enough mistakes with the one I had. I certainly didn't want to repeat them with another."

There was that word again. Mistakes. "What are you talking about? What mistakes?"

"This," Snow shouted, leaping from her seat fast enough to send the metal chair crashing to the floor. "We have nothing in common, Caleb. We're from two different planets, and I don't mean that Mars and Venus crap." She waved a hand between them. "You come from money, I come from nothing. You're college-educated, and I'm not. You think life is one playdate after another, when I know it's hard work."

Caleb had never seen Snow this passionate about anything. She'd never even raised her voice in all the time they'd been together. Which was one of the reasons he'd been so confused when she disappeared. They hadn't even had their first fight yet.

"I have nothing to do with the fact that my family is wealthy. You don't get to pick which family you're born into, Snow. And don't give me that crap about a college education. You're one of the smartest people I know."

The compliment took her by surprise. "Really?" she asked.

"Yeah," he said. "Really. And so I haven't pinned down a career. I work. I do things. I know life isn't easy."

Shaking her head as if to break a spell, Snow returned to looking agitated. "That doesn't change the facts."

"You mean the fact that we're married?"

"That's a technicality," she said, dismissing his words.

Caleb pinched the bridge of his nose. "Pretty big technicality, don't you think?"

"One that can be easily fixed."

He opened his eyes to see Snow standing before him, hugging herself as if she might break apart otherwise.

"Are you saying you want a divorce?"

Lifting one shoulder in a half shrug, she said, "Don't you?"

A divorce had never entered his mind. Okay, that was a lie. After six months with no word, he'd agreed to let his mother have the papers drawn up, mostly to stop the nagging. But he never really planned to use them. Not if he could help it.

"No," he said. "I want my wife back. Why else would I be here?"

"But . . ." she started.

"There is no *but*, Snow. I made a vow," he said, pointing to the ring on his finger. "For better or worse. And so did you." Caleb's parents may not have faith that he could make a commitment and stick with it, but in this he would prove them wrong. He and Snow would make their marriage work, but Caleb couldn't do this alone. Marriage required two participants. "You got spooked. Fair enough. So we start over. Come home and we'll work this out."

Snow backed way. "This will never work. That's proof of it."

"What's proof?" he asked. "What are you talking about?"

Pulling her coat on the rest of the way, Snow said, "Look around, Caleb. This is a business. *My* business. I'm not walking away from it."

Registering his surroundings for the first time since he'd chased her into the room, Caleb took in the shelves of dusty knickknacks. The cracked vases, water-marked tables, and stacks of faded fabrics. Nothing looked as if it was worth much.

"You can sell this one and we'll open another back home," he said, presenting what he thought was a perfectly reasonable plan.

"Baton Rouge *isn't* my home," Snow argued. "Ardent Springs might not be my forever home either, but I've made a place here. I've worked my butt off to build this shop, and I'm not about to hand that over to someone else."

Caleb tried not to panic. He wasn't giving up his wife, and she wasn't giving up this dinky town. There was only one solution. At least until he could convince her to come home with him.

"Fine," he said. "We'll live here."

Chapter 3

Snow tilted her head. "What did you say?"

"You heard me. If this is where you want to live, then I'm good with it."

A new panic raced through Snow's system. Caleb may be Southern, but contrary to what many believed, growing up in the South did not make a person "country." Snow had grown up in a small town. She was used to the slower pace and nosy neighbors. Her husband lived in cities. With malls and skyscrapers and things to do. Caleb was not the rural type.

"You're not kidding, are you?"

"Nope," he said. "Not kidding."

Now what was she supposed to do? Their location had not been the only reason their marriage had been a fiasco. There was his father and the hateful words she'd overheard the night she left. Not until her parents came to visit did the McGraw clan, Caleb included, learn that

Snow's father was half black, landing Snow squarely and immediately in the undesirable category.

After one of the most uncomfortable dinners in the history of family meetings, when he'd assumed Snow was out of earshot, Jackson McGraw had demanded that Caleb get rid of her at once. Her husband's response had been that a divorce would mean giving Snow half of everything. No, "But I love her." No, "I won't give her up."

Only that he had to protect the McGraw fortune.

Staring at the floor, Snow said, "I heard you."

"You heard me what?" he asked.

Pushing the hurt away, she answered, "I heard your response to your father when he declared my mixed blood a taint to your family line." She looked up in time to see Caleb's blue eyes flare wide with surprise. "You said a divorce would allow me to take half of everything. You couldn't jeopardize the McGraw money by divorcing the girl who tricked you into believing she was white."

Though the last part had never passed his lips, Snow knew the thought must have crossed his mind. His flip response to his father proved it.

Caleb ran a hand through his thick hair, glancing to the ceiling as if praying for a plausible excuse.

"I don't want your money, Caleb," she said.

"I never said you did." He blew out a breath and added, "I had no idea you heard that conversation, but you need to understand why I said what I did. And the way I said it."

"Oh, I understand," she said, turning her back to her husband. "And I feel the same way. As I said, this marriage was a mistake."

"Snow, my father speaks one language, and that's money. If I'd have made some romantic protest about our marriage, he would have laughed in my face and had lawyers on the phone by morning. The only way to change his mind was to make him believe that a divorce would cost him a substantial amount of money." The chair rattled as Caleb rose and crossed to stand in front of her, looking Snow in the eye as he continued. "It was the first thing that popped into my head. I'm sorry that you've thought all this time that I really meant those words."

She wanted to believe him. Staring into his face, she looked for anything that would give him away, that would prove he was manipulating her and only saying what she wanted to hear. But sincerity shone in those blue depths.

She'd been wrong, but there was no way Snow could have known that. Especially since she'd left instead of sticking around to confront him. But that one overheard conversation wasn't the only problem with their marriage; it had simply been the breaking point for her. There were still the vast differences in their families and background. Their utter lack of compatibility. And her absolute certainty that she could never fit into Caleb's world.

"We're still too different, and that isn't going to change in a new ZIP code."

In his typical stubborn way, Caleb said, "We aren't that different."

"Yes, we are." Too many times in their short relationship, Snow had given in to Caleb's obstinate positivity. His refusal to hear anything he didn't believe to be true had frustrated her to no end. If she had tried to tell him there were problems, long before that awful last night, he'd have argued that they were fine. End of conversation. Much of the time, talking to her husband felt like talking to a wall.

"We both like country music," he offered, as if stating some arbitrary interest would prove his point.

"I don't like football," Snow rebutted.

Caleb hesitated. "You don't like football? But you watched all those games with me."

"I was trying to be supportive," she answered.

Looking slightly off balance, Caleb said, "That's fine. A lot of women don't like sports."

Snow lifted one brow. "I didn't say I don't like sports. I like to watch tennis. And ice skating."

Her husband looked as if she'd set a carton of sour milk on the table. "I'm not sure ice skating qualifies as a sport."

"It's in the Olympics, Caleb."

"True," he conceded. "So we watch different sports. We agree on other things."

The man would fight with a stump. "Like what?"

The twinkle returning to his eye, Caleb stepped closer. "There's one area where we're very compatible," he said.

Snow held up a hand palm out. "Stop right there, McGraw. That's what got us into this mess in the first place."

"This is not a mess," he said, pulling her hand against his chest until she could feel his heartbeat against her skin. "This is a marriage that has been on hiatus for far too long."

As his face came down toward hers, Snow's brain fought to retain control. If her body took over this argument, she'd find herself stripped to her striped socks and moaning on the desktop in a matter of minutes.

As desperation danced down her spine, inspiration struck.

"I'll make you a deal," she said, marching backward until she was out of his reach. "I'll give you one month."

Caleb's lips were still puckered as he blinked her way. "What?"

Snow brushed a curl out of her face, then quickly tucked the shaking hand behind her back. "You can live here with me, in Ardent Springs, until November thirtieth. That gives you exactly one month to prove that we should stay married."

Rising to the challenge, as she knew he would, Caleb said, "I doubt it'll take a month, but I'll agree to that."

"There's a condition," she added, certain he would never agree to what she was about to propose.

Wearing a smile of premature victory, he said, "What's that?"

With a deep breath, Snow blurted, "There will be *no sex*."

Now she was fighting dirty.

"What kind of a condition is that?" They were good in bed. Hell, they were great in bed. Why mess with the one thing they had going for them?

"You don't like my terms, you know where the door is."

Caleb held silent, gauging how serious she might be. Damn if she didn't look really serious. He needed to make up for that stupid conversation with his dad, but how could he do that if she wouldn't let him show her how sorry he was?

"We need to talk about this," Caleb said.

"You say we belong together. *Rationally* belong together." Snow tapped a finger to one temple. "Lust is what got us into this situation, and you know it. We're aware that there's no problem in that area, so we'll take that element off the table while we figure out the rest."

"You can't take sex off the table."

"I just did," she said smugly. "Ready to walk now?"

This was a test. She was trying to make him admit defeat before the battle had even begun. Fine. He'd give her this one, but there were ways of making her pay.

Sliding on his best smile, Caleb said, "I can go without if you can, darling." He'd gone without for a year and a half. What was one more month? At least that's what his upper brain was thinking. The lower brain had reached the limits of its patience about a week after Snow had left.

So he'd call her bluff, but if Snow thought he was going to make this easy, she was wrong. He'd seen her reaction when he'd brought up that old leather chair. She was as hot for it as he was, and that was a card he'd play as often as possible.

"Good," she said, looking less sure of herself. "Then we have a month until this farce ends. If you'll excuse me, I need to finish closing my store."

"Wait a minute," he said. This wasn't all going to be one-sided. "I have a condition of my own."

Snow tossed the coat she'd removed over her desk. "And what is that?"

"No calling our marriage a farce. You have to give this a fair try, Snow." Showing more vulnerability than he liked, Caleb added, "You owe me that much."

She agreed with a nod, an unspoken apology flashing over her features.

As he watched her recount the drawer and complete her paperwork, Caleb let the relief come. He'd found her. She hadn't left him for another man, and she'd agreed to give him a chance. Caleb had a month to bring his wife around to seeing things his way, and whatever it took, he'd do it. He had to or else go home, get a divorce, and prove his parents right.

That was not an option.

"I'm parked around the corner," Snow said when she'd finished her closing paperwork. She flipped the switches that darkened the store except for the counter area, which remained illuminated. "You can follow me to my place."

Caleb shook his head. "I don't think so. Call me crazy, but I'm not giving you the chance to drive off in heaven knows what direction. You can ride with me."

Snow bristled as they stepped through the exit. "I can drive myself."

"Yeah," he said as she locked the door. "Right across the state line. My Jeep is half a block down in front of the diner. Let's go."

She held her ground, staring hard but holding her tongue. He stared back, letting her know he could be as stubborn as she was. When Snow huffed and marched off toward his Jeep, Caleb enjoyed the minor victory.

Under normal circumstances, he'd have opened Snow's door for her, but she was inside and in a full pout by the time he reached the vehicle. So long as she was going in the direction he wanted, Caleb saw no reason to look like a fool chasing her down the street.

As he climbed behind the wheel and latched his seat belt, Snow asked, "Why do you drive this thing?"

Caleb stared at her. "What's wrong with my Jeep?"

"You're rich, Caleb." Snow tugged the seat belt strap over her right shoulder. "This thing must be like ten years old. Why don't you drive something a rich guy would drive? Then maybe women like me wouldn't be so surprised to learn you come from money."

Since when did having money become a bad thing? "This Jeep is *thirty* years old, and it's in mint condition. I drive it because I like it." This Jeep carried some of the few positive memories Caleb had of family bonding, albeit bonding with an uncle instead of his father. Speaking of . . . "And my father is rich, I'm not."

Her brows shot up. "You have a trust fund."

"So I'm not poor," he conceded. "And I didn't hear you complaining about me having too much money when you were buying a new wardrobe back in Baton Rouge."

Not that he cared about Snow buying new clothes. As far as he was concerned, she could buy anything she wanted. But he'd spent enough years taking shit for his upbringing, which he'd had no control over, to let her throw it in his face now. And it wasn't as if he'd intentionally kept his bank account a secret until they were married. The subject never came up.

Snow's jaw twitched as she stared out the windshield. "Follow Main down to Butler, then make a right."

Caleb put the Jeep in gear and did as ordered. He didn't like arguing about money, and fought the urge to apologize for his words. But if she'd left him because of his money, how was he supposed to fix that? Give all his money away and become penniless? Then what kind of a life would they have?

"Turn left up here on Fair," Snow said after he'd made the turn onto Butler. "The house is the third one down on the right. Pull into the drive and go all the way back."

As he followed her directions, Caleb's jaw dropped. The white Victorian was huge. The sweeping front porch with its ornate rail ran the length of the structure, and his headlights illuminated a row of rockers to the right of the front door.

This place was straight out of the antebellum South and screamed old money. What kind of a game was his wife playing?

"You live here?" he asked, the questions building in his mind by the second.

"Pull to the left in front of the garage," she said, ignoring his inquiry.

The garage, a three-car monstrosity, looked as elaborately decked out as the house. He'd bet his inheritance that the building had been a carriage house long before anyone had heard of Henry Ford.

Following Snow's lead, who'd bolted from the Jeep the moment he'd cut the engine, Caleb stepped onto the gravel drive, then threw his head back to see the entire house. It was at least three stories, maybe four including an attic, which this place probably had. Didn't they keep the kids up there in the old days?

It wasn't until Snow said, "In here," that he glanced down to see her passing through a garden gate toward a one-level extension on the back of the building.

He caught up and followed her up the stairs, expecting to step into a large kitchen. Instead, he entered what looked like a small room that progressed into a kitchenette area straight out of a decorating magazine. An old-fashioned stove sat on the left wall. Along the back was a counter with a centered sink and two windows above it. The only cupboards were those beneath, and all Caleb could think was where would you put stuff?

The kitchen back home was larger than these two rooms combined. Everything in sight was white, except for the occasional touch of color. A red apple orchard sign on a shelf over the kitchen windows. Blue canisters along the left side of the counter. A green throw over the short white couch, and a burst of flowers in the painting to his right.

"What is this place?" he asked, confusion clouding his brain. He couldn't make a connection between the large house he'd parked behind and this miniature space.

"It's where I live," Snow said, dropping her coat and bag over a white wing-back chair. "Miss Hattie lives in the house, and she rents this apartment to me."

"Miss Hattie?"

"The Silvesters have lived on this property since the 1850s," Snow said. "Miss Hattie is the last of the line."

"Right." Caleb looked for a place to drop his bag and settled for a spot not far from the door. "It's nice." *Tiny* was the word that came to mind, but he didn't want to give her the impression that her apartment wasn't good enough for him. Just because it was smaller than the bedroom he grew up in didn't mean he couldn't adjust.

"I like it," she said, conveying the message that she had no intention of leaving it anytime soon.

They stood in the middle of the room in awkward silence until Snow said, "I need to get out of this costume."

Without thinking, he asked, "Need some help?"

Snow spun. "What part of 'no sex' do you not understand?"

Caleb leaned an elbow on the top of the chair next to him. "I didn't ask to get into your knickers, darling. I simply offered to help undo a zipper." And if his fingertips happened to slide over her skin as he did so . . .

If he didn't know better, Caleb would swear Snow's eyelid twitched. "I can manage," she said, turning toward the door next to the stove, then turning back his way to ask, "How did you find me, anyway?"

"Spotted a flier in a music shop down in Nashville for some Ruby festival. One of the sponsors was Snow's Curiosity Shop." He shrugged. "Figured it was worth checking out."

"Lucky break," Snow mumbled under her breath. "I'll get some blankets for the couch."

"Uh-uh," he said.

"Excuse me?"

Glancing toward the miniature sofa on his left, Caleb said, "I'm not sleeping there. This couch is about four feet too small. I'll be sleeping in the bed."

Propping both hands on her hips, Snow glared. "You expect me to give up my bed and sleep on the couch?"

"I never said that. You can sleep next to me," he said, enjoying this saucy side of his wife.

"We agreed," she said.

"We agreed to no sex. There was no mention of not sleeping together." Caleb stepped into the kitchen and perused the contents of the skinny fridge. "We're husband and wife, and that means sharing the same bed." Turning her way, he added, "You don't think you can sleep next to me without jumping my bones?"

Her cheeks turned a pretty shade of pink. "I'm sure I won't feel tempted at all."

Chapter 4

Snow had clearly underestimated her opponent.

Sleeping next to Caleb and not having sex with him was going to test every last ounce of her willpower. She didn't know where it came from, but the man had some weird hold over her. Not that Snow would ever admit that annoying truth aloud.

But refusing to sleep with him would be a point in Caleb's favor. Reveal a weakness she had no doubt he'd capitalize on. Massaging her temples, Snow considered her options, and the only real choice she had was to buck up and do it. To crawl into bed with the man and prove that she was *not* the weak one.

Maybe she could put pillows down the center, delineating a "his" side and a "her" side. He'd likely accuse her of needing the added protection to keep her own urges in check, but Snow would argue the barrier was to keep him out of her space. Which went beyond stupid.

If Caleb wanted to invade her side of the bed, no amount of feathers would stop him. And, Snow feared, neither would she.

The sound of the microwave accompanied by loud whistling let her know he was making himself at home. The happy tune set her teeth on edge. Caleb thought this was going to be so easy. A sexy grin with a little innuendo and she'd be begging him to breach more than a measly pillow wall.

Snow's spine stiffened. Her husband-for-now was in for a surprise. Not only was she not going to have sex with him, but she would make his every waking minute miserable for the next month. Two weeks max and he'd be heading back to Louisiana.

That thought made her feel guilty. She was still processing the fact that he hadn't meant the words he'd said to his father. Not that he'd replaced them now with declarations of love and endless devotion, but there was no doubt Caleb was determined to make this marriage work, so he must care for her.

For that reason alone, she'd agreed to give this a chance, and Caleb had been right. She owed him that much. But when this fell apart, as it inevitably would, they would go their separate ways. For good. Snow had never imagined she'd be a divorcée at the age of twenty-seven, but she also never fathomed doing something as stupid as marrying a virtual stranger in Las Vegas. This was a situation of her own making, and now she had to get herself out of it.

"I don't hear any water running," drawled a deep voice through the door.

Snow jumped away from the slat of wood and shot an evil glare she wished could travel through walls. "I'm getting my clothes together," she answered, honey dripping from every word.

"Hope it's that little red number," he said. "I've missed that one a lot."

Snow jerked a pillow off the bed and threw it at the door. As expected, it didn't make a sound. She'd worn "that little red number" on their wedding night. And several times during their first month of wedded bliss, though she didn't know why she'd bothered.

Most of the time, Caleb had managed to get Snow out of her unmentionables in less time than it took her to get into them. Not that she'd complained much at the time. When he was shirtless and that light shone in his eyes, the slips of lace practically melted to the floor. The memories alone sent heat spreading through her abdomen.

When Snow realized she was fanning herself, her resolve returned. She stomped to her dresser, withdrew her most conservative pajamas, along with her least sexy pair of underwear, and headed for the bathroom.

"You're not going to win this game, Caleb McGraw," she said under her breath. "I am not going down without a fight."

"Let me know if you need me to scrub your back," Caleb offered.

Ignoring the taunt, Snow surrendered to the childish act of sticking her tongue out in his general direction. As she turned on the hot water, she sent up a silent prayer for strength. One lust-fogged rash decision would not ruin the rest of her life. And neither would Caleb McGraw.

Caleb was playing with fire, but he couldn't help himself. All those months he'd been seeing Snow only in his dreams, and the real thing was still better than anything his subconscious had created. The dark curls dancing around her face. The hazel eyes that turned gold when she was aroused. Or angry, he now knew. The slender body that radiated power and fragility while putting ideas in his head about all the ways he'd like to test both.

As he acquainted himself with Snow's kitchen, Caleb considered the night ahead. For all his taunting and teasing, he knew Snow held the upper hand in this battle. Eighteen months of celibacy needed to end, but thanks to Snow and her "conditions," that was not going to happen tonight.

Some men might have found comfort elsewhere after their wife disappeared for more than a year, with no word on when or even *if* she was coming back. Regardless of how fickle he might appear to the rest of the world, Caleb had made a vow, and that meant something.

His father had been unfaithful for years, and though Vivien McGraw kept her head held high, Caleb knew it must be a painful way to live. His mother had all but shriveled to nothing over the years, going without food to keep her figure, as if that would somehow change her husband's behavior. Playing the doting wife in front of company, but sleeping in a separate bedroom from her husband and rarely speaking or sharing a meal in private.

That was not the kind of marriage Caleb wanted, and regardless of Snow's temporary absence, if he'd climbed into another woman's bed, his marriage was as good as over whether he ever found his wife again or not. And as for her insistence that they were from different worlds, that's what had drawn him to her.

Snow was nothing like the debutantes his mother was always throwing his way. She didn't care about brand-name purses or if the salad fork was on the inside instead of the outside. She made him laugh, and best of all, she made him feel . . . normal.

Most of the people his parents knew were just like them. Shallow. Materialistic. Not to mention power hungry and bullying. Jackson McGraw could best be described as a son of a bitch, which wasn't exactly the kind of man any boy should aspire to be. Caleb knew at an early age that he never wanted to emulate his father, which contributed to his lack of settling into a career.

His father had done everything possible short of tying Caleb to a desk to make him join the company business. Though he'd eventually caved and earned a business degree, and endured several internships at various McGraw Media holdings, Caleb had put off the inevitable by living in Nashville, near his alma mater of Vanderbilt University.

His parents believed he was considering going back for his MBA, but in truth, he'd been avoiding growing up by partying his life away. Until he'd met Snow. From that New Year's Eve on, his life was changed. Which was why when Snow had disappeared, there'd been no question that he'd go after her. Finding her had become his sole mission, nullifying the voices of doubt around him.

After a year with no word, his friends told him to give up, while his mother insisted he come home. Thankfully, Caleb had been stubborn enough to ignore them all. Today, he'd found his wife. But finding her and getting her back were turning out to be two different things.

After pouring himself a glass of water, he leaned against the bedroom door, listening for movement. Seconds of silence passed before he heard a drawer close, followed closely by the creaking of the bed.

That was his cue.

Pulling his bag onto his shoulder, Caleb knocked on the bedroom door and waited for an answer. Nothing came, so he knocked again. Had she locked the door? He fought the urge to jiggle the knob and was rewarded for his patience with a muffled order to come in.

He lingered on the threshold, staring at the explosion of feminine frills bounding from every corner of the room. A long white dresser occupied the right wall, covered in trinket boxes and what looked like a strip of material straight out of a Paris fabric shop. To his left was the bed, with a white cast-iron headboard and Snow flat on her back, eyes on the ceiling, and the faded coverlet up to her neck.

For his part, Caleb couldn't get past the explosion of colors covering her body. The bed looked as if a flower shop had puked all over it. He was secure enough in his manhood to handle just about anything, but this would push any guy's limits. Pinks, purples, and blues fought for dominance. And not even a masculine blue. More like a sissified blue, as if the other pale shades had beaten it into submission.

If Caleb wasn't careful, the same could happen to him. *Not* without a fight.

"You can put your stuff in the chair over there," Snow said, nodding her head toward the far corner of the room. The term "far corner" was an exaggeration, as the room was barely big enough for the bed and dresser. Whoever had built this dinky apartment must have had a munchkin in mind as a tenant.

Once the estrogen overload simmered down, Caleb dropped his bag onto the wicker chair indicated. The flimsy thing would never hold him, which meant he'd have to sit on the bed to remove his boots. The soft mattress dipped low beneath his weight. A quick glance Snow's way revealed the blanket had been pulled higher, her eyes and nose barely visible above the lace trim.

He couldn't help but wonder what she'd opted to sleep in. When they'd been together, neither of them slept in anything. Caleb wouldn't push his luck, or his body, that far tonight, but he wasn't going to sleep in his jeans either. Carrying his shaving bag into the bathroom, he hesitated when he spotted the sink. Who would make a sink this small? There couldn't have been more than four inches between the front edge of the bowl and the end of the faucet, which looked at least eighty years old, with two four-point knobs facing forward instead of up.

Doing the best he could not to make a mess, Caleb finished his nightly business and stepped back into the bedroom. Snow feigned sleep, but he'd caught her watching him out of one eye. She was clearly trying to pretend his presence wasn't affecting her, which made this the perfect time to show his wife what she'd been missing.

The moment she heard his zipper drop, Snow sat up in the bed. "What are you doing?"

"Getting ready for bed," he said, choosing not to mention the baby duck–covered pajamas that were buttoned to her neck. If she was going for non-sexy, she'd hit the mark. "You don't expect me to sleep in my jeans."

"Then what are you going to sleep in?" she asked, regaining the blankets and hugging them against her chest.

Caleb grabbed the hem of his T-shirt. "Afraid I don't own fancy pajamas like yours," he said with a smile, and tugged the shirt over his head.

Snow tried to cover the gasp, but it was no use. His broad shoulders glowed in the soft light of her bedside lamp, rippling with every movement, making her long to run her fingers through the light patch of hair on his chest that she knew would be soft to the touch. Her mouth dried up as other parts turned moist, and Snow couldn't pull her eyes away. Her husband was gorgeous.

And he knew it.

Holding her gaze as he pushed the worn denim over narrow hips, down muscled thighs and solid calves, Caleb conveyed with a look that all she had to do was break her own rule and she could have anything she wanted. And oh did she want. She wanted this man as she'd never wanted anything in her life, but she couldn't have him and win back her future.

"That's far enough," she said, falling back onto the pillow to stare at the ceiling.

Snow turned out the light and flopped onto her side to face away from Caleb's half of the bed. She felt cool air against her back as he lifted the blankets, replaced by heat as he settled in beside her. His breath tickled the back of her neck, and she wished he'd face the other way. Of course he wouldn't. Caleb meant to make this night as difficult as possible, just as she intended to make his days a living hell.

At least they both knew what they were up against.

"Do I get a kiss goodnight?" he asked, his voice a whisper in the silent room.

Snow squeezed her eyes shut tight as a yes danced on the tip of her tongue. She could turn around and fall into him. Experience the security and protection she always felt in his arms. But that feeling is what had gotten her into this.

"I don't think that's a good idea," she said.

"Just a kiss, Snow," he pleaded. "It's been a long time."

Caleb toyed with her curls, waiting for her to change her mind. The gentle gesture weakened her resolve, and she rolled onto her back. "Why are you making this harder?"

With a deep chuckle, he said, "Something is definitely getting harder, but it's more your doing than mine."

His toe slid up her pant leg, and Snow fought to keep her knees together. "Your condition was that I take this seriously," she whispered, turning to face him. "I'm willing to do that, but you have to honor your part of the bargain. We need to know each other without the fog of sex getting in the way, Caleb. Without lust clouding up our minds."

A boyish smile lifted one side of his mouth. "Not having sex won't take lust out of the equation. Not for me. I can't imagine ever not wanting you, Snow."

The confession created a piercing pain in her heart. "You want my body. There's more to me than that."

The toe retreated to his side of the bed. "You're right," he said, taking her by surprise. Before she knew what he was doing, her husband placed a chaste kiss on her cheek and said, "Good night."

Though she should have reveled in her victory, or been relieved that he'd seen her point, Snow didn't experience either of those things. Instead, she felt . . . disappointed. Silly, since she was getting what she wanted. She rolled onto her side again, wide awake and expecting to stay that way for hours, listening to the sound of her husband breathing only inches away. But eventually, Snow closed her eyes and drifted into dreams, lured by the dark, or calmed by Caleb's presence, she wasn't sure which.

Chapter 5

Caleb woke in an empty bed, not sure where he was. Nothing looked familiar, but when he leaned up on his elbows, the scent of wildflowers danced around him.

"Snow," he said, looking around. Fear sent his heart racing.

Had she left again? Where would she go this time? Caleb jumped out of bed and was grabbing his jeans when he heard a noise from the kitchen. Like a toaster popping. He peeked through the open bedroom door to find his wife making breakfast a few feet away.

"Morning," she said, pulling a mug off a shelf above the counter. "I was going to give you five more minutes if you didn't get up on your own." Reaching for a half-filled coffee pot, she said, "Do you want milk or vanilla creamer? Afraid that's all I have. I wasn't expecting company."

Caleb shoved one leg into his jeans. "Milk is fine," he answered. "How long have you been up?"

"About an hour." He heard plates hit the counter. "I need to leave soon."

The clock on her nightstand said 7:10 a.m. "To open the store?" he asked, stepping into the living room as he pulled a clean shirt over his head.

Snow gave him a shy smile as she handed him the coffee. "No, I don't open the store until noon on Sundays. There's an auction today out at the old Brambleton place."

"That's where you get all the stuff you sell?" he asked, sipping his coffee, which was perfectly sweetened. She must have remembered how much sugar he liked.

Shaking her head, she dished eggs onto a plate. "Not always. I started as a consignment store. Locals brought in things they didn't need or want anymore, I'd sell it, and we'd split the profit." Sliding the loaded plate onto the counter, she gestured toward the fridge. "Butter for the toast is on the door."

There was barely enough room to open the fridge with Snow standing at the stove, since the two appliances were directly across from each other, but Caleb managed to retrieve the butter as well as a knife from the proper drawer. "I'm surprised a town this small could cough up all that old stuff."

"The town isn't as small as you think," she said, a tremor of irritation in her tone. "And some of that *old stuff*, as you call it, is valuable. I get customers from outside the county on a regular basis, and I earn enough to make a living."

He'd wondered how she supported herself while they were apart. When he'd met her in Nashville, she was selling Western wear during the day, singing for tips four nights a week in local bars, and booking demo gigs whenever she could. The three jobs combined hadn't been enough for her to live on her own without a roommate.

"Do you sing anywhere?" he asked. Though he hadn't known she was a singer the night they met, the first time he heard her belting out "Delta Dawn" in a dive on Broadway, Caleb had been more than impressed.

The spatula hovered over the pan as Snow hesitated to answer. "No," she finally said. One word that said a lot.

"Why not?" he asked. "You're close enough to Nashville to record a demo now and then."

"I don't sing anymore, that's all." Snow loaded the remaining eggs onto her own plate. "Once we were married and you moved us to Baton Rouge, I thought I'd miss it, but I didn't. Getting away made me realize that, though I enjoyed the act of singing, I didn't like all the hoopla that went into trying to do it for a living." Caleb didn't like the way she said he'd moved her to Baton Rouge, as if she'd had no choice in the matter. "Besides," Snow added, "running the store takes all my time."

Slicing the buttered toast from corner to corner, Caleb set a piece on her plate and another on his own. "That's a shame," he said, reading in her body language that she didn't want to talk about it.

They took their seats on the couch, as the apartment didn't allow room for a table, and ate in silence for several minutes. Caleb hadn't planned anything beyond finding his wife, and he definitely hadn't considered playing house with her the morning after. She'd been right the night before, when she said they needed to really get to know each other. Maybe if he'd paid more attention when they'd first married, he would have recognized something had been bothering her before she left.

And if she loved this store so much, then he needed to become a part of it. Time for Operation: Getting to Know Each Other to begin.

"Tell me about the auction. Are we looking for specific items?"

Snow nearly choked on her eggs, taking several seconds to cough them out of her windpipe. "Did you say *we?*" she asked once she could speak.

"Yeah, *we*," he said. "Did you plan to leave me here while you went to the auction?"

"If you're worried that I'll disappear again—"

"That's not what I'm worried about. It's clear I wasn't enough to keep you in Baton Rouge, but I can see what this store means to you." Lifting his coffee for a drink, he added, "I know you won't leave it, even to get away from me."

"I'm not sure how to respond to that."

Caleb had hoped she'd refute the idea that he wasn't enough, but he should have known better. "No need," he said. "We have a month to get to know each other. We'll start with me watching you work." The words came out harsher than he'd intended.

"You make it sound like I'm applying for a job."

"I'm the one who's having to fight to stay on here."

"A marriage isn't a business exchange," she snapped.

"It isn't something that you quit without notice either." This was not how he'd wanted the morning to go. Caleb set his plate on the coffee table and leaned his elbows on his knees. "I don't know what you want from me, Snow, but I'm doing my best. Tell me how this is supposed to go and I'll make it happen."

Dabbing the corner of her mouth with a napkin, Snow kept her eyes on her plate. "I don't know what to tell you. That's the problem."

Taking a deep breath, he leaned back on the couch and took a different approach. "Then let's decide what we're going to tell people."

"What do you mean?" she asked, meeting his eye.

Caleb scratched the stubble on his chin. "How long have you been in this town?"

"Since June of last year."

So she'd been here almost the entire time. Amazing.

"And in all that time, did you tell anyone that you were married?"

Snow dropped her gaze. "Lorelei figured it out yesterday, and you confirmed it when you referred to me as your wife. But no one else knows."

"Today, you're going to walk into an auction with your husband. We both know people will have questions."

"I hadn't thought that far ahead." Snow gathered their plates and carried them to the sink. "Do we have to tell anyone anything?"

How had he not noticed how anti-conflict she was? "That's up to you, but I don't think we can avoid telling them something. And before you suggest it, I'm not going to lie."

"I wouldn't ask you to lie," she said, her tone defensive. "I'm suggesting we don't need to share all the facts . . . exactly."

Telling total strangers that his wife had run from their marriage wasn't an appealing choice to Caleb, but short of saying he'd dropped out of the sky, he couldn't think of any other answer.

"Why don't we tell them we were dating before I moved here," she said, "and that we've recently gotten back in touch."

"And now I'm living with you?"

"We dated for a *long* time. We can even say we were engaged. Oh," she said, growing excited about the story she was concocting. "We reconnected online and have been carrying on a long-distance relationship. And now you're here." Looking proud of herself, she added, "That should work."

Caleb didn't like having to pretend he wasn't yet married to his wife, but this could play into his favor. The town would see them as lovebirds planning a wedding. And maybe that's what they needed. Once Snow admitted they were good together, he could give her the real wedding she deserved.

"I'll go with that," he agreed, stepping into the bedroom for his boots.

When he returned with his keys, Snow was waiting by the door. "I'll drive."

"But I always drive," he said. Caleb couldn't remember the last time he'd occupied a passenger seat.

"I like driving," she said. "You don't always have to be the one behind the wheel. And besides, I know where we're going."

His sense of chivalry prickled. "You can give me directions."

Snow stared at him with her hand on the doorknob. "Caleb McGraw, you can ride in my car with me driving, or you can stay here. Or," she added, "you can go home. Those are your choices."

He didn't like any of those choices. "I can let you drive," he grudgingly agreed. "It's not a big deal."

As she opened the door and waved him through, she said, "You're not *letting* me do anything. Let's be clear about that."

Arguing was getting him nowhere, so he held his tongue and stepped past Snow onto her tiny porch. Once outside, a wave of pure satisfaction washed over him. Caleb waited at the bottom of the steps for Snow to lock the door. When she turned, reality struck. The look on her face was priceless.

They'd left her car in town the night before.

Caleb pulled his keys from his pocket, saying, "Good thing I brought these with me." He held the passenger door for his wife, who climbed inside without a word. Not that he needed her to tell him what she was thinking. The tic of her jaw said it all.

Finally. He'd won a point.

Snow had never considered herself a competitive person, but the hint of even a minor defeat left a bitter taste in her mouth. She should have insisted on driving herself home the night before. Did he really think she'd lead him on a high-speed chase?

He probably never thought she'd disappear into thin air two months after their wedding, so maybe his suspicious nature was justified.

As the Brambleton house came into view, Snow realized they'd made the entire trip in comfortable silence. She'd been irritated when they'd left her place, but there was something calming about sitting next to Caleb. A sense of security, as if she could relax because she wasn't on her own. That sense of feeling protected had been a big draw for her. Few men she'd come across in her life had carried the kind of confidence and strength that emanated from the man in the driver's seat.

Maybe that was the problem. He made her feel too comfortable. If she let her guard down completely, and then everything fell apart, where would she be? And deep down, she knew things were bound to fall apart. Caleb was the very definition of too good to be true.

Except for his annoying little quirks. Like insisting on being the big man behind the wheel.

A crowd had already gathered on the front yard of the estate. The items would likely be auctioned from the front porch, but not until potential buyers had the chance to examine the merchandise. Snow almost hated to think of the items that way. These were likely family heirlooms. Pieces that had sentimental value to someone, and that had each absorbed the history of its owners. Sometimes she could look at a piece and a scene would unfold in her head.

Ladies drinking tea and sharing the latest gossip across a Seymour card table. A lonely little boy hugging his Steiff teddy bear as he watches his parents drive off to some society gathering. Or a teenage boy in the seventies huddled over his grandfather's old Fender guitar with dreams of being the next Jimmy Page.

Years of being dragged through endless flea markets with her grandmother had given Snow both an extensive knowledge of anything old, and a love of the stories the antique pieces could tell. Granny Cameron had worked in a fine old house when she was young, and she'd been responsible for polishing the furniture that had been built before the Civil War. Sometimes it seemed as if Granny were a walking history book, and she'd passed the knowledge, along with a desire to learn more, down to her granddaughter.

"Is there something in particular we're looking for?" Caleb asked as they approached the crowd in the yard.

Snow kept her voice down so no one around them could hear the items she had her eye on. "Three things," she said. "An old dresser I can make into a bathroom vanity. The old mantelpiece, if they put that up. I'm not sure they will." She already had a buyer for the mantel, so hope sprang eternal. "And lace doilies."

Caleb stopped walking. "Doilies?" he asked loud enough for all around to hear him.

She couldn't stop the eye roll. Tugging Caleb away from the others, she scolded, "Keep your voice down or I'll have a bidding war on my hands."

Her husband looked clueless. "Bidding war? Over doilies?"

Nitzi Merchant, the high school secretary, smiled from across the lawn. Snow knew that Nitzi would be her biggest competitor for textiles. "Word has it a Brambleton ancestor was known for her handmade lace doilies. There might be kerchiefs, too. A textile like that, made over a hundred years ago, could bring in a nice profit."

"There's a market for doilies?" he asked, still incredulous.

"I knew it was a mistake to let you come." The doors had been opened while Snow attempted to educate Caleb, and the crowd was already filing into the house. Snow hurried to catch up. "Just be quiet and stay out of my way," she said.

Guilt set in the moment the words were out. Caleb had done nothing to deserve her temper, but she was already getting curious stares from the locals. Knowing the questions would come, and she would soon be the subject of town gossip, put Snow on edge. She'd worked so hard to blend into this town, which wasn't easy for a woman with olive skin and a mass of dark, curly hair.

Auctions were always an adrenaline rush, but today felt heavier. As if there were more at stake than winning an item or two. The reason was obvious. Thanks to Caleb, the perfect little life she'd created in Ardent Springs was about to go out the window.

The need to deal with their impromptu marriage had loomed somewhere in her future, and Snow was realistic enough to know this day would come. But that didn't make her any less resentful of his sudden return to her life.

"I'm sorry," Caleb whispered in her ear as they reached the front door. "I didn't mean to mess anything up."

Hesitating on the threshold, she gave her husband a weak smile. "I know. I'm sorry, too. But this is really important to me." She offered the thin lie to cover how she really felt. Not that the auction wasn't important, but her business wouldn't fold if she left the Brambleton house empty-handed.

Her status in Ardent Springs was the real issue.

Something Snow hadn't realized she cared so much about. What she had here she'd created on her own. Now, with Caleb's arrival, her life could unravel like a sweater with a loose thread. One wrong move and . . .

Snow reined in that thought. This was a temporary blip in her plan. In a few weeks, Caleb would see they were a bad match.

"Where do you want to start?" Caleb asked, drawing Snow back to the moment. He was glancing at the flier in his hand, then up at the array of rooms jutting off the foyer. "The stairs are blocked, so if they're bringing out a dresser, it must be down here somewhere."

Caleb looked like a man on a mission, and Snow's guilt increased. He was so determined to make this work. She almost wished it could.

Almost. But then she remembered their two months of awkward, uncomfortable marriage and regained her sanity. Not that every minute of their marriage had been bad. When they were alone, Snow could ignore the reality of her surroundings, and Caleb's upper-crust status.

She'd let her heart rule her head and all but convinced herself that he really was the one.

And then they would leave the sanctity of their room and the censure and snobbishness of his parents would all but suffocate her. The fancy dinners, always endured in private dining rooms, given the McGraws couldn't possibly be expected to mix with the regular folk, made her food taste like cardboard as she struggled to choke it down and pretend she didn't hate every passing moment.

Caleb had been blind to his parents' true nature. Or he'd been ignoring it for so long that he didn't see it anymore. Though he was miraculously down-to-earth and open-minded, there were moments she feared he would eventually grow to be more like them. Once he took over the family business, who was to say he wouldn't become another version of Jackson, the ruthless company leader with little concern for anything other than his own pleasure and the bottom line.

Fears she would never speak aloud. Whether he ever turned ruthless or not, Caleb would someday be in charge of the vast family fortunes, and Snow would be expected to continue the tradition of influential yet obedient matriarch. A role she never could or would want to play. Especially not after seeing what the position had done to the mean-spirited woman who was Vivien McGraw.

Shaking herself back to the present, Snow examined her surroundings and picked a direction. "The ladies' parlor is to our left," she said, examining the layout on the bottom corner of the flier. "We'll start there."

Chapter 6

Passing through the open pocket doors, a sliver of excitement shot down Snow's spine when she spotted the white mantelpiece leaning against the wall. The entire facing had been removed, and carefully from the looks of it. She couldn't be sure of its age, but the house dated back to 1898. Snow checked the sheet of paper in her hand. The mantel had been installed in 1909.

Perfect.

"Hey," Caleb said, pointing toward the object of her desire.

Snow slapped his hand down. "I see," she said with a low growl. The man could not follow instructions to save his life. But the motion brought a problem to her attention. Keeping her voice down, she said, "You need to take off your ring."

"What?" Caleb said.

"The ring." Snow cut her eyes toward the offending appendage. "We're keeping the married part secret, remember? You need to take off your ring."

"So you know," he mumbled while removing the thin band, "I've *never* taken this off." Caleb shoved the ring into his pocket as he said, "I see the same can't be said for you."

Her guilt level shot to eleven with that direct hit. "I didn't want to explain to people why a married woman was living among them with no husband."

Rubbing the spot where his ring had been, he said, "I guess I should consider myself lucky you didn't tell people I was dead."

Even Snow wouldn't go that far. "Could we keep moving, please? We have other items to find."

They passed through the door in the far corner and stepped into the dining room. The lace doilies had been spread out along the right side of a buffet. Snow put on her best poker face as she examined the pieces—definitely old, some discolored, but others were in excellent shape.

Leaning close to her ear, Caleb whispered, "This is good, right?"

Snow nodded. "Not as good as I'd hoped."

Then he elbowed her and said, "What about the painting?"

Following the direction of his less-than-subtle nod, Snow located the large painting of a ship. It looked like some paint-by-numbers thing.

"What about it?" she asked.

"We need to get that."

By Snow's estimation, the painting might bring in twenty dollars, and fifteen of that was for the frame.

"I don't think so."

Caleb remained undeterred. He leaned close, examining the signature. "I'm serious. This has to go on the list."

"Uh, no. That would be a waste of money."

If a grown man could have a conniption, Caleb had one in that moment. "It's a William Norton."

"A what?" Snow stepped around her husband and squinted at the unreadable signature. "I can't make that out at all."

"My father has a William Norton on the wall in his office. He paid ten thousand dollars for it, and it's smaller than this one."

Snow's heart dropped. "Are you making that up?"

Caleb twitched. "Why would I make that up?"

The twitch became contagious, as it was now pulsing in Snow's left eyelid. She looked around to make sure no one could hear their conversation. "You're sure? That signature is really hard to read."

"I am," Caleb said with confidence. "My father loves to brag about his trophies. His Norton is the one he talks most about, and that is definitely Norton's signature."

Ten thousand dollars would allow Snow to make upgrades in the store that she'd been dreaming about. And she could set up Lorelei's baking café in the back corner right away, instead of waiting until spring.

"Mr. McGraw, you may have just earned your keep for the week."

"Happy to be of service," Caleb said, "Mrs. McGraw."

"I can't believe the painting was that easy. Are you sure it's authentic?" Snow asked, after winning the Norton with almost no competition.

None of the other attendees seemed to know what they were looking at, as Snow had won the bidding at a low three hundred dollars. Whoever was running the auction should have done their homework and known the history and value of every piece up for sale. Especially on such an old estate.

Caleb wasn't an art expert, but the chances someone had faked a Norton that ended up in this old house seemed slim. He had no doubt the signature matched the piece on his father's wall. "Here," he said, pulling out his phone. "We'll look it up and I'll show you."

"It seems too good to be true," Snow whispered as Caleb tapped the Google app on his phone. He typed the artist's name along with the words "seafaring painting" into the search field. Several images popped up in the results, none identical to the picture they'd purchased today, but at least three were similar. "These are all in museums," he said, turning and lowering the phone so Snow could see the screen. "Here's one that sold at auction last year for eight grand, and it's at least half the size of ours."

"Ours?" Snow said, her brows riding her hairline, but she couldn't hide the grin.

Caleb tucked a wayward curl behind her ear. "You wouldn't have bid if I hadn't been here to educate you on the hidden treasure hanging in front of your nose."

With a gleam he hadn't seen in more than a year, she said, "True. You did come in handy today. I guess I'll keep you around a little longer."

"It's cute that you think you can get rid of me," he replied with a wink.

Snow's grin fell away. "And we're back to reality," she said, turning around to face the house.

His runaway bride may have been clueless about the painting, but Snow had knowledge to spare on almost everything else in the auction. She'd gotten the dresser she wanted, which wasn't as old as most of the other items, but that made it perfect for the transformation she had in mind. As Snow pointed out, cutting up a true antique would be a shame, but the less-dated piece would find new life and new purpose when she was finished with it.

"The textiles aren't as nice as I'd hoped," Snow whispered. "Nitzi Merchant is probably going to put up a fight, so if the bidding goes above fifty dollars, I'll let her have them."

"Are you sure?" he asked. "What about that mantelpiece?"

"I'm not willing to pay much over one hundred for it, since I won't get more than two fifty on the resale. But I'd hate to see it sold for scrap and end up in someone's wood heap."

"You know of anyone else who would want it for the same reason you do?" Caleb eyed their fellow attendees. They all looked easy enough to haggle with. If necessary, he'd buy the mantel from whoever won the auction and surprise her with it.

The auctioneer's voice boomed from the porch, announcing the final round was about to start. "We're about to find out," Snow said, holding her paddle tight and focusing on the man at the front.

The lace bits came and went. The price hit sixty in no time, and Snow dropped out. Three items later, the final target on her list came up as two large guys hauled the mantelpiece onto the block. The bidding started at fifty and went slow until a new bidder joined the fray at the eighty-dollar mark. Snow faced off with the determined contender until the asking price hit one fifty and she gave up. Caleb fought the urge to find the winning bidder and punch him in the nuts.

The asshole got the prize at one seventy-five, and Caleb leaned down to whisper in Snow's ear, "You should have kept bidding."

She shook her head. "By the time I cleaned it up and got it fit for sale, I'd have lost money."

"So now it's firewood?"

Snow shrugged. "Can't win them all."

This was a concept Caleb had never embraced. "I would have covered you."

Snow shook her head but kept her eyes on the porch. "This isn't your business, and I don't want your money."

"*You* are my business, and my money is your money."

Snow spun fast enough to force Caleb to take a step back. "I said I don't want your money. I mean it. That's not why I married you."

Caleb felt as if he'd landed in quicksand. "I told you, I know that. But that doesn't change the fact that you're my wife, and what's mine is yours."

Cutting off the conversation, she snapped her mouth shut and turned her back on him.

"Our final item," the auctioneer bellowed, "is a 1956 Ford F-100 pickup truck. Who'll give me five hundred?"

Caleb hadn't noticed a truck on the flier. He followed the auctioneer's gesture to the left and spotted the neglected antique pull into view on the back of a flatbed hauler. Primer gray, with a busted back window and two missing wheels, the pickup was a thing of beauty.

A little paint, probably a new engine, and some TLC would bring this baby back to life.

Someone in the crowd offered up the five hundred, and Caleb swiped the paddle from Snow's hand and indicated he'd go to six hundred.

"What are you doing?" she said.

"I'm buying that truck," he answered, as if his intention wasn't clear.

The other bidder went up to eight hundred, and a rush of adrenaline shot through Caleb's system. He took the bid to one thousand. Uncle Frazier would never forgive him if he didn't bring this treasure home.

Caleb spotted his opponent fifteen yards to his right, standing inches over most of the crowd. He wore a ball cap turned backward, and some kind of tattoo circled the forearm waving the paddle. No doubt some country bumpkin who intended to strip the thing for parts. Over Caleb's dead body.

He flashed the paddle to make the twelve-hundred-dollar bid.

"Caleb," Snow snapped. "Knock it off."

"That's a 1956 Ford," he said. "Even in the condition it's in now it's worth five grand."

Snow tried to tug the paddle from his grasp, but Caleb held tight. "Let Cooper have the truck," she said, still tugging.

"Why?"

With desperation in her eyes, she said, "Please. Don't do this."

Against his better judgment, he let her have the paddle. His opponent offered up fifteen hundred, and Caleb ignored the auctioneer's call for sixteen.

"Sold!" echoed over the crowd, and Caleb's jaw clenched. It killed him to let the truck go, but he couldn't ignore Snow's heartfelt plea.

"Who is this Cooper guy?" he asked. "What is he to you?"

"What?" she asked, amber eyes going wide. "Cooper Ridgeway is nothing more than a friend to me. He owns the garage in town and his entire life revolves around cars. He's probably had his eye on that truck for years, and it wouldn't be fair for you to swipe it out from under him just because you have more money."

Hovering inches above her nose, Caleb said, "If I wanted to throw my money around, I would have raised the bid to five thousand right away. If your goal is to make me feel like a rich asshole, then congratulations. You've succeeded."

⤴

She'd wanted her husband to hate her, and Snow was certainly succeeding. Too bad the victory felt more like she'd kicked a sack full of kittens than something worth celebrating.

He was so . . . Caleb. Confident. Pompous. Determined to have anything that caught his fancy. What would he have done with that truck, anyway? She didn't have a garage to put it in, and her husband wasn't exactly a workbench and power tools kind of guy.

A tense silence followed them to the cashier's table, where Snow paid for her winnings. She'd feared Caleb would try to pay, but he'd maintained a distance while she settled her account.

Snow turned from the table and nearly plowed into Spencer Boyd.

"Whoa," Spencer said, steadying Snow by her upper arms. "You okay?"

"She's fine," Caleb said, stepping close enough to brace her against him.

Heat shot up her cheeks as she felt her husband's body tense against her back. Part of her appreciated the protective move, while another drowned in mortification. This was not the time to make a scene. Snow looked up to see the usual smile on Spencer's face.

"You must be Caleb," he said, extending a hand to the man crowding her. "I'm Spencer Boyd. I believe you met my fiancée yesterday."

Oh, no. Lorelei must have told Spencer that Snow's husband had shown up out of nowhere.

"Yes, this is Caleb," she said, as the men shook hands. "Can we step over here for a minute?" A crowd had gathered around the cashier area, and Snow didn't want anyone overhearing if Spencer brought up the marriage part. She directed the two men to a space near the back of the house, not far from the tow truck that held the old pickup.

Once they'd found a secluded spot, she said, "What exactly did Lorelei tell you?"

Spencer rubbed his chin. "She mentioned the Vegas wedding part, but left the rest to speculation." One side of his mouth curled up. "You know how Lorelei is. I'd be prepared for a lot of questions later today."

Caleb remained silent, presumably still pouting about their earlier argument.

"I'll deal with Lorelei, but Caleb and I would like to keep the husband and wife part to ourselves for now. We'd prefer the locals think we've been having a long-distance relationship and now we're doing a trial run on the in-person thing."

"We're engaged," Caleb said.

Snow shot her husband a dirty look. "Fine," she agreed. "We're engaged."

"Might want to get a ring," Spencer interjected.

"What?" Snow said.

Spencer nodded toward her ring finger. "This town is both nosy and suspicious. If you want them to believe your story, I'd get a ring."

She had a ring, of course, but it was a wedding band. They'd meant to add an engagement ring, but never found the time in the two months before Snow left town. The truth was, Caleb had tried several times to drag her to a jewelry store, but Snow always found a reason to put him off. She knew he'd want the biggest and most expensive one, and she wasn't ready to put that kind of a rock on her hand.

"She'll have one," Caleb said. "Thanks for the tip."

"No problem." Turning to Snow, Spencer said, "Sorry about the fireplace thing."

"*You* bought the mantel?" Her opponent had been in the front of the crowd, too far ahead for Snow to see from the back.

With an apologetic smile, he said, "It's the only reason I'm here. We're creating a seating area in the lobby of the Ruby, and that piece is exactly what we need."

Snow couldn't complain about that. "I was worried whoever bought it would turn it into kindling," she said.

"The Ruby?" Caleb asked.

"A group of locals is working to restore the old movie theater in town," Snow explained. "Spencer and Lorelei are on the committee handling the renovations."

Caleb lost some of his pout. "I'd be interested in hearing more about the project."

"We're always happy to have a new volunteer," Spencer said. "The next meeting is Friday night at Lancelot's Restaurant. We're rolling out the next phase of the plans, so any input will be welcome."

Snow didn't like the idea of Caleb inserting himself into the community. This was a temporary stay. He wasn't supposed to make friends or join committees.

"I don't know if we can make it," Snow said.

"We'll be there," Caleb spoke over her.

As the pair stared each other down, Spencer said, "I'd better head in for the mantel. You two have a good day. And Snow, don't be afraid to tell Lor to mind her own business."

Before she could respond, Spencer melted into the crowd. "Why did you say that?" she asked Caleb. "You don't know anything about restoration."

"Yes," he said. "I do. Did you say the store opens at noon?"

Thrown off by the change of subject, Snow hesitated before answering. "What? Yes. Noon." She looked at the time on her phone. "Crap. That gives us less than an hour. And I forgot to ask Spencer if he'd haul the dresser over to the store."

"We can get it."

Snow shot Caleb a puzzled look. "What are we going to do? Strap the thing to the roll bars?"

"I'll take you to the store, then rent a truck in town and come back for the dresser."

"That's crazy. Spencer can get it. He's picked items up for me before," Snow said. "He won't mind."

Caleb gave her a hard look. "*I* mind."

She took a deep breath and prayed for patience. "I appreciate that you want to do this, but you've already been a big help today. As you said, I never would have bought that painting without you." She looked around for a mission to send him on. "Why don't you check out the truck while I get the painting, and I'll meet you at the Jeep." She used a tone reserved for encouraging toddlers to eat their brussels sprouts. "I won't be long, I promise."

Before he could argue, Snow hustled along the front of the porch and charged into the house looking for Spencer. She found him in the parlor wrapping the mantel in bubble wrap.

"There you are," she said. "I forgot to ask you something outside."

Spencer taped down a piece of packing material. "What do you need?"

"I bought a dresser, and I'm hoping you can bring it to the store for me."

"I can do that," he said. "I'll get Coop to help me load it up as soon as I'm done here. Do you have the receipt?"

"Oh," Snow said, figuring out which sheet in her hand went with the furniture. "Here you go."

Shoving the slip in his back pocket, he said, "It'll be there this afternoon."

"Thanks." Snow hesitated before moving on to get the painting. "This is going to seem . . . odd," she said, "but I don't want Caleb getting too involved with things here in town. He probably won't be around for long, so there's no point, really."

Taking a break from the wrapping, Spencer said, "Does Caleb know he won't be around for long?"

"Well," she hemmed, "he and I don't quite agree on the length of his stay."

"Right." Spencer unrolled another strip of wrap. "That doesn't look like a guy who's leaving town anytime soon. At least not without taking his wife with him."

Snow surveyed the area for potential eavesdroppers. "Shh . . ." she said. "I told you, I don't want anyone to know we're married."

"Sorry," Spencer apologized. "But if the guy wants to help out with the Ruby, I'm not going to turn him away."

Was every man trying to make her life more difficult?

"Fine," Snow snapped. "I'll see you at the store this afternoon."

As she reached the entrance to the dining room, Spencer called, "Snow?" She turned with a huff as he said, "That guy isn't giving you up without a fight. Good luck getting rid of him."

Feeling more fragile than she had in months, Snow said, "Ignore the possessive act. Caleb doesn't love me."

"You could have fooled me," Spencer replied.

Chapter 7

Considering her low opinion of him, Caleb was starting to wonder if he would ever win Snow back. And since when did having money make you an automatic asshole? Their relationship had been all but perfect until she disappeared, or so he'd thought. Clearly he'd been wrong. Something happened during those two months in Baton Rouge, and he was going to have to figure out what if this was ever going to work.

In addition to getting to know her, he'd have to either read Snow's mind or coax the truth out of her, neither of which he had any inkling how to do.

So he focused on something he could understand, which was the prize in front of him. As he eyed the pickup that should be his, he tried to be a good sport. He couldn't have started on the truck until this situation with Snow was resolved and they were back in Louisiana. And he doubted Uncle Frazier would wait for him. Then again, he could probably park it somewhere locally until they were ready to go home. Maybe the old woman who owned the house would let him rent one of the garage stalls. There likely wasn't anything in there, anyway.

All of this was giving Caleb an idea. Snow hadn't wanted him to deprive this Cooper person of the truck by outbidding him. But that didn't mean Caleb couldn't buy the truck from him outright, especially if the guy got significantly more than he paid for it.

"Hey there," Caleb called to the man with half his body tucked into the engine area of the old pickup. "She's a beauty."

The new owner's head popped up to look down at Caleb. "Not yet she isn't, but she will be." The man's green eyes glittered with glee at his new toy. Caleb knew that look meant trouble. This wasn't going to be easy.

Still. Everyone had a price. That was Jackson McGraw's number one lesson in life.

"It's going to take some serious cash to get her into shape." Caleb used the back tire of the hauler to join his adversary on the flatbed. A glimpse through the passenger window revealed tears in the bench seat, but the emblem was intact on the large steering wheel, and the dash looked good.

"Time and money," the stranger said, wiping his hands on a stained rag he'd pulled from his back pocket. "I think I can handle it." The man had Caleb by a couple of inches in height, but they were roughly the same size otherwise. Though the grease stains under his opponent's nails said Snow wasn't exaggerating about Cooper's love of cars.

Caleb was dealing with a true gearhead. The situation grew bleaker by the moment.

Cutting to the chase, Caleb said, "I could take her off your hands right now. Save you the hassle."

Closing the hood, Cooper said, "I appreciate the offer, but no thanks." In a surprise move, he then extended his hand. "Cooper Ridgeway. I own the garage in town, and I admire a man who knows a prize when he sees it. Not everyone would recognize the potential in a piece like this."

Accepting the handshake, Caleb conceded the battle. "It was worth a shot," he said. "I'm Caleb McGraw, and I'm really pissed right now that I let this baby get away."

"You a friend of Snow's?" Cooper asked.

"I am," Caleb answered, resenting the lie he was about to tell. "She's my fiancée."

Cooper's brows shot up. "Fiancée? That's news."

"I'm sure it will be." No one had approached them since they'd arrived at the auction, but Caleb had caught the curious looks. "I got in last night. It's been a long-distance thing."

"Congrats," Cooper said. "So you restore cars?"

"Not for a while," Caleb answered, happy to be back on safe ground. "Bought my '85 Jeep seven years ago and brought her back to life. My uncle is the real enthusiast. I've helped him with a '55 Bel Air and a '67 Stingray."

"Nice. You should come by the garage sometime. I've got a '62 Thunderbird hardtop that'll make your mouth water."

Caleb nodded. "I'd love to see it."

Cooper jumped off the hauler, and Caleb followed suit. Cooper asked, "You looking for a job?"

Getting a job hadn't occurred to him, but punching a time clock might win him some points with Snow. "Are you hiring?"

Cooper shook his head. "Afraid not, but Lowry Construction is looking for help if you have experience."

He'd swung a hammer once or twice in his life, but construction in November didn't sound appealing. "So I look like a construction guy?" Caleb asked, curious about the assumption.

The amiable mechanic didn't seem fazed. "You look like a guy wanting work, and construction is about all you'll find around here. Unless you want to drive a county or two over and apply at a factory."

There were limits to what Caleb would do to impress his wife. Factory work, which he knew to be hard, long, and underpaid, went beyond that limit.

"I'll keep both in mind." He gave the truck one last shot. "You sure you won't part with this heap?"

"If you wanted it this bad, you should have outbid me, bud," Ridgeway said as they walked down the driveway.

"The wife didn't want me bidding on anything that wasn't for the store," he said, slipping his hands into his pockets.

Cooper glanced over. "You call her 'the wife' already?"

Maintaining this story was going to be tougher than he realized. "It's all a matter of paperwork, right? Once she says yes, you're as good as hitched."

"Not me, bro," Cooper said, shaking his head. "I've got an out until the preacher says, 'I now declare.'"

"You walking down the aisle anytime soon?" Caleb asked, assuming the mechanic's intended would frown on his attitude.

"Heck no. I haven't won the right girl yet."

With a pat on his new friend's back, Caleb said, "I suggest when you find her, you keep the 'out' thing to yourself."

The pair stopped near the Jeep. "Sound advice, I'm sure." Then Cooper spotted something over Caleb's shoulder. "Here comes your girl, and she looks like an angry hornet hunting for a butt to sting." As he backed away, he added, "You might want to think about an out yourself."

Snow did look mad about something. She also looked hot as hell with the color high in her cheeks and her eyes snapping. Nope, Caleb didn't need or want an out. But he did need to figure out how to get this woman back in his bed.

Snow was still fuming over Spencer's comments when she met Caleb at the Jeep. He'd been talking to Cooper, who'd walked away before she was close enough to hear the conversation.

"What were you talking to Cooper about?" she asked, allowing him to take the painting and slide it into the backseat.

With a noncommittal tone, her husband said, "Nothing important. He invited me to check out his garage."

Another invitation. What was wrong with these people? They'd made her fight for every inch of acceptance, but Caleb waltzed into town and out came the red carpet. "Why would you visit his garage if you don't need anything fixed?"

Caleb sighed as he held the door for her. "We're boys," he said. "We bonded over old cars. It's like finding the guy on the playground who has the same ball glove you do."

This entire conversation was proof that boys never grew up. She waited for Caleb to climb into the driver's seat before asking, "So you made a playdate?"

"We didn't get that specific, but I'll make sure you don't need me before I head over." He started the engine. "Cooper said if I'm looking for a job, I should try Lowry Construction. You heard of them?"

There was no way she'd heard him right. "Why would you be looking for a job?"

"You keep saying I don't do anything. If you want a working husband, I'll be a working husband."

"But you aren't even going to be here long enough to need a job." What was she saying? The man had enough money to buy half the town. He didn't *need* a job regardless of how long he was staying. "You've been here for less than twenty-four hours and you're acting as if this is your new home."

"My home is in Baton Rouge, but you're here. So for now, home is here."

The girlie part of her turned mushy upon hearing that absurd statement. Caleb was trying to charm her into lowering her guard. Con her into believing that this reunion was romantic and noble and not about filling in the hole she'd poked in his ego by daring to leave him. She wouldn't be surprised if some of his determination stemmed from proving something to his parents. He'd married the last girl they'd pick for him, and she was ruining his little rebellion.

"Yes, I've heard of Lowry Construction. The owner is Lorelei's father," she said, refusing to address his "home is where my wife is" sentiment. "But what do you know about construction?"

The Jeep was running, but Caleb didn't put it into gear. Instead, he stared out the windshield, shaking his head in what looked like amazement. "I've handled a hammer enough times to help frame a house with no problem. I also like to restore old cars, and I'm interested in the preservation of old buildings, something my family has supported in the Baton Rouge and New Orleans areas since before I was born."

Snow managed a surprised "Oh."

"You said I don't know you, but it seems to me you've got that backwards."

Feeling defensive, Snow went for sarcasm. "I can't help it that we were too busy having sex to have actual conversations."

"Your favorite ice cream is pistachio," he said.

"Excuse me?" What did ice cream have to do with this?

"Your favorite food in the world is your grandmother's fried chicken, which is breaded, not battered. You have a tiny scar on your bottom lip from falling off a stool when you were two, you love the Beatles, and your favorite actor of all time is Paul Newman."

"How do you—" she started, but Caleb was on a roll.

"You hate Birkenstocks, anchovies, and people who talk during a movie. You sometimes hate your hair, you purr when I slide my fingertips up your bare spine, and your astrological sign is Taurus, which probably explains a lot about this entire situation."

He'd done it. Caleb had shocked her speechless. Snow didn't even remember them talking about half of those subjects, but little snippets began to float through her mind. Quiet talks after their lovemaking.

Exchanging silly stories over breakfast, usually while they were still naked. How had she forgotten so much?

"I didn't realize—"

"I was paying attention, Snow. We were never just sex for me."

Now who looked like the asshole? Snow didn't know what to say, but she couldn't keep pretending they were strangers. "We'd better go," she said. "I need to open the store."

"Right." Caleb shifted into first gear. "The store."

Several miles of silence later, as they rolled into downtown Ardent Springs, Snow said, "Chocolate is your favorite."

"My what?" Caleb asked, parallel parking in front of the store entrance.

She put her hand over his on the shifter. "Chocolate is your favorite flavor of ice cream. And you like action movies, especially ones with car chases." Her smile was meant as an apology. "I remember now."

Dropping a kiss on her nose, he said, "Took you long enough. Do you want me to hang out here today?"

Scrunching up her face, she said, "Not really. You'd be bored out of your skull within an hour."

"What time do you close?"

"For the next couple weeks it's five on Sundays, then I'll extend the hours as we get closer to the Christmas season."

"Okay, then." Caleb opened his door. "I'll carry the painting in and see you at home later."

For the first time in eighteen months, Snow would finish the day by going home to her husband. The thought appealed more than she was willing to admit. Maybe convincing Caleb that they were wrong for each other would be easier if she convinced her heart first.

Snow was relieved to have ten minutes before the clock would strike noon and the second half of her day would begin. The first part had already been more than she could process. Caleb had helped her find a deal that could take her shop to the next level, but he'd also bounced among arrogant, spoiled, and possessive. Not to mention his penchant for winning over the locals with no effort whatsoever. If they knew he was filthy rich and had done nothing to earn a penny of it, they wouldn't be so inviting.

Dropping her head into her hands, Snow hated that the previous thought had even entered her mind. His parents had turned their noses up at her lack of money and substance, and she was doing the same thing to Caleb for the opposite reason. He was right—a person didn't get to choose the circumstances into which he was born. Holding his trust fund against him was no better than all the prejudice she and her family had endured over the years.

Granted, Caleb could walk away from the money, but why would he? It wasn't as if the elder McGraw had made his fortune selling drugs or something. As far as Snow could tell, the man was a workaholic who put his business dealings above all else. Including his son.

Her husband was a good man, a product of his upbringing, and so far out of her sphere that even if she wanted them to live happily ever after, they never could. The mere thought of going back to Baton Rouge made her want to run again. But she wasn't running anymore.

Snow had found a life here in Ardent Springs, and it did not include a husband. That meant Caleb had to go. She had to *make* him go. She'd cried for a week after leaving him a year and a half ago, and she would likely cry again when they ended for good. But cutting things off as quickly as possible would prevent her losing her heart completely. At this stage, she might recover. If Caleb kept giving speeches like the one he'd laid on her today, Snow was a goner for sure.

Self-preservation could be a powerful motivator. And right now, Snow was desperate for any kind of lifeline.

"Snow, are you in there?" yelled a voice through the back door, followed by three hard thumps.

Lorelei.

"I'm coming," she yelled back, crossing the storeroom to unlock the door. "Why didn't you come to the front?" Snow asked as Lorelei stepped inside.

"I tried, but it was locked."

Snow checked the clock on her desk—12:02 p.m. Crap.

"Sorry. I was distracted and lost track of time."

Lorelei followed Snow as she headed for the front door. "Does the distraction have anything to do with, say, your incredibly hunky husband?"

"Lorelei, I—"

"Not that I blame you for not getting any sleep last night. Holy heck." The blonde made a purring noise. "Don't get me wrong. Spencer is hot, and I don't want anyone else, but girlfriend, that man of yours is smokin'."

Snow ignored the bubble of pride that formed in her chest. "Yes, Caleb is pretty to look at, but I got plenty of sleep last night." Slept better than she had in months, but she ignored that fact as well. At this rate, she'd be the queen of denial in no time.

"You mean you didn't—" Lorelei stepped in front of Snow, putting her back to the front door before the lock could be turned. "Are you telling me you didn't jump that man's bones as soon as I locked this door for you? You're welcome for that, by the way."

On a sigh, Snow said, "There are . . . issues." She reached for the lock, but Lorelei blocked her again.

"You mean he can't . . ." Her friend held up one finger, bent at the knuckle.

"No!" Snow exclaimed. "Caleb can get it up just fine, thank you very much. Now let me unlock this door."

Lorelei finally moved. "You know, if you'd gotten laid last night, you might not be so grumpy today."

With an evil glare, Snow said, "When you rolled into town in June, did you jump Spencer's bones right away?"

The sheepish look said it all. "That was different. Spencer and I weren't married. And we had things to work out."

"Exactly," Snow said. "Caleb and I have things to work out. And if everything goes to plan, he'll be leaving town soon."

"You're leaving town?"

"Of course not. I said *he'll* be leaving town. A-*lone*."

"Oh." Lorelei grew serious. "You're talking divorce. So this is more than some lovers' spat."

"Much more," Snow answered. "Caleb and I don't fit together. We'd known each other only two months before waking up in a Vegas hotel suite wearing matching rings. It's all a lust-hazed blur when I think about it now."

"I don't blame you on the lust thing. That boy is—"

"Please stop pointing out how hot my husband is," Snow said, pulling the cash drawer from the safe. "I'm aware. But there's more to marriage than sex."

Lorelei leaned an elbow on the counter, balancing her chin in her palm. "Were you drunk?"

"Excuse me?" Snow blinked in confusion. "Was I drunk when?"

"The night you got married."

"No," Snow said. "I'd had a glass of wine, maybe."

"Then if you didn't want to get married after knowing him for only two months, why did you?" Lorelei gave a quick shrug. "There had to be a reason, and it doesn't sound like he forced you into it."

Caleb hadn't forced her into anything. Snow took the treacherous journey back in time to the night she and her hunky boyfriend had sprinted to the nearest wedding chapel, high on young love and the giddiness of total freedom. She'd felt like they owned the world that night. Like there was nothing that could break them apart.

And then something did.

Within a week, they were living in Baton Rouge and Snow's world went from perfection to a bad dream. Caleb seemed as happy as ever, doting and generous, but Snow had become a whirling mass of insecurity and panic.

It was no wonder she'd bolted the way she did. The real mystery was what took her so long.

"Did he refuse to give you a divorce before you left?" Lorelei asked, dragging Snow back to the present.

Keeping her gaze from meeting Lorelei's, she said, "I didn't ask for a divorce."

"Then what reason did you give for leaving?"

Keeping her voice low, Snow answered, "I didn't give any reason."

The blonde leaned forward. "So you what? Said good-bye and drove off?"

She'd thought answering to Caleb had been hard. Snow leveled her shoulders and prepared for Lorelei to think the worst of her. Goodness knew she didn't like herself very much right now, and regardless of the circumstances in which she'd found herself, Snow sure as heck couldn't justify her actions.

"I didn't say good-bye. I waited until he was asleep, and then I left."

Lorelei stood straight. "Just like that? No warning? Not even a note?"

Snow shook her head.

"Wow," Lorelei said. "That's—"

"Cowardly," Snow finished for her. "Not to mention rude, idiotic, and immature."

"I was going to say gutsy."

Not the reaction Snow expected. "Gutsy?"

"Men don't like it when they don't get a say in things. How long ago did you get up the nerve to tell him where you were?"

"I didn't tell him. He found a flier for the Ruby festival down in Nashville and caught the Snow's Curiosity Shop mention. He didn't even know for sure it was me, but he drove all the way up here to find out." As she heard herself explain it that way, Snow realized how far Caleb had gone to find her. And not just geographically. "If I'd gotten the tip that he was coming, I could have hidden somewhere and let you pretend to run the store."

The bells jingled over the door as the first customers of the day strolled in. The two older women lingered in the jewelry section near the front. Dropping her voice, Lorelei said, "How would you have gotten a tip?"

Snow leaned close and said, "His mother."

"What?" Lorelei asked, jerking back. "You got his mother to work against him?"

"Trust me," Snow said, "she was more than happy to have me out of Caleb's life. She caught me the night I left and gave me an e-mail address to contact her when I landed somewhere. As she put it, when Caleb finally agreed to divorce me, they'd need an address to send the papers."

"And she kept your secret all this time?" Lorelei asked, fascination dancing in her eyes. "That's wild."

For the first six months, Snow had been certain Caleb's mother would fold and spill her whereabouts, but the woman was more ruthless than she let on. Vivien McGraw—bone thin, always smiling, never angry or flustered—was in reality a mean woman with a heart of stone. Snow wanted to believe the McGraw matriarch's motives were to protect her son's heart, but deep down, she knew it was all about the family. Keeping up appearances. Maintaining their high standards.

"She did," Snow said. "In exchange for sharing my location, I made Vivien agree to send the occasional message to my family. If Mom didn't know where I was, she didn't have to lie to Caleb if or when he asked her if she'd heard from me. But I couldn't leave them wondering whether or not I was okay either. Vivien wasn't my favorite choice for messenger, but I had no other options at that point."

Lorelei shook her head. "To save your parents from having to lie, you let his own mother betray him. And I thought Hollywood had the drama."

Betray was such a harsh word. It wasn't as if Snow had paid her to keep silent. Or even had to twist her arm. "However it went down, Caleb is here now and I have to convince him that we aren't right for each other."

"How is that going?" Lorelei asked.

Pushing unruly curls back from her face, Snow said, "Rocky at best. I set the condition that we wouldn't have sex in the next month, and I thought that would send him running."

"He agreed?"

"Yeah." She still couldn't believe that tactic hadn't worked.

Following a low whistle, Lorelei said, "That boy is determined. And I don't know how you're going to hold out for a whole month."

"Sadly, neither do I."

Chapter 8

Caleb wasn't sure what to do with himself. He'd considered checking out his temporary new town, but driving around alone held no attraction for him. He'd rather explore the area with Snow. Let her show him around and share whatever it was that drew her to this place. As far as he could tell, Ardent Springs was a sleepy little metropolis with a bustling downtown and not much else. The proximity to Nashville kept the town from being remote, but without a business or family in the area, he didn't see much of a reason to stick around.

As he parked the Jeep outside Snow's apartment—or rather *their* apartment for now—he was surprised to see one of the garage doors open. The walls were lined with shelves, most holding neatly organized paint cans, canvases, a few easels, but there was no vehicle. Seemed a waste of space. This garage was made for cars, not paintbrushes and dirty rags.

"You got a reason to be nosing around my property?" Caleb spun to find an elderly woman nearly his own height staring at him through the biggest pair of sunglasses he'd ever seen. She wore a ball cap, an over-sized blue robe-looking thing that buttoned up the front, and a pair of regular glasses dangling from a string of beads around her neck.

Caleb didn't make a habit of checking out older women, but it was impossible not to notice that this one desperately needed to put on a bra. Everything was sitting around waist level.

"I'm Snow's hus—" he started, then corrected himself. "Fiancé. Snow's fiancé. Are you Mrs. Silvester?"

"Since when does Snow have a fiancé?" she asked, dragging out the last word into several syllables.

That was a good question. They hadn't discussed a time line for this bogus engagement, so Caleb decided to wing it. "Since two weeks ago."

His interrogator looked him up and down. "How long have you been in town?"

He was tempted to tell the busybody it was none of her business, but the impression she was digging for answers in protection of Snow kept him polite. "I got here yesterday," he said.

"But you asked her to marry you two weeks ago." The words were more statement than question. Her top lip curled as if she'd tasted something bitter. "What'd you do? Ask over e-mail or something? What kind of a boy asks for a girl's hand like that?"

She had a point. Caleb cursed his quick answer and resented Snow for making him lie like this. "Not exactly," he said, stalling to come up with a better story. "We talked about it over the phone and then agreed that I should come stay for a while to see how things go." What a load of bull. He only hoped he'd remember all of this to get the story straight with Snow later on. "I haven't actually gotten down on one knee and made an official proposal yet."

"What the hell you waitin' on?"

Caleb went with the first thought that entered his head. "I don't have a ring."

That put a hold on the rapid-fire questions. The woman slid her sunglasses to the end of her nose. "You're certainly pretty enough for my girl. What do you do for a living?"

Refusing to throw another lie on the metaphorical pile, Caleb said, "I'm between jobs at the moment."

Gray brows shot up. "At least you're honest." With a tilt of her head, she added, "Louisiana boy, aren't you?"

Impressive. "Yes, ma'am."

"You're lucky," she said, sliding the glasses back up. "I have a soft spot for Louisiana boys." Turning on her heels, she said, "Follow me." Caleb was so surprised, he didn't move for several seconds, until she turned and barked, "Don't be dillydallying now. We've got work to do."

Too stunned to argue, Caleb shuffled across the driveway, following Her Geriatric Highness through the garden gate and toward the side of the big house. "You *are* Mrs. Silvester, right?" he asked as he caught up to her.

"I am not and never have been Mrs. anything. Call me Miss Hattie." She floated up the six steps to reach the porch without touching the hand rail. "First, we'll take care of the ring situation." Resting her hand on the screen door handle, she removed the sunglasses, sliding one stem into the top of her robe thing—Caleb wasn't sure what to call the outfit other than shapeless. "I assume you're staying in the apartment with my tenant. You young folk might take this sort of thing lightly, but in my day, a woman didn't live with a man without first getting the ring *as well as* the vows spoken in front of the preacher." Opening the door and waiting for Caleb to hold it, she said, "I'll let the second part slide, but insist on the first. You have a problem with that?"

Since they'd already said their vows, be it in front of an Elvis impersonator instead of the traditional preacher, Caleb saw no reason to argue. "No, ma'am. But I can take care of the ring part myself if you'll point me in the direction of a good jeweler."

"Nonsense," she said, charging into the house. "I've got the perfect bauble."

Was she suggesting he take a ring from her? That was out of the question. "Mrs. Silvester . . ."

"That's Miss Hattie, and don't worry, I'm not giving you anything for free," she said, stepping up to a table in the foyer and dropping her hat and glasses on the marble surface. "The only kin I have is some distant cousin in Chattanooga who likely wouldn't know an heirloom from his hairy bottom. I'd rather sell a piece to you than see it end up in a pawn shop."

"But, ma'am . . ."

"Snow deserves the best, and what I'm offering is better than anything you'll find for several hundred miles," she said. "You want your wife to have the best, don't you?"

Yes. Yes he did. But this still seemed wrong.

"Are you sure about this?" he asked, knowing how closely his mother protected the jewelry that had been handed down through generations of McGraws, dating back to pre–Civil War days. "You don't even know me."

"What's your name?" she asked.

The question took him off balance. "Um . . . Caleb," he said. "Caleb McGraw."

"Nice to meet you, Caleb," Miss Hattie said with a hand extended. Manners made him accept the shake without thought. "Now we know each other. And we both care for Snow, am I correct?"

"Of course," he said without hesitation.

"Then it's settled. Let's get that sweet little thing a ring."

Thirteen thousand dollars. Snow leaned back in her chair, staring open-mouthed at her computer screen. The only painting by William Norton that was close to the size of the one she'd bought had sold at auction the year before for thirteen thousand dollars. Her eyes cut over to the new treasure and all she could do was smile. This lucky find was going to change her life, and she had Caleb to thank for it.

They'd need to find the right auction. And have it checked for authenticity, of course, but Snow believed she was looking at the real thing. The temptation to keep it danced along her brain. She, Snow Cameron, the lowly peasant with the tainted blood who wasn't good enough for his son, owned a painting more valuable than Jackson McGraw's. What would the blowhard say to that?

Not that she was bitter or anything. She already had Jackson's most valuable possession—his son. Too bad the old man couldn't see past his bank account to recognize that Caleb was the real prize.

That thought straightened her spine. Caleb *was* a prize. And he deserved a woman of equal value. Snow was smart enough to know she wasn't worthless, but she wasn't on her husband's level either. Since she had every intention of letting him go, Snow opted not to think about her marriage.

For today, she would wallow in her William Norton victory and plot out exactly how she'd use her future profits to improve the store.

Snow opened a new document in her computer and typed SHOP IMPROVEMENTS across the top at the same time the store phone sitting next to her keyboard began to chirp. Without checking the caller ID, she answered, "Snow's Curiosity Shop, how can I help you?"

"Is my son with you?" demanded the chilly voice on the other end.

"Hello, Vivien," Snow said, refusing to hop to attention like a trained puppy.

"Answer the question," the Southern diva snapped. "Is he there?"

"Not at the moment, no. But yes," Snow confessed, "Caleb is here in Ardent Springs."

"How could you let this happen?"

"Me?" Snow exclaimed, then glanced around the store and lowered her voice. "You were the one in charge of the smoke signals. Why didn't you warn me he was coming?"

"Because I didn't know," she muttered. "He sent me a text yesterday morning that he'd found a lead and was leaving Nashville, but there were no further details. He refused to answer my messages."

Maybe Mama McGraw didn't have her boy on as tight a leash as Snow had thought.

"There wasn't much I could do," Snow said. "He walked into the store out of nowhere. Other than feigning amnesia, I was out of options."

"I should have known this would happen," Vivien said, more to herself than to Snow. "I'm assuming you both agreed the marriage is over. When is he coming home? I'll set up a meeting with our lawyer. The divorce papers were drawn up months ago, so the process shouldn't take long."

A cold, stabbing pain hit Snow in the gut. The papers were ready to go? Was that Caleb's doing?

"I don't know when he's going home," she said, ignoring the ribbons of doubt clawing to take hold. "According to my husband, this marriage is salvageable." Apparently, like a car or an old building. Maybe Snow should hit up Buford at the hardware store for a tub of spackle.

"What are you talking about? *You* left him. He didn't hear from you for nearly two years." Her mother-in-law's voice dripped with icy incredulity as she reiterated every one of Snow's sins. "How could he *possibly* want to stay married to you?" she finished.

Snow asked herself the same thing, but she wasn't about to share that fact with Vivien McGraw. "Maybe for the same reason he married me in the first place," Snow said, prepared to lie to save her own pride.

"Oh, please," Vivien huffed, impatience clear in her tone. "Once he stops thinking with his libido, Caleb will see reason."

It was a wonder Caleb carried any kindness at all after being raised by this heartless woman. Of course, Vivien was smart enough never to reveal her true self to the men in her life. From their first encounter, Snow had marveled at how tightly Vivien spun her wicked web of fake Southern charm and empty maternal preening. The moment she'd caught Snow sneaking out of the house, the mask had dropped and Vivien had held no compunction about letting her son's fleeing wife know exactly what she thought of her.

The fact that Caleb's mother had been willing to pass messages on to Snow's family with complete anonymity was her only saving grace. But then, the longer Snow's whereabouts stayed secret, the closer Vivien came to wiping Snow out of her family for good.

"Your son doesn't see it that way." Snow couldn't help herself. As much as she knew Vivien was right, she couldn't stand to admit as much. Not to this horrible woman.

Silence prickled through the line, raising goose bumps along Snow's arms. Her mother-in-law was a formidable opponent. A woman unaccustomed to being crossed.

"How do you think my son will feel when he learns that you used his own mother against him?" Vivien asked, the threat unmistakable.

"I didn't use anyone," Snow answered, struggling to keep the panic from her voice. The guilt was harder to ignore. "Everything you've done was of your own choosing."

"That's your word against mine, now, isn't it?"

The betrayal would kill him. Even if he gave Snow a chance to explain, the truth was still ugly and hurtful.

Her position achingly clear, Snow said, "Your son will be home before Christmas. You can start your proceedings then."

Vivien's voice lost a bit of its edge. "This is the best for all involved. I assume you'll no longer need my assistance in contacting your parents?"

"No," Snow said. "I'll contact them directly from now on."

As she spoke the words, all feeling left her body. This was what she wanted—Caleb out of her life for good. So why did she feel as if she was losing something all over again?

"Snow?" Vivien said, sounding once again like the dictator she was. "Don't do anything foolish."

"Good-bye," Snow said, ending the call without waiting for the other woman to respond.

Closing her eyes, Snow took several deep breaths, willing the tears away. Once she regained control, she opened the phone line and entered a number she hadn't dialed in eighteen months.

⁓

"Are you sure this is the one?" Caleb asked, turning the tiny ring between two fingers to catch the light. Hattie had put him in a small ladies' parlor before disappearing up the stairs and returning moments later with a cream-colored jewelry box.

"I'm sure," Hattie said, balancing the box on her lap. "That ring has Snow written all over it."

The round diamond, held in place by four prongs and accented by six smaller stones on each side, *was* dainty, understated, and beautiful. Just like his wife.

"The band is platinum," Hattie explained. "Aunt Edith gave it to me when I turned sixteen. Her first husband had been killed in World War II, and when she remarried, her second husband gave her a new ring." The older woman's voice turned wistful. "I think seeing this in her jewelry box every day reminded her of Uncle Harry and what she'd lost. They'd been so in love, those two."

Caleb had no doubt he could afford whatever price Hattie asked, but now he knew there was sentimental value involved. "I don't want to take something so personal," he said. "I'll make a trip down to Nashville tomorrow."

Hattie waved his words away. "I'll hear nothing of the sort. That ring is meant to be worn, not sit in a box forever. Besides," she added, "I can't take it with me."

From what little time he'd spent with Hattie Silvester, Caleb surmised she was as healthy as he was. But not all ailments were obvious. "Are you planning on meeting your maker sometime soon?" he asked.

Shaking her head, she said, "My luck, I'll still be kicking around this old place twenty years from now. That doesn't change the fact that Snow deserves this ring."

The delicate piece continued to sparkle as he held it closer to the window. "What do you want for it?"

"It's worth about five thousand," Hattie said, shrugging as she answered. "Give me whatever you can afford."

Caleb could afford twice that much. "How do you feel about monthly payments?" He'd simply pay the small amount for the first month or two, then hand over a large check before he and Snow left for home.

"Like I said, pay me what you can afford." The older woman placed several small satchels back in the long jewelry box and latched the intricately decorated lid in place. "Say, do you know anything about the newspaper business?"

Considering his father owned three of them and he'd interned at each, the answer was obvious. But again, he didn't know what story Snow wanted him to tell. This lying business was more trouble than it was worth. Which was why he'd never made a habit of it.

"I know a little, I guess," Caleb said, deciding that understatement was better than a lie.

"Good." Hattie set the jewelry box on the desk and scribbled something on a piece of paper. "Be at this address at nine tomorrow morning."

Caleb took the note and read 121 Second Avenue North. "What is this?" he asked.

"You want a job or not?" she asked.

He'd told Snow he'd get a job, and working for a newspaper was better than slinging a hammer, but Caleb didn't know what Hattie expected him to do. Journalism was not his arena, but the paper could be hiring a delivery boy for all he knew.

"I appreciate your help, but I don't know what you're offering. And you don't even know if I'm qualified."

She once again waved his words away. "You'll be fine. Now we have more work to do," she said, charging out of the small sitting room.

"Excuse me?" Caleb said, following after her.

"It isn't often I have a little muscle around here," she said over her shoulder. "Keep up and we'll earn you the first installment on that ring before the day is out."

Chapter 9

"Mama, if you'll just listen—"

"Don't you *Mama* me, young lady. Do you know what you put your family through? We were worried sick." Snow had hoped that after eighteen months Roberta Cameron would be too happy to hear from her to launch into a full-on scolding.

Snow had hoped wrong.

"Running away from a good man like that. Leaving us behind to look like fools, trying to make excuses for our daughter's rash behavior. I *know* I taught you better than that. I have never been so humiliated in my life."

No concern over what had driven Snow to her "rash behavior," as Mama called it. No sympathy or compassion for the daughter who'd been distraught enough to stay in hiding for more than a year. None of that maternal stuff for Snow's mother.

"I shouldn't have taken off like that," Snow said, "but I had a good reason. Aren't you at all interested in why I left?"

"Do you know that boy has called me every month like clock-work?" Roberta asked. "I could mark it on my calendar and know exactly when I'd hear from him. But I never knew if or when I'd hear from my daughter."

Pounding her head on the wall behind her, Snow said, "I sent messages, Mama. I even sent presents on holidays and birthdays. You knew I was okay the whole time."

"As if a pretty teacup would make up for not having you here." That teacup was Wedgwood, for Pete's sake. "If you wanted to leave that boy, though heaven only knows what woman in her right mind would, you could have come here."

"I needed to go somewhere that Caleb couldn't find me," she said. "We aren't right for each other, Mama. Getting married was a mistake, and I couldn't spend one more minute in that house."

Snow had hit her limit of toxic hatred from her in-laws, both back at the time and now.

"Marriage isn't an easy thing, Snow. You had to know that."

If anyone knew that, it was Snow. A child didn't grow up in the Cameron household, with the screaming and fighting, empty cupboards and an emptier house, without learning that lesson. Somewhere around the age of ten, she'd started questioning why her mother stayed.

Her parents may have been in love at some point, but they sure didn't like each other. Zeke Cameron was a man with too much pride who couldn't keep a job long enough to fill out his first time card, and he had little patience for a wife who pointed out his faults on a daily basis.

"I don't have any illusions about marriage," Snow said. She hadn't been given enough time to even think about marriage before she and Caleb had tied the knot. "But I refuse to stay in a situation that isn't right."

Her mother's voice sharpened. "How could you know if it was right or not? Did you even give it a chance? Two months? You think two months is time enough to know anything?"

"Fine," Snow said. "I screwed up. I can't go back and change it now. I'm sorry that you were worried. I'm sorry that you were left to explain my actions. I never meant for anyone to have to speak for me."

"That's why you stick around and speak for yourself." The voice on the other end finally softened. "Are you really okay, honey?"

This was the mother Snow needed.

"I am. Well, I'm working on it. Caleb found me yesterday."

"I'm glad," she said. "Now you kids can straighten this mess out."

"There's nothing to straighten out, Mama." Snow kept her voice low as she smiled at a customer passing the counter. "He's old Baton Rouge money, and I'm no Birmingham money. He's upstairs, I'm downstairs."

"Don't you ever talk like that. I may have cleaned houses a time or two, but this isn't the nineteenth century. You're just as good as those McGraws." Her mother huffed. "Better if you ask me. I like that husband of yours, but his parents are another story."

And therein lay Snow's problem. Caleb and his parents were a package deal. She couldn't have one without the other two, and she couldn't bear life with the other two.

"Caleb seems to agree with you," Snow said. "He thinks we can make this work, but he's wrong. He'll realize that before Christmas, and when he agrees to end this marriage once and for all, I'll let you know."

"Give it a chance, baby. That boy cares about you."

If only things were that easy.

Shifting the subject away from her tattered marriage, Snow said, "I'm sorry I won't be able to come see you for a while. I run a store here in Ardent Springs, and it's impossible to get away during the holiday shopping season."

"You run a store? As in manage it?"

"No, I own it," she said. "It's called Snow's Curiosity Shop, and Grandma would love it. Everything from art deco jewelry to antique furniture and fabrics. A lot of it is on consignment, but I keep an eye on auctions and estate sales to fill in the rest."

"You did all this on your own?" her mother asked, the wonder in her voice heightening Snow's pride.

"I did. It's something special, Mama. Maybe you all can come up and see it sometime."

"We'll see," she said, though her tone gave a clear answer. "Your father's health isn't that good, and money's tight."

"What's wrong with Daddy?" Snow asked, fear jerking her upright. "Is he okay?" The man may not have been a great breadwinner, or all that touchy-feely, but he was still her father.

"Don't get yourself worked up. His lungs just aren't as strong as they used to be. Doc thinks the fumes from his years of house painting are to blame."

Sometime during Snow's high school years, her father had started his own house painting business, and thanks to being his own boss, stuck with it. He never made much money, but being his own man had made him easier to live with.

"Maybe I can come down between Christmas and New Year's," Snow said.

"You and Caleb are always welcome."

"Mama . . ."

"Like I said, just give him a chance. The fact that he's there should tell you something, baby. That boy's a keeper."

That boy needed to go home. Alone. And by Christmas, Snow would make sure he did.

Several hours later, Snow parked her red Nissan next to Caleb's Jeep in front of Miss Hattie's garage, but she didn't bother getting out. Instead, she stared unseeing through the windshield, contemplating how to handle the next few minutes. She'd agreed to Caleb's terms. He had a month to change her mind. Only no matter how he tried, Snow would have to let him go. Which had been her intention all along, but when she was with him, her determination wavered.

And this had been the reason she'd run away in the first place. Snow knew, with every ounce of her being, that she and Caleb were not meant to be, but then he'd smile or say the right thing and her misgivings went right out the window. If she'd told him she was unhappy, he'd have convinced her things would get better. If she'd asked for a divorce, Caleb's easy charm would have had her begging to stay before she'd known what she was saying. She couldn't reason with him, and she couldn't keep her heart out of the equation when he was around.

But in the end, she couldn't hurt him. Not the kind of hurt that would come with learning his own mother had kept her secret. When Snow had been certain that notice of the end of their marriage would come in the mail at any time, she didn't have to think about the mess she'd created. Regardless of what some Louisiana law said, she'd had no intention of taking a dime from Caleb. She only wanted to give him his life back and let him move on to find the right girl.

The society princess who would give him perfect babies, throw perfect dinner parties, and please his persnickety parents.

Vivien McGraw likely had a batch of Southern debutantes ready and willing to fill Snow's shoes. Picturing her husband showing off his new bride—tall and slender with the body of an underwear model, waves of blonde hair dancing around her shoulders, and proof of pedigree in her dainty clutch—made her nearly toss what little salad she'd managed to swallow for lunch.

Snow's grandmother's voice echoed through her mind. "Rip it quick and sure, baby. Draggin' it out only makes it worse."

That's what she needed to do. Walk inside and send Caleb back where he belonged. This one-month thing had been pointless from the start. She'd revert to her original plan. Be impossible to live with until he couldn't hit the road fast enough.

Her mind set, Snow climbed out of the car, marched through the garden gate and up her porch steps. He'd left the light on for her, something that softened the girlish section of her brain. She hardened her heart. A little light didn't mean anything. Caleb needed to go.

With one final deep breath for courage, Snow opened and stepped through her front door ready to be the shrew of all shrews. Except there was no one in sight. It wasn't as if her apartment was so big that Caleb could hide somewhere. His Jeep was outside, so he had to be here. The scent of something spicy and mouthwatering filled her senses, pulling Snow toward the kitchen.

Lifting the lid on the pot simmering on the stove, she couldn't believe her eyes. How did Caleb know how to make chicken and dumplings?

"Hattie sent that over," Caleb said, startling Snow into dropping the lid with a clang.

She looked up to find him standing in the doorway to her bedroom wearing nothing but a towel around his hips. Her heart rate skipped to double time as heat danced up her spine.

"You talked to Hattie?" she asked, struggling to keep her eyes above his chin.

"Spent the day with her," he said. Noticing he was dripping on the carpet, he added, "Hold on. I need another towel."

You need to get some freaking clothes on, Snow thought, leaning on the counter for support. Her knees didn't seem up to the task of keeping her upright. Closing her eyes tight, she mumbled, "I can do this. Just stay strong, Snow. Stay strong."

The words weren't really helping, but she repeated them silently all the same. Caleb emerged from the bedroom once again, this time with another towel around his neck that he was using to squeeze the water from his hair.

"That's an interesting landlady you have there," he said, crossing to the counter as if he weren't half-naked and they were some happily married couple who did this every day.

"Landlady?" Snow asked, her brain not functioning on all cylinders.

Caleb retrieved a glass from the second shelf. "Miss Hattie. The woman in the big house attached to this one?"

"Right," Snow said, stepping into the small living room in the hopes that more distance between them would cool her awakened libido. "Miss Hattie." The distance helped enough for his previous statement to sink in. "Wait. You spent the day with Miss Hattie?"

"Not voluntarily," he said, pouring himself a large glass of milk. "Not at first, anyway."

Snow removed her coat and threw it over the back of a chair. "Are you saying my landlady forced you to spend time with her? I find that hard to believe."

Hattie Silvester, as far as Snow knew, had little time or patience for the males of the species. Why Caleb, a complete stranger, would be an exception to the rule was beyond Snow. She could see a younger woman fawning over his pretty face, but not Miss Hattie.

"*Forced* isn't the word I'd use. More like . . . steamrolled." Caleb flexed his shoulders, which caused the towel to dip half an inch lower on his hips.

Snow's mouth went dry.

"She caught me in the driveway when I came back after dropping you off," he said, "and the next thing I knew, I was hauling paint cans and canvases up and down her stairs."

None of this was making sense. The part about Hattie steamrolling someone computed just fine, but Caleb? And him doing manual labor? There was no way. Then again, maybe if the man in her kitchen would put on some clothes, Snow could think straight.

"Did you tell her who you are?" Snow asked.

"About that," Caleb said after taking a drink of the milk. "We need to get this story straight. I don't like lying to people, especially not someone like the nice old lady next door."

Oh no. "What did you tell her?" Snow demanded, charging back into the kitchen.

"Relax," he said, setting his glass on the counter. "I said I was your fiancé, but then she asked since when. I panicked and said two weeks."

If he hadn't insisted they include the engagement part, the time frame wouldn't be an issue. "What did Hattie say?"

Caleb crossed his arms as he leaned a hip on the counter. "She did the math and assumed I'd asked you to marry me over the phone or e-mail."

"This is a complete mess," Snow said.

"I fixed it," he argued, holding his hands up in front of him. "I told her I hadn't done the official down-on-one-knee proposal thing yet because I don't have a ring."

Snow tapped her foot against the weight of mounting lies. The life she'd built was being twisted into some crazy work of fiction. How was she going to unravel all the lies after Caleb left? Would she even remember them all?

"You need to go," she said, panic fogging her brain. "This marriage is over."

Chapter 10

Caleb stepped toward his wife. "Excuse me?" he said, certain he'd heard her wrong.

"I can't do it," she said, her voice rising several octaves. "I can't keep pretending like this."

Making up a story had been her idea. He'd been willing to tell the truth, even knowing that he'd look like the hapless jerk who couldn't keep track of his own wife. Or that locals would assume he'd done something to send her running. What a few strangers thought of him didn't mean anything so long as he had Snow back where she belonged.

"We don't have to lie," he said, taking her by the arms. "Snow, baby, calm down. It's going to be all right."

"No, it isn't," Snow growled, pushing against his chest. "And I don't want to calm down. You can't charm us out of this mess."

Now he was really confused. "This isn't a mess," he said, determined to remain calm. "This is our marriage. We haven't done a great job of it so far, but we'll figure it out."

Snow stomped into the bedroom. "When is it going to sink into that thick skull of yours that I'm not right for you?" she asked, turning and throwing the jeans he'd left on the bed at his chest. "We're not *right* together. There's no fixing us, Caleb. There never should have been an us to begin with."

Ignoring the jeans that puddled onto the floor in front of him, Caleb kept his voice calm. "What happened to the Snow I left at the store this morning? Where is all this coming from?" He'd suspected there'd been more to his wife's leaving eighteen months ago than she'd admitted to so far. Now he was certain. "Help me understand what's going on."

Shaking her head, Snow said, "I keep messing up your life."

"No," he said, stepping over the jeans and taking her in his arms. "Don't say that."

"It's true," she mumbled with her face pressed against his chest. Her tears warm on his skin. "How do you not hate me?"

In their short time together, Snow had never struck him as emotionally erratic. They'd been back together less than twenty-four hours, and trying to follow her moods was like being stuck in a pinball machine. "Honey, I could never hate you."

"Oh, yes, you could," she said. "You have no idea what I'm capable of."

Pulling back far enough to look her in the eye, Caleb pressed damp curls away from her face and smiled. "I promise you, there is nothing you can do that will change how I feel about you. My being here right now should be proof of that."

Snow sniffled. "But you don't know everything."

He placed a kiss on her forehead, then one on each eyelid. "Whatever I don't know doesn't matter. We're going to be fine," he said, giving in to temptation and dropping kisses along her jawline.

"We aren't going to be fine," Snow said, even as she slid her hands into his hair. "We're prolonging the inevitable."

"You can say that until you're old and gray," he mumbled, rubbing his thumb along her bottom lip. Her full lips were one of the first things he'd noticed about his wife. Lips that were made for kissing. "But I'll still be right here."

To seal the promise, Caleb did what he'd been dying to do since he'd walked into her little shop on the corner the day before. He slid his lips across hers as his arms tightened around her tiny waist, lifting her off the floor. To his great relief, Snow welcomed the advance, wrapping her arms around his neck and kissing him back. Caleb had thought to go slow, to ease his way in and savor every second.

But Snow wasn't interested in slow and easy. She wrapped her legs around his hips, sending his towel to the floor as her mouth opened over his. She tasted like sugar and tea and he couldn't get enough. She flung the towel he'd draped around his neck to the floor and tightened her hold as Caleb took three steps and pressed her back against the wall.

When he deepened the kiss, Snow arched against him, a soft cry echoing around them. *This* was where they were good.

"Caleb, we can't," Snow said, pulling back and pushing against his shoulders. "This is wrong."

"There's nothing wrong about this," he said, nipping at her bottom lip.

Snow put two fingers over his mouth as she pressed her head back against the wall. "Please," she said, the desperation in her voice enough to drag him out of the fog. Her eyes were pleading as she said, "Don't make this harder than it already is."

He didn't know what she meant. Keeping his hands off of her was the hardest thing he'd ever done. "I want you, Snow. And I know you want me."

"We agreed," she said. "This isn't going to help us figure things out."

Caleb exhaled and let Snow's feet touch the floor. He was hard as a rock and letting her slide down his body wasn't helping him gain control.

"I need a minute," he said, his eyes closed as he stepped back to give her space to leave.

"Caleb," Snow said, her voice soft and apologetic. She waited for his eyes to open and meet hers before she said, "You'll understand this someday."

He didn't feel all that understanding at the moment. "I doubt it," he said, stepping into the bathroom and closing the door behind him.

Snow sat tucked into the corner of her couch, knees to her chest, staring at Caleb's boots by the door. The last ten minutes played through her mind over and over. She didn't even recognize the woman playing her part. The goal had been to make her husband want to leave, but without warning she'd shot right over to psycholand.

If he walked out of the bedroom carrying his bag and heading for the door, she would not be surprised. Part of her wanted to explain. To apologize, but for what? For screaming then crying then climbing him like a woman desperate for the last coconut on a deserted island? Caleb was right, she wanted him as much as he wanted her. And she'd almost given in.

She *still* wanted to give in. To kiss Caleb until he forgot how much she'd turned his life upside down. But they'd have to come up for air sometime. And her secret would still be there. The threat from his mother would still be hanging over her head. No matter what, Caleb could never learn the truth. Not because he'd never forgive her, but because she wouldn't hurt him like that.

It had been bad enough explaining everything to her mother, who was relieved to finally hear Snow's voice, but disappointed in the choices her daughter had made. Snow didn't tell her mother everything. She didn't want her to know about the tainted blood comment. Nor did she admit the messages her family had received in the last year and a half had come through Vivien.

The fewer people who knew that tidbit the better.

One thing was for certain. The idea of the one-month trial period would end tonight. Even Caleb wasn't optimistic enough to think anything could change between them now. If he chose to stay the night, Snow would sleep on the couch and try not to think about watching him drive off in the morning.

She was contemplating how little sleep she would get when Caleb stepped out of the bedroom. He was wearing gray sweatpants with a black T-shirt. His feet were bare and his hair still damp. Without a word, he sat down beside her on the couch.

"You okay?" he asked, which was the last thing Snow expected him to say.

"I'm not sure," she answered truthfully. She didn't know what end was up at this point. "I'm sorry," was the only thing she could think to say.

Caleb leaned forward with his elbows on his knees as he scrubbed his hands down his face. "What happened after I left you at the store this morning?" He turned her way, blue eyes intent. "We were good. Something changed that."

Snow yearned to tell him the truth, but while relieving her conscience would take the weight off her shoulders, knowing the truth would only hurt Caleb. Protecting him was the least she could do.

"I called my mom today," she said, wanting to tell him something. "She was pretty upset."

"You haven't called her all this time?" he asked. "I checked with her every month or so, and she said all she could tell me was that you were okay."

He'd called her mother every month. Snow couldn't believe he'd never given up.

"I sent messages through a friend." She shrugged, shame washing over her as she added, "I didn't want her to have to lie to you. If she didn't know where I was, then she didn't have to lie."

A tear slid down her cheek, but Snow ignored it. Why hadn't she recognized what she was doing by asking his own mother to lie to him? Snow had been so desperate to get away, she hadn't thought of anyone but herself.

To her surprise, Caleb leaned back and took her hand. "I need to understand why you ran away, Snow. Tell me what I did to make you go."

She squeezed his hand, unable to resist the source of strength. "I told you—"

"No," he cut her off. "Don't give me the not-compatible crap again. In the four months we were together, we never argued. If there was something wrong, you should have told me."

Pulling her hand from his, Snow shifted until she was facing him and tried to explain. "Caleb, life is one easy day after another for you, but that isn't reality. Not for all of us. If I had told you I had concerns, you would have said everything was fine. Brushed it off as nothing we couldn't deal with, but your idea of dealing with something is ignoring it."

Tilting his head back, Caleb spoke to the ceiling. "You really don't think much of me. It's a wonder you married me at all."

"You're a great guy, but—"

"But I'm a shallow jerk who never listens to you."

"That's not—"

"When?" he asked, draping an arm across the back of the couch. "When did you tell me you had concerns and I didn't listen?"

Snow racked her brain searching for an answer. In truth, she'd kept much of her thoughts to herself during their brief time together. "I said I was worried that the houses we were looking at were too much for us."

"And I said once we had kids, they wouldn't feel so big."

"But we never talked about kids."

"Of course we did," he said. "When we talked about the house."

Shaking her head, Snow said, "We didn't talk about the house either. You said we're going here and we'll have kids, but I never said anything. I didn't feel like I had a vote."

Caleb rubbed the stubble on his chin, looking as if she'd landed a right hook. "You don't want kids?"

"That's not what I'm saying." Snow closed her eyes and tried to find the right words. "I went from enjoying dating a new guy to being that guy's wife. It's a miracle we didn't both suffer whiplash from how fast things happened. Sneaking away wasn't the right way to handle the situation, but I was running on instinct, and all I knew was that I couldn't get my bearings and I couldn't stay."

"I never had any doubts," Caleb said. "I didn't think you did either."

With a sad sigh, she said, "I'm not sure *doubts* is the right word. We were still getting to know each other when we landed in Vegas. I never considered we'd come back married."

"You say that as if I dragged you to the chapel."

"I take full responsibility for getting caught up in the whirlwind and going along with it. It wasn't until the dust settled that I realized what we'd done. That's when the panic set in."

Rubbing the top of her knee, he said, "I'm sorry that you went through that alone. And that you thought I wouldn't listen to you."

In Snow's experience, men didn't apologize often. She was relieved to have her misgivings finally out in the open, and that Caleb understood that they'd made a mistake. This was the closure they needed.

"I'm sorry, too," she said, some of the suffocating weight she'd been carrying for so long lifting away.

"At least now we know what we need to do," Caleb said, taking this much better than she'd expected.

"Yes, we do." Finally, they were both on the same page.

"We have to go back to dating."

Snow threw her hands in the air, which Caleb fully expected.

"Hear me out," he said, leaning forward. "You're saying that since we cut to the chase too fast, we should call the whole thing off. But who's to say if we'd kept on dating for, say, six more months, that we wouldn't still be married right now?"

His wife didn't have a ready answer for that one.

"We can't go back and change what we did," he added, taking advantage of Snow's silence. "But we can go ahead and do the part we skipped."

Thin brows narrowed over her golden eyes. "You're trying to confuse me. Unless you have a time machine, we can't change anything."

"Not change," he clarified. "Think of it as completing the middle step."

She jerked back. "You're calling a do-over?"

It was Caleb's turn to throw his hands in the air. "I'm saying we go back to dating."

"But we're married," she argued. He wasn't sure if she was playing slow on purpose or trying to throw him off.

Regardless, he was certain this was the answer.

"Listen to what I'm saying." Caleb pressed a hand on each side of Snow's knees and held her gaze. "You said we went from newly dating to man and wife."

"Yes, we did. And that's why—"

He held up a hand. "Hold on. We can fix that by going back to dating."

"Meaning get a divorce and then date each other?"

Caleb smiled. "According to the people in this town, we aren't married."

Another furrowed brow. "Then you're suggesting we pretend we're not married, which is what we're already doing. Which means we have to lie to everyone."

"Look," he said, rising to his feet, "we both know that we could end this marriage with a couple signatures on a document and no one in this town would ever be the wiser. Add the fact that we've been apart a hell of a lot longer than we were ever together, and regardless of our legal situation, we aren't a married couple at all."

"I'm not sure," she said, "but I think you just agreed with what I've been saying for the last twenty-four hours."

"I do agree," Caleb said, watching suspicion cloud Snow's features. He was determined to make her see that they could still make this work. All they needed was a little time. "Right this minute, maybe we aren't two people who should be married. But," he added, "if we continue dating, picking up where we left off before the Vegas trip, we could get there."

"So we not only lie to other people, but lie to ourselves." Snow shook her head. "You're grasping at straws, Caleb."

Dropping onto the couch, he asked, "Before that trip to Vegas, did you want out?"

Her jaw tightened. "No."

"So you liked me?"

"Yes," she conceded, "but I'm struggling to remember why at the moment."

Twisting a curl around his finger, Caleb said, "I liked you, too. And I still do. Based on what just happened in the bedroom, I'd say we still have a spark."

Snow pushed his hand away and tucked the curl behind her ear. "We always had a spark, Caleb, but sexual chemistry isn't enough to build a marriage on."

"We have more than that, and you know it. This morning, after the auction, you felt it, too." Caleb took her hand in his. "Let me remind you, Snow. Let's see what would have happened if we'd never boarded that plane."

She didn't look happy, and she sure didn't look like a woman about to change her mind. But then she shook her head. "I knew this was going to happen."

"Is that a yes?" he asked, hope filling his chest.

"We go back to dating. We talk about kids and life and where we each see our lives going, as if we never took those vows," she said. "Are you sure that's what you want?"

"Yes," he answered, feeling the sweet thrill of victory.

"But what if we don't see our lives going in the same direction? Are you prepared for *that*?"

He wanted to tell her that of course they'd see things the same, but that would mean he really was the guy she'd described. The one who didn't listen and dished out platitudes that meant nothing. Though the words tasted bitter on his tongue, Caleb said, "If we don't see our lives running together, then we'll go our separate ways. That's the deal."

As she had that morning, Snow visibly relaxed. The girl he'd whisked off to Vegas was back.

"Okay, then," she said with a nod, "we're back to dating. But there's one issue."

After gaining so much ground, Caleb didn't like the step back. "What's that?"

"We weren't living together before we left for Vegas."

"Right," he agreed. This was a bump he hadn't seen coming. "But we were spending so much time together that we were *practically* living together."

Snow hemmed and hawed over that statement for several seconds. "I suppose it would look odd to the locals for me to bring you here on the premise of getting engaged, but then make you stay in a hotel or something."

"Considering you left with no warning, sent me on a wild-goose chase, and then dragged me up to this hole-in-the-wall town to find you?" he said. "A little room and board is the least you can do."

"Hey, now," Snow said. "We're pretending none of that happened, remember?"

"Now who's looking for a do-over?" he asked with a smile, happy to be standing on lighter ground. "As of right now, we're a couple who really like each other, who've been conducting a long-distance relationship." Holding up one finger, he added, "Which is technically true."

Snow picked up the story. "But now we're considering something more permanent, and you've come to live with me so we can see if we really are cut out for each other."

"Again, all true," he said. And if they were still in the considering stage, he could keep the ring to himself until the time was right. Snow deserved a real proposal. A story she could tell their children someday that was more than them sitting on a couch after a fight and him sliding a ring on her finger for looks alone.

Brushing his damp hair off his forehead, Snow said, "Then I guess we have a plan." She still looked like a woman waiting for the sky to fall, but at least she wasn't demanding he get out. "Now, are those dumplings as good as they smell?"

A smile split his face as a warmth spread through his chest. "I was waiting for you to get here to find out."

"I'll get the bowls," she said, hopping off the couch.

Caleb watched his wife go through the motions of dishing up their dinner, her moves graceful and compact. Tonight had been a close call. If he wasn't careful, Caleb would find himself eating crow and having to admit that his parents were right. That he was a spontaneous fool who leapt before thinking.

Going forward, Caleb would make sure he listened to everything Snow had to say. Though he had a funny feeling that picking up on what she *didn't* say would be the real challenge.

After dinner, during which she'd managed to stay relaxed through sheer force of will, Snow slid off to the bathroom for a long, hot bath. Caleb's determination was hard to resist. He'd said, in no uncertain terms, that there was nothing that would make him change his mind about wanting to be with her. Short of her carrying another man's child, of course. Which was crazy. At least she hadn't screwed her life up *that* bad.

They'd been crazy for each other before the trip to Las Vegas. And though she'd blamed her spontaneous marriage on mind-numbing lust, the truth was she had liked him. Liked Caleb, the man. The guy who surprised her with flowers for no reason. The one who gave the most amazing foot massages and listened to her talk about her day as if he really cared.

He'd been dependable, coming to her rescue when her car got a flat. And the time she'd tried to make him Granny's fried chicken and started a fire. Her then-boyfriend had known exactly what to do, bounding into action and saving the day.

It seemed Caleb was always saving the day for her. And now he was determined to save their marriage by offering to date her. The truth was, he was offering to court her. To earn the vow she'd made to love and cherish him 'til death did they part. What woman would turn down a man willing to go to such extremes to get something he legally already had?

A woman who cared enough about him to let him go.

Nothing would change with a few dates. The holiday season was coming, and Snow would be busy. So she'd play along, biding her time until he finally admitted the truth. And then she would send him home to his mother and sign when the papers arrived.

Chapter 11

Caleb parked along the curb in front of the address Hattie had given him, not sure what to expect. A one-level, white stone building bore the words THE ARDENT ADVOCATE etched into the thick glass insert in its front door. Seemed like a solid name for a town paper.

"Welcome to the *Advocate*," said a guy in a black polo strolling past the office foyer. "Someone will be with you in just a minute." The man proceeded to disappear down the hall to Caleb's right.

For some unknown reason, Caleb was nervous. He knew everything about the newspaper business except writing the actual stories. He understood circulation, layout, and had assisted in creating an online presence for two of his father's papers. The only reason he didn't work for his father full-time was because that was exactly what his father wanted.

Jackson McGraw expected his son to live under his thumb, follow his orders, and be groomed as his successor. Only Caleb knew that the life his father envisioned would be hell.

Jackson, barely fifty years old, maintained his health meticulously. The man would likely remain at the helm of McGraw Media for another thirty years. If Caleb ever had designs on taking over, he'd have to pry the company from his father's cold, dead hands. For him, the prize wasn't worth the price.

Unfortunately, he had yet to find an alternative to his father's plan, which infuriated the elder McGraw to no end. And was apparently an issue for his wife, as well.

A door near the window was open, and a female voice filled the tiny space, yelling, "Son of a biscuit eater!" The outburst was followed by a loud bang and the words, "Stupid drawer."

Caleb stepped closer to the window, not sure how to proceed. A glance to his left revealed a long, empty hallway with Hattie nowhere in sight. Not that he even knew if Hattie had intended to be here.

"Hello?" he said through the open window. "Is this the newspaper office?"

"Well, it ain't NASA," replied the brunette rubbing her knee. Then she looked up, and her brown eyes went wide. "Hellooo, sailor," the middle-aged woman drawled. "What have we here?"

Caleb honestly couldn't tell if the question had been posed to him or not. "Hattie Silvester told me to be here at nine this morning, but she didn't give me a name for who I'm supposed to meet."

The office lady's jaw dropped. "You're Hattie's boy?"

"Uh . . ." Caleb hedged. "No. I just met her yesterday. She seemed like a nice lady, but if she's senile and this is all a joke—"

"Miss Hattie called this morning and said she was sending a nice boy over to see Wally. Honey child," she added, her voice dropping low as she stepped up to the open doorway, "you are not what I expected."

And this entire encounter was not what Caleb expected. "Did you say Wally?"

As the woman stared at his shoulders as if sizing up their load-bearing capacity, Caleb guessed her to be in her upper forties, maybe.

He'd never been much good at guessing women's ages. Her dark hair was piled high on her head, but several pieces had come loose to dangle around a pretty face that sported a hefty layer of makeup.

She swiped away a strand that had slipped over her brown eyes and smiled with a mouthful of straight, white teeth. The belted flannel shirt covering her floor-length red dress accentuated an hourglass figure, but the look in her eyes gave him pause. He'd avoided enough man-eaters in Nashville to recognize a leader of the pack when he saw one.

"I'm Piper," she said, "Piper Griffin." The hand she extended was turned palm down, as if she expected him to kiss her knuckles. Caleb gave it a quick shake.

"Can you tell this Wally person that I'm here?"

"Of course," she answered, then mumbled, "God bless Miss Hattie."

Caleb was used to women having a positive reaction to making his acquaintance, but he'd never felt as much like a side of beef as he did in that moment. Hopefully, whatever Hattie sent him here to do would not require further interactions with Piper Griffin.

Snow opened the store Monday morning with heavy resignation. All she had to do was endure the next few weeks, if it took that long, being friendly enough to make it look as if she were making a real effort, while highlighting all the reasons that she and Caleb should go their separate ways. She would also have to resist a full-out wooing from a man who had the unnerving habit of making her forget all of those reasons.

In fact, this morning, she wasn't sure she could come up with a list of five. But then Snow didn't need a list. Vivien McGraw had made sure of that.

After their talk the night before, Snow had worried that Caleb might once again try to eliminate the no sex agreement, but he'd surprised her by not even bringing it up. In truth, she'd been a tiny bit disappointed that he hadn't at least tried to kiss her again. When they'd been dating, rare was the night that didn't include a passionate interlude. But then, Snow reminded herself, this was what she wanted. No sex to cloud her judgment.

When she'd woken in Caleb's arms with something poking her backside, she'd been half tempted to roll over and break her own rule. But Caleb respected their deal, dropping a kiss on her temple and padding into the bathroom. Snow had cursed herself and her stupid ideas, spending her last few minutes in bed thinking about anything other than the virile man currently portraying a saint in her powder room.

"Based on that look," Lorelei said, walking up to the counter, "you either came to your senses and got lucky, or you didn't and have resorted to naughty-smile-inducing fantasies."

"Is your love life so boring that you have to live vicariously through mine?" Snow asked. "If so, I feel sorry for you."

Lorelei chuckled. "Don't feel sorry for me, girlfriend. Spencer is determined to show me all that we missed out on during our twelve years apart." Her eyes took on a far-away look. "What that man can do in a shower should be an Olympic sport."

Snow would never be able to look Spencer in the eye again. "I give," she said. "No, I did not get lucky. Yes, I was thinking about it. End of conversation."

Following her Monday morning routine, Lorelei proceeded to set out her newest batch of sugary goodness. "At least you're entertaining the notion, which is more than you seemed willing to do yesterday. What changed?"

Embarrassed by her erratic behavior, Snow kept the details to a minimum. "I had a bit of a meltdown," she said, slipping around the counter to help Lorelei set up. "Two days ago I had this nice little life I'd created for myself. I had no past, and definitely no dark secrets for the gossip lines. Then Caleb strolled into town and *boom*. Reality hit like a freight train."

"You can never outrun your past," Lorelei said, arranging slices of nut bread on a round platter, then placing a glass dome over them. "Trust me, I tried."

Lorelei was proof that a woman's past could be overcome. Or at least not stand in the way of future happiness.

"How did you do it?" she asked. Snow had witnessed Lorelei's triumph over the town that had branded her persona non grata once upon a time, but didn't know how exactly she and Spencer had found their way back to each other. Snow had never mustered up the nerve to ask about the intimate details.

Lorelei moved on to arranging gingersnaps. "In our case, I was the problem. I'd always had a chip on my shoulder, and when I came back from LA, my self-esteem was in the crapper, to put it mildly." The cinnamon wafers were pushed to one side to make room for the sugar cookies. "I don't think Spencer and I are unique. You have to fight and talk and fight some more. In the end, he stood by me, and that woke me up."

Snow didn't know what to say. Part of her felt bad for prying into her still-new friend's personal life, while another lamented the fact that Lorelei's explanation didn't help her own situation in the least. She and Caleb were from different worlds, whereas Spencer and Lorelei had very similar experiences. And knowing that she wasn't the wife he needed had nothing to do with Snow's self-esteem. Theirs were more circumstantial problems, not emotional roadblocks.

"Do you love him?" Lorelei asked, taking Snow by surprise. They'd thrown the L-word around during their brief marriage, but Snow was never sure if she was saying it because she meant it, or out of obligation. Married couples were supposed to say "I love you," right?

The realization hit that in all his pleading and negotiating, Caleb hadn't uttered the four-letter word even once.

Wanting to be honest, with Lorelei and with herself, Snow said, "I care about him. I think, before I left, that I was falling for him."

"Whoa." Lorelei set her sheet of cookies on the counter behind them. "You married a guy without knowing if you loved him?"

"I told you," Snow said, feeling defensive, "we got married in Vegas. It wasn't planned, and we sure as heck didn't put much thought into it."

"Getting married isn't about thought, it's about feelings."

Grabbing a handful of chocolate chip cookies, Snow returned to the dessert display. "You sound like a greeting card."

"And you're dodging the issue." Lorelei put her hand on Snow's wrist and waited for her to make eye contact. "Do you *love* him?"

Buying time, Snow arranged the cookies, and then she stepped back, brushing the crumbs from her fingers. "The truth is, I've spent eighteen months trying *not* to love him. It's taken him less than forty-eight hours to undo all my hard work."

This was a confession Snow neither liked nor had intended to say aloud. If anything, admitting this particular truth was the most danger-ous thing she could do. Not saying the words meant she could pretend her heart could still be saved.

"Oh, sweetie." Lorelei put her arm around Snow's shoulders. "If it makes you feel any better, I had twelve years to get over Spencer, and you see how well that worked out."

"Has anyone told you that you suck at this sort of thing?" Snow asked, desperate to lighten the mood. Lorelei squeezed her shoulders tighter before returning to the treats. "We did have a good talk last night," Snow said. "We came to an agreement about how to proceed."

"Good for you," Lorelei said. "I'm still deep enough in the mushy-love stage to want everyone to be as happy as I am."

"I didn't say we agreed to stay together," Snow clarified. "Caleb has this crazy idea that we can fix all our problems, or at least get around my misgivings about our marriage, by going back to dating."

"Now you lost me." A cookie broke in Lorelei's hand, and she said, "Oh darn. Now I'll have to eat this one." She held out half to Snow.

"If we must." Snow couldn't turn down even a piece of a Lulu's Home Bakery cookie. "He lost me, too, when he made the suggestion, but it kind of makes sense. We dated for two months and found ourselves married. Before we call the whole thing off, Caleb suggested we pick up where we left off before that ill-advised trip to Vegas. Since no one in town knows we're actually married, besides you and Spencer, we can return to dating and see how things go."

"Isn't that called a do-over?"

"Yes, but considering how crazy the rest of our relationship has been, I agreed to give it a try. Or pretend to, anyway."

"So no matter what happens in the next few weeks, you won't change your mind and stay with him?" Lorelei asked.

Vivien's threat loomed in the air like an ax about to drop.

"I won't change my mind," Snow said. She couldn't, even if she wanted to.

"I would call you stubborn, but that would make me the pot and you the kettle, I suppose," Lorelei said, winning points in the support area. "So what's he doing today, anyway? I half expected him to be here with you."

"He's doing something for Miss Hattie," Snow said, still confused that the older woman had Caleb taking orders. "She caught him lingering around the house yesterday and put him to work." Caleb hadn't said exactly what he'd be doing today, but Snow assumed he probably wouldn't know until he reported for duty.

"Is she still as eccentric as she used to be?" Lorelei asked. "When I was a teenager, she scared the bejeebers out of me. And that's saying something, since I fancied myself the ultimate rebel-without-a-clue."

Snow didn't know what kind of person Miss Hattie had been during Lorelei's youth, but she liked what she knew of her now. "Colorful clothes. Never wears a bra. Big sunglasses with straight-brimmed ball caps. She's never been anything but sweet to me," Snow added. "I like her."

"I only ever saw her at church," Lorelei said, placing the last of the pumpkin bread on the display platter. "Her sweater sets were more colorful than most of the other ladies, but ball caps were never part of the ensemble. I remember her mouth looking pinched, as if she'd sucked a lemon seconds before sliding into the Silvester pew. And she always sat alone. I kind of felt bad for her back then."

If there was one thing Miss Hattie would not tolerate, it was anyone's pity. Snow didn't need to know the woman for decades to be certain of that. "She's blunt, but kind. She has a dry sense of humor. I think you'd like her."

"But would she like me is the question."

Maybe Lorelei still held some lingering insecurities where the Ardent Springs community was concerned.

Wadding up the plastic wrap that had covered the cookie tray, Snow said, "She'd *love* you."

Lorelei smiled. "If she keeps that man of yours out of your way, I say we give her free cookies for a year."

Chapter 12

In complete contrast to Piper Griffin's overzealous welcome, Wally Dupuis greeted Caleb with the warmth of a New England flagpole in mid-January. At first, Caleb feared he might have unwittingly stepped in something based on Mr. Dupius's facial expression upon first meeting. Yet after several minutes in the man's presence without a shift in the puckered lip and pulled brow, Caleb concluded this must be his interviewer's normal look.

And it hadn't taken long to realize he was, indeed, in the midst of an interview. With tiny round glasses perched on the end of his bulbous nose, the newspaper's managing editor, as was proclaimed across his office door, fired off the typical interview questions, until Caleb interrupted him.

"If you don't mind my asking," Caleb said, leaning forward in his chair, "why exactly am I here?"

Bushy gray brows drew together. "You don't know what job you're applying for?"

The tone of the question set Caleb on edge. "I helped Miss Hattie around her house yesterday afternoon, and she asked me to report to this address at nine this morning. That's the extent of my knowledge."

Wally sat back, his expression relaxing into something less . . . offended. "I should have known," he said, sliding the glasses up a long forehead to perch atop his nearly bald head. "Hattie didn't tell you anything about why she sent you?"

Caleb shook his head. "Afraid not."

"That woman should come with a warning." The reading glasses hit the desktop. "We're looking for a salesman, Mr. McGraw. Do you know anything about selling advertising?"

Though he'd worked the numbers, knew the sales structure and terminology, Caleb had never actually worked in the sales department of any of his father's papers. He'd been groomed as future owner and leader, not the man on the ground shaking hands and making deals. Still, that didn't mean he couldn't do the job.

"I know about points, and how to calculate column inches. I'm sure you have a reference available with a breakdown of your basic pricing structure. Do you have a graphic artist on staff, or are customers required to submit their own artwork?"

"That's more than most strangers off the street walk in knowing, Mr. McGraw. Seems odd that a minute ago you were clueless and now you're talking pricing structure."

With a smile, Caleb said, "I never claimed to be clueless about the business. I simply didn't know if Miss Hattie sent me here to deliver papers, scrub the floors, or write up obituaries. She only asked if I knew anything about newspapers. When I said I did, that seemed to be enough for her to send me here."

Wally rocked back in his chair. "Where did you learn about newspapers?"

If Dupuis didn't make the connection between his last name and McGraw Media, Caleb didn't see the need to enlighten him. For once, he would land a job on his own merit, and not due to the power behind his name.

"Did some internships in college," he answered. "My experience is more on the financial side, but I had to understand the sales department to analyze the numbers."

Caleb heard the words come out of his mouth, all of which were true, but he wondered why he was bothering. Since when did he want to work in sales? He'd set out to get a job in town to make Snow happy. To prove he could be focused and useful, and selling ads did sound better than slinging a hammer, but Caleb had made a concerted effort to avoid working in the newspaper industry. He'd turned down every job his father offered, determined to find his own path.

This little windowless office stood as one of the many indicators that the *Ardent Advocate* was in no way competing on a mass-media scale. Working construction would have been temporary. What was wrong with selling ads instead? A hint of guilt entered the equation at the idea of taking an offered job with the intent to resign in a matter of weeks.

Caleb could see the wheels turning in the man's head as Wally tapped a pen on his blotter. But were they turning in his direction? "The position would pay a base salary plus commission to start." That answered that. "You'd shadow Gerald for the first couple weeks before we send you out alone."

The men Caleb had dealt with through his father wore suits that cost more than Mr. Dupuis likely made in a month. And he'd held his own with all of them. Handling a few local business owners should be no problem at all. Still, to appease his conscience, Caleb said, "How about a trial period? You see what I can do, and I decide if selling ads is something I want to do."

Not that he doubted Dupuis would be more than happy with his performance at the end of the trial, but this left Caleb an opening to walk away knowing he was honest from the beginning. Mostly.

"Well," Wally said, "you already have the owner's approval, so now it's a simple matter of paperwork."

He'd met the owner? Caleb shuffled through his morning and cringed. Piper Griffin owned the paper? "I didn't realize when I met her that she was the owner of the place."

Exiting his chair, the editor motioned for Caleb to precede him into the hall. "Hattie's family started this paper back in 1927. I'm surprised she didn't tell you."

Hattie? The eccentric old lady with the cat paintings and wild clothes owned a newspaper?

"Not knowing why you were here explains the jeans," Wally continued as they strolled down the hall toward the front office Piper had occupied. "You won't need a suit and tie, but khakis and a polo shirt is sort of the uniform for the sales team. Though *team* is a bit of an exaggeration. Gerald and Piper handle all the selling, and with Gerald retiring at the end of the year, you can see why we're in a pinch to fill the spot."

Caleb filed the issue of working on a team with Piper to focus on the bigger problem. The paper needed a permanent replacement for this Gerald person. There was nothing permanent about Caleb and Ardent Springs. "About the trial period—"

"No worries," Wally said, stepping into the office across from the building entrance. "We'll give it a shot, and if it doesn't work out, no hard feelings. Eleanor," he said, turning to a woman behind the desk, drawing Caleb's attention to the stranger in the room, "Mr. McGraw here needs to fill out an application and a new hire package. He'll be working with Gerald for the next couple weeks to learn how things run around here."

"Bless your heart," the stranger said, flashing a sympathetic smile as she glanced over the cat-eye glasses perched on the bridge of her nose. "You're a daring soul."

Not the "welcome to the company" he was expecting.

"Let's not scare him off on the first day." Wally slid his hands into his pockets, which emphasized his protruding middle. "Gerald Nichols has been with the *Ardent Advocate* since 1960. There isn't a person in this town he doesn't know. He either went to school with them, coached them in Little League, or attended their baptism as an honorary grandparent. Since selling is all about relationships, that makes him the best around."

"He's also the crankiest SOB this side of the Mississippi," Eleanor said. "And that nicotine gum isn't doing squat to soften his disposition."

Rolling his eyes, Wally sighed. "Gerald's a longtime smoker. His wife, Dolly, finally had enough and said it was her or the cigarettes, so he's trying to quit. It's been a transition for all of us."

If Caleb wanted to spend his days with a hateful old man, he'd go to work for his father. "Are you sure—"

"Gerald is a great guy," Wally said, cutting him off again. "Everybody loves him. You'll be fine." Moving faster than he had since Caleb met him, the editor shuffled out of the room. "Eleanor, you can take it from here."

The blonde stuck a pencil in her hair bun as she rolled to a file cabinet behind her and withdrew a long manila folder. "You will be fine," she said. "Really. Have you ever worked in sales before? You can't be but twenty-five or so. You fresh out of college? Though if you are, I don't know what you're doing in this little town of ours. What brought you to Ardent Springs, sugar?"

Caleb didn't know which question to answer first, so he took them in order. "No, I've never worked in sales, and I'll be twenty-nine this month. Not fresh out of college." He ignored the final question.

"Oh," Eleanor said, her moment of supportive enthusiasm wavering. Her voice dropped to a whisper as she leaned his way. "Not that I condone fibbing, but in this case, I highly suggest you not tell Gerald that. He'll chew you up and spit you out if you do. Use that pretty face of yours to charm the customers and he won't be any the wiser."

This was not how Caleb imagined his day would go when he'd parked in front of 121 Second Avenue North. Pride alone kept him from walking out the door without looking back. He didn't need some old codger making his life miserable, but he'd taken the job now. Quitting before he'd gone on his first sales call would be the cowardly thing to do. And Caleb was no coward.

As Eleanor showed him to an empty desk in the back corner of the office, which was really two offices combined, a deep voice echoed from somewhere down the hall.

"Who washed my goddamn coffee cup?"

Handing him a pen, Eleanor said, "And that's another thing. Don't ever wash Gerald's coffee cup. He doesn't like that."

Great, Caleb thought. What the hell had he gotten himself into?

By noon Snow had scheduled a consultation with an art dealer out of Nashville, who sounded skeptical about the authenticity of her painting, but she'd agreed to travel to Ardent Springs to see this miracle find for herself. She'd also answered two inquiries about the handsome man who'd accompanied her to the auction the day before.

Social media had nothing on small-town gossip lines. Busybodies had been passing along rumors and conjecture far and wide long before the term *going viral* was even a concept. Snow usually observed the speed with which news spread in her adopted town with rapt fascination, until the news involved her personal life.

Now this small-town quirk didn't seem so quaint.

Nitzi Merchant had been the first to ask, when she'd stopped in to put her new bits of lace for sale in her booth. The doilies were priced at more than they were worth, but Snow knew full well that Nitzi always started high before making drastic price cuts, which led the customers to feel as if they were getting a deal. The practice was as old as time, and Nitzi knew how to make it work in her favor.

To Snow's surprise, the second inquiry had come from Priscilla Winkle. The first lady of Ardent Springs didn't have much time for Snow after she'd befriended Lorelei Pratchett, against whom the Winkles had waged some kind of personal vendetta. Priscilla's daughter, Becky, was best described as Lorelei's arch-nemesis, but Snow had never liked the snarky blonde with the bouffant hair.

When Mrs. Winkle had approached Snow near a stack of vintage suitcases she'd been straightening and asked whom she'd been with at the auction, the woman's tone implied that said man might be new meat for the local marriage market, and therefore her daughter's next matrimonial victim.

"He's my fiancé," Snow had informed her. "We've been in a long-distance relationship for a while and have decided to take things to the next level."

Though she'd been reluctant to use the engagement element, seeing Priscilla's dull blue eyes go wide with surprise made Snow feel as if she'd won a contest. The conversation hadn't proceeded far beyond that point, as Mrs. Winkle lost interest the moment she heard Caleb would not be courting her daughter.

It wasn't until she'd finished her peanut butter and jelly sandwich that Snow experienced her third surprise encounter of the day, when Piper Griffin blew into the shop for their regular Monday meeting.

Piper was Snow's sales rep from the *Ardent Advocate*. The middle-aged brunette dressed too young for her age, wore enough perfume to gag a moose, and could sell space heaters in the Bahamas. She'd been harassing Snow to increase her ad budget for three months.

If the painting turned out to be authentic and worth as much as Snow hoped, Piper might get her way.

"Am I glad Halloween is over," Piper said, sliding behind the counter and lifting a plateful of cookies from a lower shelf. They'd made a deal long ago that Snow would always put a select number of cookies aside for these visits, since Lorelei's goodies rarely lasted past lunchtime. "Now we can get on with my favorite time of year." Piper popped a piece of gingersnap between her deep-red lips and talked around the morsel. "The Christmas shopping season."

Snow noticed that Piper did not state that *Christmas* was her favorite time of year. So much for the reason for the season.

"We're still weeks away from Thanksgiving," Snow reminded her rep. She wouldn't exactly call them friends, since Piper was only interested in the commission she could make off Snow's advertising, but they did speak at social functions, on the rare occasion they crossed paths. So she was at least a friendly acquaintance.

"Pish posh." Piper shooed the facts away. "I've bought four presents already, and if you don't want people taking their business online, you need to remind them why they should shop local."

And how she should do that was to buy a bigger ad. "Are you doing the Buy Local promotion again? That did well last Christmas."

The paper had created a full-page ad the previous year dedicated to encouraging readers to invest their hard-earned money into local businesses, instead of driving down to Nashville to hit the big stores, or making the majority of their purchases on the Internet. Each local business had the opportunity to contribute a relatively small amount to be included in the promotion.

Piper finished off a chocolate chip cookie before responding. "We're definitely doing that again, but it's going to take more than your name included in a mass ad to let our readers know of the treasures you have here." The empty plate returned to the shelf as Piper added, "You've got one-of-a-kind stuff in this place, Snow. And a much bigger inventory than you had this time last year. People need to know that."

Snow supposed she was right. Though the shop benefited from its central location on the corner of a major downtown intersection not far from the town square, which, ironically, was round, there was less foot traffic in the winter. Buyers needed a reason to visit the store.

On a sigh, Snow said, "Why don't you draw me up some sort of Christmas marketing plan and we can talk about it."

Pausing in brushing crumbs from her cleavage, Piper looked up. "Are you serious?"

With a nod, Snow said, "I am. I'm not promising I'll spend a lot, but you're right. I need to advertise more, especially this time of year."

"Brilliant!" Piper exclaimed, throwing her arms in the air. "I'll have a full plan drawn up for our meeting next week."

Snow had half expected the saleswoman to demand they sit down and work something up right then. "Oh," she said. "Okay. I look forward to seeing what you come up with."

"You're going to love it. Now I have to get back to the office." The flamboyant woman shifted her abundant hips through a narrow opening between two large displays. "A new guy started at the paper this morning, and he is delicious." She glanced at her phone. "He's following Gerald around, and that means they'll do a midday check-in within fifteen minutes. Bless that old man's heart, you could set your watch by his schedule."

This sounded like good news to Snow. Another new arrival might take the gossip heat off of her and Caleb.

"A new guy as in a new hire, or new to town?" she asked, hoping it was the latter.

Piper tapped her chin. "I've never seen him before, so I'm thinking new to town, but I didn't get as much time with him as I wanted. He's young, tall, and hot as all get-out," she said. Piper wiggled her brows. "And no wedding ring. That means he's fair game."

A trickle of concern danced along Snow's spine. That description matched her husband to a tee, but then young, tall, and hot weren't exactly specifics.

"How was he dressed?" Snow asked, hoping against hope the answer would not be jeans and a red button-up shirt.

Warming to her topic, Piper said, "Oh, honey, let me tell you. The boy fills out a pair of jeans like he was born to wear them. I made sure I got a good look, and I'd bet my best push-up bra that you could bounce a quarter off those cheeks, and I don't mean the ones above his neck. The red button-down was simple enough, but accentuated those broad shoulders to the point that I nearly wept." With a wink, she added, "If I have my way, that boy will be the present under my tree, and wearing nothing but a red bow I plan to untie *real slow*."

Snow was too stunned to say any of the million things running through her mind. A wave of jealousy smacked her like a bucket of ice water, while anger bubbled up over Caleb not telling her he was taking a job with the local paper. He hadn't even mentioned the newspaper.

Was he planning to surprise her? *"Hi, honey, I'm home. Guess what I did today? I got a job!"*

And was Snow supposed to be happy? Relieved? Proud of her ultra-rich husband sinking low enough to take a salesman position with a paper that would be a joke in his father's media conglomerate world?

She was torn between ripping Piper's eyes out for fantasizing about her man, and the urge to follow Piper back to the paper and order her husband to go home.

As Snow stewed, Piper stepped through the front door into the November sunshine, yelling, "See you next week!" She was off to see her client's tall and hunky husband, who had apparently failed to mention he had a wife. Or a fiancée, rather, since they were keeping the wife thing a secret. For now.

In that moment, Snow wanted nothing more than to claim Caleb as her own. To make sure every woman within a hundred miles knew the gorgeous man with the tight jeans and blazing blue eyes was very much *off*-limits.

Instead, she went back to straightening her suitcases and simmered, grinding her jaw tight enough to rub her teeth to dust. Mr. McGraw would have some serious explaining to do to Mrs. McGraw this evening.

Chapter 13

By three in the afternoon, Caleb was in dire need of a shower, and he never wanted to see a cup of coffee again in his life. He'd witnessed Gerald Nichols drink from some of the nastiest cups on the planet. At one tire joint in town, the sales manager pulled a used paper cup from the bottom drawer of an old metal desk and proceeded to fill it with what could best be described as black sludge. Then he drank the concoction without so much as an eye twitch.

Of course, a man who smoked as much as Gerald probably didn't have any taste buds left. Hence, Caleb's need for a shower. He smelled as if he'd been stuck in a chimney for a week.

They'd been on the road all day, with one brief stop at the office for lunch. A meal that consisted of Gerald putting down his cigarette long enough to chow down a roast beef sandwich he'd brought from home, and Caleb attempting to keep at least three feet between himself and Piper Griffin. He'd swear the woman had four hands. When he couldn't scoot his chair over any more without putting himself into the hallway, Caleb mentioned that he couldn't wait to get home and tell his fiancée all about his new job.

That seemed to slow Piper's attack, but not end it. She dropped the not-so-subtle hint that a man was free until the vows were spoken, and it had taken everything Caleb had not to confess the truth right then and there.

"That was our last call of the day," Gerald said, as the pair climbed into his white 2000 Buick. Caleb wondered if the interior had been black upon purchase, or if all the smoke accumulated over fifteen years had turned it that way.

The last call had been with an insurance agent more interested in talking about sports than advertising. Caleb's new mentor had convinced his client to double his holiday ad spending from the previous year. Insurance wasn't exactly the type of business that experienced a boom from Christmas shopping, but that hadn't stopped Gerald.

The man might be as old as dirt, smoke two packs a day, and drink the most disgusting coffee ever brewed, but he knew how to sell advertising.

"Do you typically visit five clients a day?" Caleb asked, adding to the mental notes he'd been taking. "How far in advance do you set up these appointments?"

Gerald shook his head after lighting another cigarette. "I see the same clients on the same days at the same time every week. There is no appointment setting."

He'd heard of a stringent schedule, but this seemed extreme. "What about new clients?"

The driver turned to blow smoke out the window before answering. "In case you haven't noticed, Ardent Springs isn't very big. The concept of new clients doesn't come into play much." Asking his first somewhat personal question of the day, Gerald said, "How long have you been here?"

"Since Saturday afternoon," Caleb answered. "I came to live with my fiancée." When he'd mentioned the word during lunch, Gerald didn't seem to notice.

"I thought you were making that up to get Piper off your tail," he said, revealing the older man paid more attention than he let on.

Caleb shook his head as he leaned toward his open window, desperate for clean air. "No, I was serious. We haven't made it official, with rings and all, but Snow and I are together."

Gray brows shot up a long forehead. "Snow of Snow's Curiosity Shop?"

With such an unusual name, Caleb would have thought the answer was obvious. "One and the same."

A low chuckle filled the car. "That should make your life interesting."

"How so?" Caleb asked, curious what Gerald Nichols might know about his wife.

Tipping his ashes out the window, Gerald gave Caleb a bright, denture-perfect smile. "Snow is Piper's client. I believe they have a standing Monday visit."

Caleb hadn't told Piper who his fiancée was, and he hadn't told Snow he was taking a job at the paper. Mostly because he wasn't aware of the fact himself when he'd left the house this morning.

"Do you think . . . ?"

"Oh, I'm sure of it," Gerald said, looking more entertained than he had all day. "If I know Piper, and I should since I've worked with her for fifteen years, you might want to pick up flowers on your way home."

"Right," Caleb said. "I might do that."

Snow's afternoon had bounced between fleeting images of Piper Griffin bouncing spare change off her husband's bottom, and a nearly uncontrollable urge to call said husband and tell him exactly what she thought of his new situation. The biggest thing keeping her from making the phone call was the fact that Snow had no idea how she felt about anything at the moment.

The day had started well enough. She had a plan. Her life would be back to normal before Christmas. But then Snow had learned that Caleb spent the day putting lusty fantasies into the minds of who knew how many Ardent Springs residents of the female persuasion. A revelation that turned Snow a shade of green she neither welcomed nor liked to acknowledge.

But dammit, she was jealous.

This was her husband's fault. Not that she ever truly forgot his physical attributes, but he'd made her like him as a person. To appreciate his strength, sense of humor, and gentle nature. If he were nothing more than a pretty face, she wouldn't be wanting to punch Piper Griffin in the throat right now.

Oh, yes. Caleb was definitely to blame.

Arriving home at the end of her day, she was prepared to let her husband have the full brunt of her disapproval, until she entered the apartment and the scent of fried chicken filled her senses. Not just any fried chicken, but Granny's fried chicken.

This meal could not have come from Miss Hattie.

"Am I smelling what I think I'm smelling?" Snow asked, dropping her purse into a chair and then tossing her coat over the back. "There's no way you've made Granny's fried chicken." Even as she said the words, Snow's mouth watered.

"Hey there," Caleb said, turning from the stove and dropping a kiss on Snow's cheek. He was wearing the frilly yellow apron that had been hanging on the pantry door when Snow moved in. The man was wearing a freaking apron. "I doubt it's as good as the real thing," he said, "but I followed the recipe exactly. So you think it smells like your granny's version?"

Smelled like it. Looked like it. If it tasted like it, Snow would happily renew their vows tomorrow.

"But how . . ."

Caleb placed a juicy-looking drumstick on a plate next to a mound of green beans and a large helping of mashed potatoes. "I called your mom."

"Mama gave you Granny's recipe? That recipe has never been shared outside the family."

Her aproned spouse looked her way. "I *am* family, remember?"

Snow cringed at having to be reminded. "Right. But still . . . You know how to cook?"

"I cooked for you when we were dating," he replied, sliding a sizzling thigh next to the leg. "We need to work on that selective memory of yours."

When they were dating, Caleb often made breakfast, but making scrambled eggs and toast was much different from making one of Granny's recipes. It had taken Snow years to get her fried chicken even close to Granny's, and hers never smelled this good.

"There's cooking, and then there's *cooking*," Snow said, leaning over the plate Caleb slid down the counter to make room for the next one. She closed her eyes and was sucked back in time, standing on a chair in Granny's kitchen, begging for an early taste. "You've been holding out on me."

Handing her a fork and napkin, Caleb said, "In my quest to figure out what I wanted to be when I grew up, I did a semester at culinary school. I guess I retained more than I realized."

This man was full of surprises. "You never told me that."

"I would have," he said, lifting both plates and motioning for Snow to sit down in the living room, "if we'd kept dating. So, now that we're back to dating, I'm telling you."

As she mindlessly followed Caleb's direction, her brain struggling to process this new tidbit about her significant other, Snow spotted a beautiful arrangement of flowers on the coffee table, flanked by tall taper candles. She recognized the candleholders from Miss Hattie's dining room.

"I'd prefer an actual table, but since there's no room for one of those in this little space, the coffee table is the best I can do."

Flowers. Candles. Her favorite meal.

Caleb knew she knew.

Instead of sitting down, Snow faced her doting husband with hands on her hips. "Why didn't you tell me you were taking a job at the paper? You didn't even tell me you were applying."

"Please," Caleb said, "sit down and let me explain." His calm tone put a damper on Snow's anger. When she did as asked, he said, "Thank you," and handed her the full plate of food. "Yesterday, Hattie asked if I knew anything about the newspaper business, and when I said I knew a bit, she told me to report to an address at nine this morning."

"So this is Miss Hattie's fault?" Snow asked, amazed that he would shift the blame to an innocent old woman.

"Not fault, but her doing, yes. She gave me the address but never said why I needed to be there. I figured it had to do with newspapers, but not actually working for one. I could have been hauling stacks of papers off a truck for all I knew."

Snow felt her shoulders relax. The explanation made sense. And Miss Hattie did have a way of parsing out information. "You had no idea? None at all?"

"None." Caleb loaded green beans and potatoes onto his fork. "I didn't even know who to ask for. Turns out, the local paper, which Hattie owns . . . Did you know she owned the paper?"

"No," Snow said. How had she missed that in all the town gossip?

"Well, I didn't either," Caleb said after he'd chewed his food. "Turns out, the chain-smoking sales manager, who as far as I can tell has been around since possibly the Civil War, is retiring at the end of the year."

"And you're going to take his place?"

"Not as a manager. At least not to start." Caleb kept his eyes on his plate as he said, "It's a trial period right now. They get to see if they like me, and I get to see if I like them."

Snow pushed off thinking about his new roots in her town long enough to take her first bite of chicken. By all that was good and holy in this world, Caleb's chicken was as delicious as Granny's. Maybe even better. She'd have felt guilty for entertaining such a disloyal thought, but her taste buds were running the show, and they felt no remorse whatsoever.

"By that look on your face, I'm guessing the chicken is good?" Caleb asked.

"Words cannot describe how good this is." Snow dragged her mind back to the subject at hand. Caleb had mentioned a trial period. Eventually becoming a manager . . . "Wait. Did you let them think that you're staying in Ardent Springs?"

Caleb shrugged, continuing to avoid eye contact. "I didn't make any long-term promises."

"But you didn't tell them that you have no intention of keeping this job." Snow set her plate on the table. "What are they going to do when the other guy retires, you leave, and they're stuck with no one to fill the position?"

Snow would have enough explaining to do as it was, without Caleb pretending to become a permanent part of this community.

Stabbing three green beans in a row, Caleb pointed his fork Snow's way. "The better question is, why are you acting as if my leaving town is a foregone conclusion? What do you know that I don't?"

Caleb wasn't sure where the question had come from, but by the look on Snow's face, there was definitely something he didn't know.

"I don't know anything," Snow answered, regaining her dinner and sitting back on the couch. She kept her eyes on her plate as she said, "We both know this isn't your kind of town. You said so yourself. Baton Rouge is your home."

"I also said that wherever you are is where I will be. You're here, so I'm here." Caleb assured himself that Snow was the only reason he was developing a connection with the area. He didn't want to leave *her*. The town had nothing to do with it.

In a low voice, Snow mumbled, "It isn't as if I'm the only woman in town who's interested."

"What's that supposed to mean?"

"Nothing," Snow said, her voice higher than usual as she continued to avoid his gaze. "It just seems as if you've made a powerful impression on one of your coworkers."

So Piper did say something. Gerald was a smart man.

"I assure you," Caleb said, loading his fork with potatoes, "I did nothing to encourage the woman."

Snow's eyes went wide. "So you know Piper wants you?"

The woman had done everything but write her number across his palm. Of course he knew. "She wasn't exactly subtle, but I barely spoke to her," he defended. "And it doesn't matter what Piper wants, she's not getting anything that involves me."

"She said if she has her way, you'll be under her tree come Christmas morning wearing nothing but a bow." Snow tapped her fork on her plate. "And I have a pretty good idea where she'll want that bow."

Unless his ears were deceiving him, his wife was jealous. The night was suddenly looking up. "Nothing but a bow, huh?"

A wadded-up napkin flew his way. "Wipe that smug look right off your face, Caleb McGraw. That woman is at least twenty years older than you, and if word around town is true, she's pretty free with her bows, if you know what I mean."

There was nothing unattractive about Piper Griffin on the surface, but Caleb wasn't interested in becoming any cougar's boy toy. Besides, he was married. Maybe their little game of pretend had Snow forgetting that part.

Caleb set his plate on the table and reached for his wife's. Her body tensed as he set her plate next to his.

"I had eighteen months to find another woman if I'd been so inclined," he said, looking into obstinate gold eyes. "I don't want Piper Griffin or anyone else. I want you. And as much as it strokes my ego to know that you're jealous, I need you to believe that."

Snow rubbed a finger along his knee. "I'm not jealous. The way she talked about you made me want to smack her is all. An urge I'm not proud of, nor do I like it." Rolling her eyes, she added, "So maybe I did get a little jealous."

The confession could not have been easy for her, which made Caleb more determined to reassure her.

Nudging his wife's chin up, he asked, "Did you tell her that I belong to you?"

Snow shook her head.

"Next time," he said, leaning close, "feel free to stake your claim. Because I'm yours, Snow. All yours."

Unable to help himself, Caleb pressed his lips to hers. He kept the pressure light, letting her know that he was a patient man, but that didn't mean he didn't want her in every way. When she slipped her arms around his neck and pulled him closer, his intentions went to hell and his instincts took over.

Before Caleb knew it, Snow was pressed into the pillows, her body half under his. She tasted like buttery panko crumbs and strawberry lip gloss. His fingers slid beneath the hem of her shirt, garnering a purr from deep in her chest as Snow threw a leg over his hip and writhed up, pressing their bodies as close as their clothes would allow.

Seducing his wife hadn't been on Caleb's agenda for the evening. He'd agreed to her no sex condition, and defaulting now would strengthen her assertion that their relationship was based on sex alone. But how was he supposed to resist when she set him on fire and gave no signs of stopping?

Trailing kisses along her neck, Caleb breathed deep of honeysuckle and woman as he fought for control. If this kept up, he'd be a dead man before the month was up.

"I missed this," Snow said, rewarding him with another hard-won admission. Trailing a delicate finger across his brow, she made no move to extricate herself from beneath him.

"Me too." As much as his body demanded he take her right there, Caleb kept his tone casual. "I would have told you about the job if I'd known ahead of time. And I'm sorry you had to learn about it from Piper." With a half grin, he added, "But I'm glad she got us to this."

Pushing against his shoulder, Snow sat up. "This isn't how I saw our evening going."

Caleb handed over her plate, then picked up his own, but he remained pressed along Snow's side on the couch. "You're cute when you're jealous," he said.

That earned him an elbow to the ribs. "Can I ask you one thing?"

"Sure," he answered, biting into his chicken breast, which didn't taste nearly as good as his wife's lips.

"If you wanted a job in the newspaper business, why didn't you take one when your father offered?"

Setting down his fork, Caleb wiped his mouth before answering. "If I'd taken a job in McGraw Media, it would have been me cashing in on my name. The son getting a high-level position because his daddy runs the company. But here," he said, "I got offered a job for no reason other than I knew a bit about the business and was willing to give it a try. Whatever I accomplish at the *Ardent Advocate*, for however long I'm there, will be my own. Not because Daddy gave it to me, but because I earned it."

Caleb surprised even himself with his answer. He'd been running on the belief that refusing to work for his father stemmed from an aversion to being under the old man's thumb. But maybe it had more to do with earning his own way. Being his own man. Selling ads for the *Ardent Advocate* wasn't anything major, but Caleb *had* enjoyed the day. Other than the fog of smoke he'd had to endure.

"So you have a job," she said, twirling a green bean on her fork. Not a flicker of excitement stirred in her tone.

He nodded. "I do."

They continued to eat in silence until Caleb said, "We're doing pretty good at this dating thing." He watched for her reaction out of the corner of his eye.

Stabbing a green bean, she said, "Sure. We're doing great."

Chapter 14

"You're never going to believe what she said!" Snow yelled as she burst into the apartment, throwing her purse and coat on the couch on her way to the kitchen.

By Thursday, she'd grown used to finding Caleb whipping up some delicious dinner for the both of them. Snow learned quickly that a mouthwatering meal could be a sensual experience, and watching her husband work around a stove was a complete turn-on. The combination of food and virile male was putting a dent in her determination to send her husband packing.

In truth, everything Caleb did turned Snow on. From the smile he gave her in the mornings, to the way his coin-bouncible cheeks looked in a pair of black boxer briefs.

"Who?" Caleb asked, wiping his hands on the new, manly gray apron she'd bought him. "Who said what?"

"The appraiser," Snow answered, dragging her mind away from the image of her husband in nothing but the apron. An image that traipsed through her brain with unnerving frequency of late. "It's real. And it's valuable," she said, resisting the urge to kiss the cook. "God bless William Norton and your good eye."

When she thought about the things she could do with the amount of money this painting could bring, Snow wanted to dance a jig.

"I'll take equal credit with Mr. Norton, sure. But how much are we talking?" he asked.

Snow contemplated her answer and with a smile said, "How about, make-Jackson-McGraw-jealous money."

"Then it *is* worth more than Dad's?"

"According to Ms. Bolliver, I shouldn't take less than thirteen thousand for it, but she believes it would go even higher at auction."

"Woo-hoo!" Caleb exclaimed, lifting Snow into a spin. Her laughter echoed off the black-and-white tile before he planted a hot kiss on her lips. Caught off guard, Snow held tight to Caleb's shoulders as she kissed him back, ideas about how they should celebrate coming to mind.

Very naughty ideas.

When her husband broke the kiss and flashed a grin that made her toes curl, Snow almost suggested they take things to the bedroom. Instead she said, "Put me down," in a voice that betrayed his true effect on her.

Snow's weakened state was completely Caleb's fault. He'd been planting sexy thoughts in her head at every turn. In addition to the amazing meals, he'd adopted the habit of walking around half-naked at every opportunity. And then there were the more subtle tactics—leaning a little too close, rubbing a little too much, touching a little too often. All the things that dating couples did. And in order to keep up the pretense of giving their relationship a chance, Snow had to endure the torture.

Something that would be easier to do if she hadn't begun to really like him. As a person and a friend. Even a roommate. He had yet to master the seat-down thing, but Caleb didn't leave shavings around the sink and only forced her to watch sports on certain occasions. Like when his Saints played on Monday night.

By the middle of the second quarter, Snow had been yelling at the refs right along with him. Turned out football wasn't so awful to watch after all.

Instead of dropping her as quickly as he'd swept her off her feet, Caleb lowered Snow slowly, keeping their bodies in contact the whole way. By the time her toes touched the floor, Snow was ready to climb back up and take a second ride.

"So what's next?" he asked, desire evident in the darker shade of his eyes.

"What do you mean?" Snow asked. She couldn't stop staring at his mouth. Remembering how it felt, and not just against her mouth. "What do you want to do?"

If ever there was a rhetorical question.

Caleb chuckled, and Snow felt it ripple down her spine. "I mean with the painting."

Blinking in confusion, Snow tried to remember what painting they were talking about.

"Oh," she said, stepping back. "The Norton." Bracing a hand on the edge of the sink, she looked anywhere but at her husband. "I don't know. I guess I'll put it in an auction."

"You have to make sure it's the right auction. With the right buyers."

"Yes, that's what Ms. Bolliver said." Snow drew a glass off the shelf and filled it with tap water. She was in dire need of a drink, though she wished there was something stronger than water close at hand. "She's going to keep an eye out for me and let me know when the right opportunity comes up."

"Then it sounds like you're in good hands." Something spattered behind him, and Caleb swung to the stove. "You distracted me, woman," he said, flipping two beautiful salmon filets.

"Sorry," Snow said, "but I couldn't wait to share the news."

Pulling her against his side, Caleb set the spatula on the counter and tested each filet with the tip of a finger. "I think I saved them," he said. Then he gave her waist a squeeze. "I'm proud of you, darling."

"Thanks," she said, leaning her head against his shoulder. "I would have missed that painting if not for you."

"Then it's a good thing I was here." He kissed her hair as his thumb rubbed the skin above her jeans, increasing Snow's heart rate. "You ready to eat?" Caleb asked as he shifted the pan to a cool burner.

Snow sighed and reminded herself that this was nothing but pretend. At the end of the month, she would send Caleb on his way. She had to. Better to break her own heart than let Vivien break them both.

"I'm ready," she said. "I'll get the plates."

"You almost ready?" Caleb asked for the second time, peeking into the bedroom to see Snow staring into the mirror at her third outfit in ten minutes. The Ruby Restoration meeting was scheduled to start in less than thirty minutes. If they were going to make it on time, they needed to leave in the next five.

"I don't know what to wear," she said, turning his way. "How does this look?"

He took in the burgundy sweater and skinny jeans, and experienced the same reaction he'd had the last two times she asked. *You'd look better wearing me.* Once again keeping the thought to himself, Caleb stepped closer to settle his hands on her hips, feigning interest in the clothes.

"Looks good to me."

The moment he touched her, Snow leaned into him. She'd been doing that more every day, which was why he made sure to touch her at every opportunity.

"You said that about the last two."

With a tug on her belt loop, he dropped a quick kiss on her lips and said, "I can't help that you look good in everything." Which she did. But that didn't mean he wouldn't prefer she take the clothes off rather than put them on.

With a dazed look on her face, she said, "Try to focus." He wasn't sure if she was speaking to him or herself. "Is this appropriate for tonight?"

Rubbing his chin, Caleb asked, "Have you ever been to one of these meetings?"

"No, but Lorelei is on the committee. I should call her." Snow reached for her cell, but Caleb cut her off.

"We need to leave in a few minutes, and Lorelei won't be able to see what you're wearing through the phone." And if she called Lorelei, Snow might learn where he planned to take her after the meeting.

Tonight was their first official date since the do-over started, and he planned to get Snow onto a dance floor. The few times he'd taken her dancing in Nashville, she'd claimed a lack of rhythm, and he'd acquiesced, not wanting to push while their relationship was still new.

The free pass ended tonight.

"I could text her a picture," Snow said, still stalling.

Caleb's brow shot up. "Are you fifteen?"

Giving him a dirty look, she surveyed the clothes scattered across the bed. "I think a nice top and cardigan would be better."

"So . . . outfit number one?" Truth be told, the little white tank had done wonders for his wife's amazing breasts. And it didn't hurt that the neckline offered him a clear view down to the lacy number beneath.

"Give me two minutes," Snow said, shooing him out of the room. If they weren't in such a hurry, Caleb would have insisted on helping her change.

Two minutes later, Snow stepped out of the bedroom wearing the burgundy sweater. To Caleb's confused stare, she said, "What?"

"Forget it." He would never understand women and their fashion struggles, so there was no sense in trying. "It's time to get this night started. The sooner the meeting is over, the sooner we start our date."

As he dragged her to the door, Snow asked, "Are you going to share the details of this date?"

"You'll find out soon enough," he said, spinning her onto the porch before locking the door. She displayed enough rhythm to make a perfect turn without losing her balance. "Now let's go before we're late."

They were down the steps before Snow realized the Jeep was running. "Were you in that much of a hurry?" she asked, jogging to keep up with him.

"I wanted to warm it up for you," he lied, then lifted his petite wife into the passenger seat and dropped a kiss on her temple. As he marched around to the driver's side, Caleb thought about warming something else up later tonight, and hoped this meeting didn't take too long.

Snow tried to focus on the meeting ahead and what it would mean for her going forward. After tonight, there would be no sending Caleb home without anyone in Ardent Springs being the wiser. Though she supposed that ship had sailed five days ago, the idea of having to put on an act as young lovers taking the next step in their relationship put her nerves on edge.

Especially since it didn't feel like an act.

Snow's libido had been arguing the case for days. Why couldn't they have sex and still go their separate ways? Why should she go without? Why deprive herself of the delectable man who'd been showing her in every way possible that he was ready and willing to make her see God?

And he could do it, too. He'd certainly done it before.

Halfway to the restaurant, Caleb's cell phone went off. "See who that is, would you?" he asked her, handing over the phone he'd pulled from his shirt pocket.

At the name on the screen, Snow's blood turned to sludge. "It's your mother," she said, her libido instantly silenced. This was why Snow couldn't have nice things.

"This night is not to include my mother." The Jeep rolled to a stop at the light at Main and Fifth, and Caleb took the phone, swiping to send the call to voice mail. "I'll call her back in the morning."

She didn't know how often Caleb ignored his mother's calls, but she hoped it wasn't too often. All she needed was Vivien getting the idea that Snow was telling him not to answer and who knew what she'd do. Or what she'd tell her son in retaliation.

"I don't mind if you call her now," she said.

"Don't be silly." He squeezed her knee. "This is our first second-time-around date. Whatever my mother wants can wait."

"Okay," Snow said, keeping her eyes on the streetlights going by as they crossed into downtown. More to herself she said, "I sure hope that's true."

As he parked in front of Lancelot's Restaurant, Caleb put thoughts of his mother out of his mind. She'd called three times this week, taking every opportunity to ask when he was coming home. He'd told her that was up to his wife, which earned him another reminder of how Snow had abandoned him and that they kept the best lawyer in the state of Louisiana on retainer for these kinds of situations. Vivien had gone so far as to say that for as much as the man cost, surely he could get their son out of an undesirable marriage.

It was at that point that Caleb informed his mother that his marriage was not undesirable. Yes, they'd had this conversation before, and

Caleb reiterated his stance—*if* he and Snow decided to end their marriage, the decision would be theirs and theirs alone. Of course, Caleb had no intention of letting that happen, so his mother could stuff her high-priced lawyer where the sun didn't shine.

"I see you're learning your way around," Snow said as she unclipped her seat belt. "You didn't need my help to get here."

Caleb nodded toward the building. "This is one of Gerald's clients. One of the only places he drinks normal coffee."

"Normal coffee?"

"You don't want to know. I've seen things this week that I can't unsee."

"Oh," she said, jerking her head back. "I don't need to hear any more."

To his delight, Snow waited for him to come around and open her door. A positive change from the Saturday before. They entered the restaurant with his hand on the small of her back, and followed the hostess to the back room. The space was mostly empty, but Lorelei and Spencer were already there.

"Hey, you made it," Spencer said, extending a hand.

Caleb accepted the greeting as Lorelei and Snow hugged. "Told you we'd be here. Are we early?"

"A bit," Spencer replied. "Meeting starts in fifteen minutes. The usual suspects typically roll in with a minute or two to spare."

"You guys look great together," Lorelei said, gaining confused looks all around. "What? They look nice," she said to Spencer.

He leaned close but spoke loudly enough for Caleb and Snow to hear. "What did we discuss about your meddling?"

"I'm not . . ." Lorelei started. "I only meant . . ." To Spencer's raised-brow look she said, "Fine. You guys ready to sit down and order?"

"We are," Caleb answered.

The foursome took their seats along the side. The room was set up with long tables arranged in a U-shape, with a podium, shorter table, and projection screen at the front. Orders were taken with pleasant efficiency, and before long the rest of the attendees filed in. Caleb recognized the woman Snow had bid against for the doilies, the owner of the hardware store, and an older couple who ran a B&B on the outskirts of town. Mike Lowry, who owned the construction business Cooper had mentioned, entered minutes before the meeting started and took a seat next to Spencer.

As Caleb ate the best catfish dinner he'd had in a while, Lorelei whispered bits of information on most of the attendees, reserving her least favorable comments for the town mayor. Based solely on the looks Jebediah Winkle was shooting her way, the civic leader didn't like Lorelei any more than she liked him.

Observing the meeting as an unbiased outsider, Caleb noticed three things—there was a power struggle within the group, Spencer Boyd was the de facto leader, regardless of who held the title, and this project was bigger than Caleb had expected.

Based on what he'd learned, the Ruby Theater deserved to be saved, if for no other reason than the fact it was built in 1937 and was still standing as a single-screen movie theater. It was as if the Ruby was the theater that time forgot. A full restoration would be a major boon for the town.

Leaning close to Lorelei's ear, he whispered, "Can I see this theater sometime?"

She leaned back and tugged on Spencer's sleeve. "Caleb wants to see the theater."

Spencer caught Caleb's eye and nodded. "That can be arranged."

Snow asked, "What's going on?"

"I asked to see the theater." Caleb kept his voice low as they'd begun to draw attention. "I have some ideas."

She blinked in surprise. "Really? Has your family helped restore a theater before?"

Caleb shook his head. "No theaters, but several churches and countless historic buildings in New Orleans, especially after Katrina."

"Oh," she said, awe in her voice.

"Don't be too impressed. My parents simply wrote a check. It's not as if they got their hands dirty."

"Are you willing to get your hands dirty?"

He smiled her way. "Maybe. We'll start with a tour first."

Snow's reaction to his answer lacked enthusiasm as she nodded and returned her attention to the speaker at the front of the room.

Snow was seriously questioning her plan. Caleb was never supposed to become part of this town. He definitely wasn't supposed to make friends. Less than a week in Ardent Springs and he already had a job and was taking a major interest in the Ruby restoration project. Or at least he might be, once he saw the place. Whatever ideas he might have, Snow hoped they would help the cause, but she didn't want him sticking around to see them through.

The only reason Snow had never joined the committee herself was because she didn't feel she had much to bring to the table. She didn't know the first thing about restoring a theater, and when the group extended the call for fundraising assistance, she'd stepped up as a willing merchant. Until Caleb came to town, she'd assumed that would be the extent of her involvement. Now she wasn't so sure.

If he made commitments before heading back to Baton Rouge, Snow would be obligated to step up in his place. She'd created this cluster of a situation, and she was quickly losing control. She couldn't exactly tell Caleb to stop talking to people because his time in Ardent Springs was temporary no matter what. Then the arguments and head-butting would start all over again.

While Caleb paid the check at the checkout counter near the restaurant entrance, Lorelei pulled Snow aside. "So?" she asked. "How's it going?"

Snow watched the young cashier blush while taking Caleb's money. "Not good," she said. "Can't you tell Spencer to ignore him or something?"

"According to Spencer, Caleb deserves a chance," Lorelei said.

"You two have talked about this?"

Her friend shook her head. "I didn't tell him that you're only pretending to give the relationship a go. I love Spence, but the man code runs deep with him. He'd tell Caleb in a heartbeat."

"He can't do that."

"I know," Lorelei said, her voice carrying a heavy dose of frustration. "But do you see how he looks at you, Snow? That isn't the look of a man planning to walk away."

"I don't need this right now," Snow said. She didn't need Lorelei voicing the doubts dancing through her mind. "We are not staying married."

"Good Lord, woman. Why not?" Lorelei's voice shot well past whisper level.

Though the question of their compatibility grew dimmer by the day, Vivien's threat wasn't going anywhere. And Snow harbored no illusion that Caleb would be content to remain in Ardent Springs indefinitely. At some point, he'd insist they go back to Baton Rouge, and Snow could not handle a rerun of that miserable episode.

"Keep it down." Sparing another glance at her husband/date, she whispered, "Whatever you do, do *not* tell Spencer anything."

Lorelei huffed as Caleb joined them and asked, "What's going on over here?"

"Nothing," they chirped in unison.

"Don't ask," Spencer said as he stuffed his wallet into the back pocket of his Wranglers. "We ready to do some two-steppin'?"

"To do what?" Snow asked, cutting her eyes to Caleb. "What is he talking about?"

"I told you there would be dancing tonight."

"I don't dance," she replied, shaking her head double time.

Lorelei took her by the arm. "Relax. It's like riding a bike. In time to the beat and with a spin here and there."

"Oh no," Snow argued, putting on the brakes as Lorelei pulled her toward the door with an evil gleam in her eye.

Caleb joined the effort and pushed from behind. "Don't worry, darling. I'm a great lead."

Before she knew it, Snow found herself being dragged through the entrance to Brubaker's Bar. She'd never been inside the dance hall before. Had avoided it in some ways because it reminded her of her singing days in the clubs in Nashville.

As much as Music City looked like the friendlier side of the business, the view from inside was as cutthroat and seedy as anything that supposedly went on in New York or LA. And the coating of Southern charm didn't make it any more palatable.

But she did miss being on stage. At least a little. After showing ID and paying their cover, the group stepped into the bar and wended their way through the crowded room. Brubaker's was apparently the place to go on a Friday night. Caleb held her hand, cutting a path for her, while Spencer led the charge in front of Lorelei. The music was so loud Snow could feel it in her chest.

Spencer found Cooper at a cocktail table on the left side of the dance floor, which took up most of the room. Couples twirled by while a small group in the center of the floor performed a line dance.

Snow had been out of the scene too long to know the name of the dance. It had always been a good thing that she was on the stage, because she was born without a lick of rhythm. During their two months of dating in Nashville, Caleb had taken her to a couple of similar establishments, but she'd gotten out of having to dance thanks to his large group of friends who exchanged partners like the local church ladies exchanged recipes.

A curvy waitress appeared out of nowhere as the men finished their inaudible greetings. "What are we having?" she asked, slapping four small napkins onto the table.

"I'll get this round," Spencer said. "Two beers here. You guys?" he asked Caleb and Snow.

"Bud for me," her husband said, then looked to her for an answer. She'd expected him to remember that she didn't like beer, and this didn't look like a wine sort of joint. "Water or soda?" he asked.

So he did remember. Snow said, "Water, thanks."

The waitress melted into the crowd as Cooper yelled, "Come on, Lorelei. They're playing our song."

Spencer threw his hands in the air as his best friend tugged his woman onto the dance floor. Lorelei blew him a kiss seconds before Cooper spun her into the mass of rotating couples.

"You gonna let him take your girl like that?" Caleb asked Spencer, who didn't look the least bit put out.

"She knows who's taking her home." He gestured toward the floor. "Don't feel obligated to keep me company. Get on out there."

Snow used to like Spencer.

"We're good right here," she said, straining to be heard over the music.

"Don't be silly." Caleb took her hands and, with a single tug, spun Snow until she was tucked against his side. "We're here to dance, woman. Let's do it."

Against her will, and protesting all the way, Snow was pulled to the floor and maneuvered into the churning throng of dancers. She stumbled twice, but Caleb remained patient. "I told you," she yelled. "I don't know how to do this."

He pulled her closer and said, "Follow my lead, darling. Just follow my lead."

Her eyes locked with his, Snow stepped off with her right, and did her best to echo his movements. After a full turn around the dance floor without a single stumble, she smiled at her partner. "I'm doing it. I'm dancing."

Caleb's eyes turned dark. "Yes, you are."

With their bodies so close together, Snow enjoyed the feel of Caleb's thighs pressed to hers. And the flex of his biceps beneath her palm. As they made a second pass around, going much slower than the other dancers, she realized the flexing of another part of her husband's anatomy.

"Sorry," he whispered in her ear. "But you're driving me crazy."

"I'm not doing it on purpose," she said, attempting to pull back. "I think it's time to get off the floor."

Her husband held tight, keeping his cheek against hers. "The song isn't over yet."

She nodded. "Right." No wonder dancing this way had been frowned upon in high school. This was practically foreplay.

Pulling her in again, Caleb asked, "When can we leave?"

A voice in her head said, *Not soon enough,* but Snow ignored it. "We just got here," she answered.

"Okay," he said, his voice vibrating along her skin. "Fifteen more minutes."

Chapter 15

After two more turns around the floor, Caleb escorted Snow back to their group to find a new person had joined the gathering. And from the looks of it, she was ready to give birth at any second. The mother-to-be stood between Spencer and Lorelei with her head bent to hear something the latter was saying. Their conversation ended with a nod before Lorelei turned to Snow.

"What happened to 'I can't dance'?" she asked.

His wife shrugged as he tucked in behind her and wrapped his arms around her middle. There was no reason for the others to witness the effect Snow had on him.

"Caleb is a good lead," she said, reaching for her water glass on the table. "How are you doing, Carrie?" she asked the pregnant woman. "I didn't know you were going to be here."

Carrie hefted herself onto a stool with Spencer's help. "Lorelei convinced me to come. I think she expects me to hit the dance floor and jar this little girl into making an appearance."

Lorelei dropped an arm across Carrie's shoulders. "The munchkin needs to get out here already," she said. "I'm dying to meet her."

As if remembering herself, Snow said, "Oh, Carrie, this is Caleb." He extended his hand in greeting, leaning close so the woman could stay upright on her stool. "Caleb is my fiancé," she added, which was the first time she'd introduced him as such. The words sounded nice to his ears, making him think maybe they had skipped something important with the impromptu nuptials. "Caleb, this is Carrie Farmer."

"Nice to meet you," he said. "Congrats on the little one. Your husband must be thrilled." The group hushed, and he knew he'd said something wrong, but wasn't sure what.

"My husband passed away a few months ago," Carrie answered, making Caleb feel like a complete jerk.

"I'm sorry—" he started.

"No," Carrie said, flashing a half smile. "It's okay. You didn't know."

"Doesn't matter," Spencer said. "This little girl is going to have more folks looking out for her than any child would want." Addressing Caleb, he said, "How are you liking things at the paper?"

Thankful for the change of subject, Caleb replied, "I like it a lot. How did I do in that sales call this week? Gerald didn't warn me I'd be the one doing the talking when we met up with you."

Spencer nodded. "Sounded like a man who knows his stuff to me. Nichols is definitely the guy to teach you the ropes. I think he's been selling since snake oil was a thing."

"I wouldn't doubt it."

The waitress returned to the table to get Carrie's drink order. Spencer spoke for her and seemed protective of the expectant mother. Lorelei didn't appear to mind. Caleb wondered exactly how close these friends were.

After taking a long draw off his beer, Cooper said, "Who am I dancing with next?"

Carrie threw her hands in the air. "Don't look at me. Unless by *dance* you mean walk slowly around the edge of the floor taking a pee break once a minute."

"This one is mine," Spencer said, sweeping Lorelei toward the hardwoods.

Cooper looked at Snow with raised brows. "Guess that leaves you and me." Glancing Caleb's way, he said, "You mind, bro?"

The look of sheer terror on Snow's face made his answer clear. "Go for it, man. But bring her back with all toes intact."

"What?" Snow exclaimed.

He dropped a hard kiss on her cheek and said, "If his hands get too low, knee him in the groin." Before she could argue, Cooper gave a "Yeehaw!" and hurried her to the floor. Caleb knew he shouldn't piss off the woman he planned to seduce in less than an hour, especially when he'd waited so long to have her. But then again, she looked so hot when she was pissed.

"That was nice of you," Carrie said, reminding him that he wasn't alone.

He gave her a crooked smile. "She'll hate me for it, but she's a better dancer than she thinks."

Shaking her head, the future mom said, "No, I meant for Cooper."

"How did I do a favor for Cooper?" he asked, the smile fading as he searched the floor for the man in question. Caleb hadn't considered the possibility that the gearhead had more than a passing interest in his wife. Several ideas for how to handle the situation came to mind, most of which involved ripping the mechanic's head off.

"Relax," she said. "I don't mean like that. He loves to dance and is always the third wheel with Lorelei and Spencer."

"Oh," he answered, continuing to monitor the space between Cooper and Snow as they passed by. "Why doesn't he bring his own date?"

"Cooper has eyes for only one girl, and she doesn't come here." Carrie kicked her feet forward and back where they hovered a foot off the floor. "She never comes to Brubaker's."

Their conversation the day of the auction came to mind, and the mechanic's answer that he hadn't won the right girl. Yet.

"Why doesn't he ask her to come?"

Light blue eyes met his with a look of gentle pity. "That's what the rest of us keep asking, but he won't do it."

Watching Cooper hoot as he twirled Snow into the back of another couple, he said, "The guy doesn't strike me as the shy type."

Carrie chuckled. "Me neither, but he has his reasons, I guess. I've been tempted to say something to her, but I'd hate if someone did the same to me."

"You know her?"

"She's my OB," the woman answered. "Needless to say, I see her regularly these days."

A mechanic with tattoos and an OB doc did sound like an odd combination. But then Snow claimed the two of them were opposites and Caleb didn't see it.

The up-tempo song faded into a slower tune, bringing Cooper and Snow back to the table. Spencer and Lorelei remained on the floor. "Here you go," Cooper said, presenting Snow like a prize. "All body parts present and accounted for."

Snow used a small napkin to dab beads of sweat from her forehead, but the grin and flush on her cheeks said she'd enjoyed the dance more than she was probably willing to admit.

"Anytime," he replied, tucking his wife against his side and whispering for her only, "How about we make this date a little more private?"

Fanning herself with the napkin, she muttered, "Are you sure you don't want me to leave with Cooper instead?"

Ignoring his wife's sarcastic comment, Caleb tossed a twenty on the table and said, "Tell Spencer and Lorelei we'll see them later. The next round is on me."

"You're leaving?" Carrie asked.

"Been a long week," he answered, extending a hand to Cooper. "If the offer is still open, I'd love to see that old Thunderbird sometime soon."

Cooper nodded as they shook. "The shop is open all weekend. Come on by when you can."

Snow blew a damp curl out of her eyes as she shot him a less than friendly look. She may have been pissed about being handed off for a dance, but he'd put a smile on her face as soon as they got home.

"Will do," he said, navigating Snow off the raised platform and toward the door.

On the outside, Snow was fuming. On the inside, she was a mass of nerves and second-guessing mixed with sexual need and the stirrings of mind-numbing panic.

"You okay over there?" Caleb asked once they'd driven several miles in silence.

"Sure," she said, the word clipped and hiding little of the turmoil churning through her system.

Would giving in really be the end of the world? Where was the harm in having sex with her husband? Even if she intended for him not to be her husband much longer. They were only dating. Dating couples had sex all the time.

Another stretch of silence before Caleb asked, "Was it really that awful to dance with Cooper?"

Holding her tongue, Snow shook her head in the negative, keeping her face turned toward the passing hickory trees. She needed them to be home so she could lock herself in the bathroom and attempt to drown the desire coursing through her.

Caleb made no further attempts at conversation until they'd parked in front of the old garage outside the apartment. As Snow reached for her door handle, he stopped her with a gentle hand on her arm. "Hey. Nothing has to happen tonight that you don't want."

Her heart cracked in that moment. She'd never wanted anything so much, or been so certain of impending danger in her life. Caleb had made his intentions clear back at the bar, and she'd said nothing. Hadn't reminded him of their deal, or ended the dance when the evidence of his condition had become obvious.

"I'm scared," she admitted in a voice she didn't recognize. Why would she admit as much out loud? Maybe all the lust that had been building over the last week had addled her brains. Of course, he didn't know what she was afraid of.

Instead of reassuring her, or offering his own fears, Caleb exited the Jeep with a sigh. Snow cursed her stupid mouth seconds before the passenger door opened and Caleb extended a hand without speaking. With a shuddering breath, she slipped her fingers into his palm, thankful yet leery of the warmth and strength she found there.

Silly ideas bubbled to the surface. If only she could keep her hand there all the time, locked in Caleb's steady grip. If only they weren't doomed from the start.

When she stepped out, Caleb didn't move, locking her body between him and vehicle. He tilted her head up with one finger beneath her chin and brushed a curl off her forehead. "What are you afraid of, Snow?" he asked, his blue eyes unreadable in the darkness.

"We haven't figured out our future yet," she said, being as honest as she could without revealing her true feelings.

"Forget the future," he said, trailing his thumb along her bottom lip. "Tonight is about two people who like each other a whole lot taking their relationship to the next level. Nothing more than that."

The knot in her stomach loosened, replaced by a growing heat lower down. "Another do-over?" she asked, amazed she managed to utter the words while he looked at her like that. Like she was the only woman in the world he would ever look at.

His mouth tilted up on one side. "Yeah," he said. "Another do-over." Her hand in his, he led her through the garden gate. On the porch, he turned before opening the door. "To be clear, there's nothing I want more than to get reacquainted with every curve and delicate crevice on your body, but I'm serious when I say you call the shots here. I told you before, we were never just sex to me."

The words were like a muzzle for the voices in her mind. Snow laid her palm along his jaw, the porch light allowing her to see the honesty in his gaze. She nodded her understanding, but he continued to ignore the key in his hand.

"But to be fair, we were really, really good at it." The half smile was back, and Snow considered jumping his bones right there on the porch. There was no reason to deny herself this man. If she had to give him up, at least she would have evenings like this to get her through the long, lonely nights ahead.

"Caleb McGraw, if you don't open that door and take me to bed right this second, I may never speak to you again."

The key was in the lock before she could blink. "Yes, ma'am."

∽

Caleb's heart threatened to beat out of his chest. So many nights he'd dreamt about this woman. Woken sweaty and shredded and longing for the real thing. Now, here she was, ordering him to make love to her.

If this was nothing more than another dream, he was going to be furious when he woke up.

They took off their shoes by the door, Snow's coming off first, but instead of moving into the apartment, she waited for him. Caleb made quick work of his boots, never taking his eyes off her. When she put out her hand, he took it and let her lead him to the bedroom. She moved like a woman who knew what she wanted. A woman who wanted him.

He'd had no idea what to say to her in the Jeep, as the girl in his passenger seat seemed like a stranger there for a few minutes. So he'd gone with his gut, assuring her that they didn't need to have sex tonight.

By some miracle, he'd said the exact right thing.

When they entered the bedroom, Snow dropped his hand and turned on the light next to the bed. He liked the idea of getting to see her as they did this. Snow stopped beside the bed, a look of uncertainty in her amber eyes. As if she'd run out of confidence on what to do next.

Pulling her close and dropping his hands to the small of her back, he said, "You're perfect," before taking her mouth with his. He could taste hints of the peach cobbler she'd had for dessert and the strawberry in her lip gloss. For months after she'd left, Caleb couldn't even look at a strawberry without experiencing an intense surge of longing.

She opened to him with complete surrender, a moan of pleasure escaping her throat. He knew exactly how she felt.

Caleb had decided, when this night finally came, that he'd go slow and make the most of every second, but Snow's moans turned to bites as she tugged on his shirt with great determination.

"Off," she said, breathless and impatient. "This needs to come off."

He pulled the cotton over his head, happy to oblige, and reveled in the feel of her slender fingers gliding through the thin hair covering his pecs. Snow took his mouth again, straining against him as if she couldn't get close enough. Another sensation he understood well. Drawing the burgundy sweater over her mass of dark brown curls, Caleb threw the garment onto the floor and filled his hands with black lace. He rubbed his thumbs across her nipples and felt them pebble against the delicate material.

"God, I've missed this," she said, climbing onto the bed on her knees. She kissed him like a drowning woman fighting for air, then pulled back. "Am I going too fast? Because this doesn't feel fast enough for me."

He couldn't help but laugh. "Like I said," Caleb answered, joining her on the bed, "you're in charge tonight. We can go as fast or as slow as you want, but if you keep looking at me like that, this could go faster than either of us would like."

Snow giggled. "Then we'll have an excuse to do it again."

"Oh, we'll do it again," he said, taking her down to the mattress. "I promise you that."

Chapter 16

How had she slept next to this man six nights in a row and stayed on her own side of the bed the whole time? Sheer stupidity was the only answer she could think of.

And then Caleb's lips trailed down her neck and she stopped thinking altogether.

One black strap slid down over her shoulder as his mouth traveled to the swell of her breast. The warmth of his breath sent shivers down her spine as he slowly eased lower and lower. If he didn't move things along, she feared she might die right there, clinging to his shoulders and melting in a ball of fire.

"Caleb, please," she murmured, arching her back.

"Please what?" he said as the other strap descended down her arm. "Tell me what you want."

She hadn't realized that when he said she was calling the shots, that he expected her to actually *call* the shots. It wasn't as if he didn't know what she wanted.

In frustration, she pushed on his shoulder. "You know," she said, her nails digging into his flesh. Why hadn't she taken off the damn bra with her shirt? She needed his lips on her. His teeth driving her crazy. She needed to get them out of these clothes.

Leaning on one elbow, Caleb pressed her curls back from her face and waited. What was he waiting for? Snow opened her eyes to see him staring back at her, desire evident in his gaze.

"Tell me what you want," he repeated. "Take the lead."

The man could steer her around a crowded dance floor, but now he wanted to follow. This wasn't how things had been between them. He'd always taken charge in the bedroom, and Snow didn't see any reason to complain when he sent her soaring every time.

But then she realized what he was giving her. She was a woman in full control. She ran her own business. She'd built her own life in a new town. She was in charge, and Caleb understood what all of that meant to her. Now he was giving her the reins to control *him*.

The surge of power from that thought alone threatened to send her over the edge. She couldn't stop the smile that curved her lips. "I want your mouth on my breasts," she said, her voice weaker than she liked. With more authority she added, "But first, I want you naked in my bed."

The admiring grin he flashed felt like a well-earned reward.

"Yes, ma'am," he said, his lower-than-usual voice vibrating through her body. Cool air drew goose bumps along her flesh as Caleb crawled off the bed, never taking his eyes from hers. With slow, deliberate movements, he undid his jeans and slid them down his powerful thighs. Grasping the headboard for balance, he pulled them off, taking his socks with them. His full arousal was evident behind the black boxer briefs.

"Wait," she said, before he could push the underwear over his hips. "Let me." A tiny voice in Snow's brain screamed, *What are you doing?*

but she stayed the course, scooting to the edge of the bed. "Come closer," she ordered, and Caleb did as asked without complaint.

She explored him first through the cotton material, fascinated by how easily she could make him moan. The sound was like a drug, and she wanted more. Much more. With a hand on each hip, she slid the waistband down to reveal the vee that made her mouth water. By the time the elastic reached mid-thigh, Caleb was trembling and a glance at his face revealed his struggle to hold on.

Once the briefs fell to his feet, Caleb shifted as if to join her on the bed. "Not yet," Snow said, her hands on his hips.

In a strained voice, he said, "I thought you wanted me naked in your bed."

Trailing a finger over the front of his thigh, she said, "I've changed my mind."

She could have sworn she heard him say, "Oh, God," as she took him in hand, but Snow was too focused on her target to be sure. He was hot and pulsing, and she realized she'd never done this with the lights on. Never explored him at her leisure. There was so much she'd been missing out on.

When she kissed the tip, his knees nearly buckled. "Snow, please." It was Caleb's turn to beg, and she decided he was probably right. This would be better with him lying down.

Scooting back, she dragged the covers down, and without a word he joined her. "Where were we?" he said, sliding a hand across her stomach.

"Where was I, you mean." Snow pushed him back with one finger on his shoulder and then scooted down on the bed. "You don't mind, do you?" she asked, glancing up from the middle of the mattress.

With a gleam in his eye, Caleb said, "I've created a monster, haven't I?"

"Is that a bad thing?"

He shook his head. "Something tells me it's a very good thing. I'm all yours, darling." His hands slipped behind his head as a smug expression crossed his face.

Snow had a sudden urge to hear him beg once more.

She kissed the tip again, then trailed her tongue down to the base. Caleb's gasp made her smile, but she didn't hesitate in taking him completely. She didn't need to see her husband's face to know the smug look was gone.

His hands gripped her hair as she began to move. Hips rose as she set up a rhythm and his breathing grew jagged and thin. When she cupped his balls, a deep growl echoed around them and his hips drove up harder. Keeping her mouth on him, Snow undid the front clip on her bra and tossed the garment to her left, not caring where it landed.

The taste of heat and salt and man filled her senses. On her knees now, Snow dug her nails into Caleb's tight ass and increased her intensity. She knew he was on the brink of snapping when Caleb pulled her up his body and said, "Now."

He rolled her to the side and had her jeans and panties off within seconds. Part of her wanted to order him back to obedience, but the truth was, she couldn't wait any longer either. When Caleb leapt off the bed, she yelped.

"Where—" she started to ask, but saw him pulling something from his bag. Now? Now was the time he had to get something out of his bag?

Caleb returned to the bed with several condoms, tossing all but one on the nightstand. Tearing the package open with his teeth, he cooperated without argument when Snow took over and slid the sheath into place.

"I thought I was in charge," she teased, relishing the feel of him hot and naked against her.

"I tried," he answered before taking her mouth at the same moment he slid a hand between her legs. When he found her hot and ready he mumbled, "Thank God" against her mouth as he drove into her.

Snow's entire world lit up at the same moment her eyes snapped shut and her body lit on fire. She stretched to accommodate him and the whole planet fell away. There was nothing but her and the man clenched between her thighs. She'd feared this wouldn't be as good as it once was, but she never dreamed it could be this much better.

"Oh, Caleb," she said as her hands slid down his sweat-slick back. "Oh my."

She felt him nod in silent agreement, his forehead pressed to hers. Snow kissed his chest and his collarbone, the base of his neck and his strong jawline. His brittle scruff scratched her delicate skin, but she didn't care. So long as she had him in her arms, and in her bed, Snow didn't care about anything else.

The thought sent a brief shiver of panic through her mind before she shut it down. This wasn't about losing her will to her libido. This was more than that.

"Snow," Caleb said, her name like a prayer on his lips. She looked up to see him watching her, his shoulders strained. He was holding back. For her.

The look in his eyes told her everything she ever needed to know, and Snow handed over her heart as she always knew she would. Tightening her knees against him, she lifted her hips, meeting him stroke for stroke. They were kissing wildly, biting and nibbling and increasing the pace until Snow didn't know if she could take any more.

With one last powerful drive, Caleb's head dropped to her shoulder as a guttural sound ripped from his chest. Snow was cresting the wave as Caleb shuddered against her. As they went over the edge together, she was already looking forward to the next round.

Caleb struggled to hold his weight on his arms. He didn't want to crush Snow, but his muscles were on fire. As was the rest of him.

"I hope you don't mind if I catch my breath before we do that again," he said, rolling onto his back and pulling his wife with him until she lay sprawled along his front. "I'm more out of shape than I thought."

Snow blew a mass of damp curls off her forehead, then dropped her chin onto his sternum. "If this is out of shape," she said, "I'm not sure I could handle you fit." The source of his ego jolted against her stomach, resulting in one raised dark brow. "Someone's caught his breath already."

He laughed, which threatened to throw her off him. Caleb caught Snow under her arms and pulled her higher on his chest. With a deep sigh of satisfaction, he twisted a curl around his finger. "I missed you," he said in lieu of the other three words brimming to get out. A temptation that took him by surprise.

There was no doubt that he cared for, and physically wanted, his wife. They'd exchanged "I love yous" after their nontraditional wedding, but neither had ever made the declaration in a moment like this. A moment, he now realized, that really mattered. What would she say if he spoke the words now? She'd pointed out that their future was still undecided. Bringing love up at a time like this would get her thinking, and that was the last thing he needed.

The precariousness of Caleb's position bore down on him. She'd run from him once, and there were still no guarantees she wouldn't call things off for good. He could refuse to accept her decision for only so long. Eventually, if she really wanted out, he'd have to honor that.

And doing so would tear him apart.

Feeling vulnerable wasn't something Caleb had much experience with. The morning he'd awoken to find Snow gone was the last time he'd felt anything akin to the uncomfortable frisson of fear currently poking at the back of his eyeballs. He'd determined right then and there that once he found her, she would never leave him again. A bold decision for someone who clearly had no more control over his wife than he did over the weather.

He didn't then. And he didn't now.

Which put a remarkable amount of power in his wife's dainty little hands.

"Earth to Caleb," Snow said. "Did I fry your brain?"

Shaking his head, he dropped the curl to wrap his arms around her. "Singed maybe," he joked, sliding the previous thoughts to the back of his mind. "The last thing I want to do is get off this bed, but there's something I need to throw away."

Her face scrunched up in the cutest way. "You go do that," she said, shifting herself onto the bed. Lying on her side with her head balanced on her hand, she said, "Don't take too long."

As ordered, Caleb crossed the short distance to the bathroom, tossed the condom into the trash, and pranced back to the bed. "Move over, woman," he said, climbing under the covers.

As she was still on top of them, Snow looked at him as if he'd forgotten something.

"What?" he asked.

"Are we going to sleep now?"

Mimicking her pose, he answered, "Not if you join me under here."

She rolled her eyes and climbed under the covers. "Now what?"

Without responding, he pinned her beneath him and proceeded to drop kisses along her jawline. "Now I have my way with you."

Snow chuckled. "Didn't you just do that?"

He looked up to meet her eyes. "Uh . . . no. *You* had your way with *me*, remember?"

"Ah," she said, nodding. "I did kind of do that, didn't I?"

"You did," he said and returned to kissing her.

Sliding her arms around his neck, she asked, "Did I do a good job?"

Again, he stopped to look at her. "Darling, you did such a good job, I'm going to let you have your way with me anytime you want from now on."

That evoked a full-out laugh. "Never let anyone say Caleb McGraw isn't a generous man," she said once the laughter subsided.

Growing serious, he said, "Only with you, Snow. Only with you." Those three words were dangerously close to the ones he was determined to keep to himself.

She sighed, toying with his hair. Her mouth opened as if to say something, but she clamped it shut.

He narrowed his eyes. "What were you going to say?"

Snow brushed off the question. "I believe you were about to have your way with me?"

Yes, Caleb thought. *Yes, I am.*

"Oh, that's right." He slid his knee between her legs. "That is what I was about to do."

Kissing her chin changed to kissing her neck and shoulders. Then lower, to her breasts. "Isn't this what you demanded a little while ago?" he asked before taking a taut nipple between his teeth. Snow writhed off the bed with a gasp. "I'll take that as a yes," he said as he moved to the other breast. He made sure to give both equal attention, moving lower once Snow's breathing became a series of rapid pants.

Her hands tangled in his hair as his tongue teased around her navel. He kissed an inch lower and Snow bent her knees, planting her feet beside his shoulders.

"Hold on, darling," he said, watching her body arch for him. "I'm about to return the favor."

Chapter 17

Snow screamed Caleb's name four more times that night. Two while he was returning the favor alone. By the time they'd fallen asleep somewhere around two in the morning, she was physically spent.

But now, in the light of day, she was an emotional wreck.

Deep down, Snow had known that sex with Caleb would tangle her heart even more than it already was. They were playing house in this tiny town, pretending that reality wasn't looming in the distance, waiting to smack them both. And what if, in the throes of passion, Caleb had said he loved her? What would she do then?

Would she admit that regardless of how the next few weeks went, they would still be signing divorce papers? Or would she continue the ruse, hoarding every touch and caress she could get? Worse yet, there was the option of saying to hell with Vivien McGraw and fighting to keep her husband. Was it worth letting Caleb be hurt to find out if he really was with her "no matter what," as he'd put it?

Stirring her tea, Snow leaned against the counter, wearing nothing but Caleb's shirt from the night before, and admitted the truth, at least to herself. There was no cure for Caleb McGraw. Even if he drove off tomorrow, she'd never get him out of her blood. Or her heart. But that didn't mean she didn't have to let him go. In fact, it made the sacrifice even more necessary.

"There you are," the subject of her thoughts said, strolling into the kitchen in nothing but his underwear. By the looks of things, he was in search of more than a cup of tea. Caleb pinned her to the counter with an arm on each side and nuzzled into her neck. "I was hoping to give you a proper good morning."

Snow leaned her head to the left, giving him better access. "I'm surprised you're up," she said. "It isn't even nine o'clock."

He leaned in, pressing their bodies close. "Oh, I'm up, darling. I'm up." His lips returned to her neck and descended down the opening of her shirt. Or his shirt, rather. "You might want to put that mug down."

Unable to resist, Snow did as he suggested, expecting him to tug her into the bedroom. Instead, he lifted her off the floor and dropped her bare bottom on the countertop.

"Hey now," she said, surprise sending her voice up several octaves. "That's cold."

"Don't worry," he mumbled, nipping at her lips. "I'll warm you up."

True to his word, Caleb chased the chill away with his hands and his mouth. Snow nearly came undone when he licked her earlobe. He held her steady on the counter as he undid the buttons of her shirt with one hand. Seconds later, cool air rushed her skin when the cotton slid off her shoulders, but once again, Caleb's heat warmed her. Sunlight streamed in through the window over the sink, highlighting the strips of chestnut in his thick hair. Snow ran her fingers over his scalp as Caleb suckled her breast, his hands kneading her hips.

Pulling her forward until she felt him pressed against her core, Caleb murmured, "I can't get enough of you." He took her mouth in a searing kiss that said all the words she needed to hear. Almost.

Snow reached to slide his underwear off his hips and was relieved to see he'd taken care of the condom issue before leaving the bedroom. His confidence should have been annoying, but knowing how badly he wanted her sent her temperature spiking. She wrapped her legs around his waist, angling to get closer. To feel him inside her.

"Now, Caleb. I need it now," she said.

Without a word, he drove into her as she arched, driving her hips forward. He set up a pounding rhythm, and she met him thrust for thrust until they were both sweaty and panting and mumbling incoherent words in each other's ears. He drove in hard, murmuring something about never letting her go, and Snow nearly shattered right there in his arms, her heart at his feet as her body took him in deeper.

Too far gone to speak, Snow rode the crest surging through her center and out her limbs. She wanted to stretch and curl into a ball at the same time. Let it go and hold it tight. When the peak hit, she gripped her legs tighter, her arms wrapped around Caleb's neck like a dying woman clinging to life. He finished seconds later, and they returned to reality together, Caleb's strong arms holding her upright as she dropped delicate kisses along his slick neck.

Their bodies still connected, Snow set her forehead on Caleb's shoulder and rolled it back and forth. Desperate to break the mood, she said, "You're going to clean this counter."

Instead of the chuckle she'd hoped to evoke, Caleb sighed and lifted her against him. "The counter can wait," he said, carrying her toward the bedroom. "I'm not done with you yet."

Caleb whistled his way through the next several days, more content with his life than he'd been in a long time. Even when he and Snow were first together, he hadn't been this happy. He had a job he liked, and was learning more about the business of selling every day. Even this tiny blip on the map was starting to grow on him. The people were nice, for the most part, even with the few typical small-town types who weren't receptive to outsiders putting down stakes.

Baton Rouge was still his hometown, but the distance from his parents made Ardent Springs that much more attractive. Unlike his mother's constant calls, Caleb's father hadn't bothered. He must have been informed by now that their son had found his runaway bride, but even that hadn't garnered enough interest from the man to warrant a phone call.

Then again, his mother called often enough for both of them. She'd called twice on Monday alone while Caleb had been on a sales call and unable to answer. In her message, she apologized for their previous conversation and promised not to discuss his ill-conceived marriage again.

Conceding a point had never been Vivien McGraw's strongest skill.

"You ready to see her?" Cooper asked, hauling Caleb from his maternal reverie.

"Yes, sir," Caleb responded, following the excited mechanic out the door.

Snow was spending the evening with Lorelei and Carrie, and she'd encouraged Caleb to explore the area. After ten days of working for the paper, there wasn't much left of Ardent Springs that he hadn't already seen. Gerald's clients stretched from the other side of Franklin Bridge to downtown and out past the fairgrounds. Which amounted to pretty much the entire town, plus a few miles outside the city limits.

So instead, he'd come to see the old Thunderbird he'd heard so much about. The owner had to finish up a quick oil change, which left Caleb waiting in the office, ruminating about the two women in his life. Parting with either of them wasn't an option. He simply needed to convince the one to tolerate the other.

Cooper escorted him around the garage to the back of the lot, where two structures filled the landscape. One large enough to house several vehicles, and the other more like a toolshed. Both looked home-made and weather-worn, but stable. They crossed to the larger building, and Caleb found himself curious as to what he'd find inside. The Thunderbird, obviously, but this wasn't the kind of building that housed a solitary vehicle. As soon as Cooper drew back the hangar-like door, his hunch was confirmed.

The space was packed with cars, old and somewhat newer models, most in the midst of a makeover or repair, and all surrounded by an assortment of parts large and small. Paradise.

"You've been holding out on me," he said, easing into the dark interior as his eyes adjusted. "What all do you have in here?"

His tour guide's attempt to look nonchalant failed miserably. "Dude, you wouldn't believe it. Old Tanner collected this stuff for years, and I got it all when I bought him out about three years ago."

"Old Tanner?" Caleb asking, squatting down to examine a radiator that looked at least a hundred years old.

"Tanner Drury. He owned the garage forever. I started working for him in high school and thought he'd never retire, but the wife finally nagged him into it." Cooper jabbed the ever-present stained rag into the back pocket of his coveralls. "Come over this way."

Contrary to the chaotic scene, a sort of method to the madness began to emerge. A wide aisle led down the center of the building, and each vehicle occupied a stall. Several were covered in old tarps or blankets, whetting Caleb's curiosity to see what treasures were hidden underneath. But Cooper was moving too fast, and Caleb didn't want to offend his host by demanding to see every cracked mirror they encountered.

He'd just have to get an invite back to dig through the rest.

Cooper stepped into a stall at the end of the aisle that looked nothing like the rest. The space around the vehicle was clean, or as clean as anything could be in an old building filled with relics, and a spotless car cover protected the large object occupying the center.

Looking like a magician about to reveal his premier trick, Cooper said, "Here she is." He grabbed the front corner of the cover and pulled slowly until the material pooled on the floor behind the back tires.

Caleb couldn't believe what he was seeing. "Dude," was all he could manage, as he inched into the stall.

"I know," Cooper said, nodding his head as if they'd exchanged some great thought.

This wasn't the typical Thunderbird model that most car enthusiasts focused on, but with such a gorgeous piece of machinery glimmering before him under the fluorescent light, Caleb couldn't understand why. Deep scarlet with black vinyl hardtop, complete with the signature "S" bar emblem along the sides, the car made his palms itch and he hadn't even heard her run yet.

"Please tell me she purrs," he said, glancing through the driver's side window.

"Of course," Cooper said with pride.

The red leather bucket seats looked fresh from the factory, and the dash sported enough chrome to be blinding. "Swing-away steering wheel?" Caleb asked.

"You know it. I don't take her out often, but there's a cruise-in down in Goodlettsville once a month during the warmer months. Since that doesn't put a lot of miles on her, I try to get down there as often as I can." He brushed something invisible off the front fender. "They hold it on Friday nights, which makes it tougher to get out of here, but sometimes I make it."

"Seems a shame not to show her off." Caleb admired the large, round tail lights that looked as if they belonged on a rocket instead of a car. "No cruise-ins here in town?"

"Nah," Cooper said. "Other than the fairgrounds, nobody has a parking lot big enough. And Mayor Winkle doesn't want what he calls a bunch of old, leaking gas-guzzlers messing up his fairground."

Caleb had yet to be officially introduced to this notorious town mayor. He also had yet to meet a native with anything positive to say about him. What he'd witnessed at the Ruby meeting hadn't left Caleb with a positive impression himself.

"Sounds like a great guy."

"Pompous asshole is more like it."

Dropping the subject of the civic leader, Caleb reached the passenger side and stepped back. "You said she was a beauty, but this is better than I imagined. A 1962 Thunderbird Landau. Amazing."

Cooper reached for the car cover, and Caleb moved to help him. "I don't know how long Tanner had her, but this turned out to be the original color. They call it chestnut brown. The only thing I had to do was a little upholstery repair, give her a tune-up, replace the tires, and apply soap and water. The rest Tanner had already done."

"Like I said, amazing." The pair tucked the cover tight under the front end. "So what's the next project?" Caleb asked, giving a fleeting look to the rest of the inventory. "I don't see that old truck you swiped out from under me."

"I told you," Cooper said, leading back to the entrance, "if you wanted that truck, you should have outbid me. I've got that one at home where I do my fun work. Next up in here will be that '57 Vette over in the corner." He pointed toward a heap in the shadows covered by a dirty tarp. The only thing showing was a smudged round headlight.

"You've got a '57 Vette under there?"

"I do." The mechanic sighed as a depressed look crossed his face. "And a ton of others waiting for attention. I either need to marry rich or win the lottery so I can spend my days fixing 'em all up."

"Now that would be a nice life," Caleb said, and he meant it. Waking up every morning, grabbing some coffee, and stepping into a well-appointed garage to work under the hood of a vintage machine sounded like a great way to spend the rest of his years. So long as Snow was along for the ride.

The men stepped into the waning sunlight, and Cooper slid the rusted door shut. "You're welcome to come down to Goodlettsville when the events start back up in the spring. If I have the truck running by then, I might let you drive the T-Bird."

A tempting offer for sure, but Caleb's first thought was that he wouldn't still be in town come spring. Or would he?

"Thanks, Cooper. I may take you up on that."

Chapter 18

Lorelei had been after Snow for days to spill all her juicy details, pointing out that the insipid grin on her face was proof enough that she was no longer sleeping chastely beside her husband. At first Snow had put her off, certain that Lorelei would not approve of her leading Caleb on when she still intended to end the marriage. But more and more Snow was starting to believe that marrying Caleb had not been a mistake.

Marrying him so *quickly* had been the problem.

And, as her mother had pointed out on the phone earlier in the day, Snow and Caleb were rectifying that particular issue by returning to the dating stage. Not that she'd planned to tell her mother about the bizarre state of her life, but as soon as Snow had heard Mama's voice on the other end, she'd spilled it all.

By the time they ended the call, Roberta Cameron was throwing around "I told you sos" and planning a big Christmas dinner to welcome home her prodigal daughter and unwavering son-in-law. Too bad Snow didn't harbor the same happy ending certainty her mother did.

"If that isn't the face of a woman satisfied with life, I don't know what is," Lorelei said, dropping into the booth across from Snow. They'd agreed to meet for dinner at the new Mexican restaurant two blocks down from Snow's store.

Mamacita's added a dose of sorely needed variety to their little metropolis—an alternative to greasy diner food, and deep-fried and gravy-covered options. Based on the tantalizing smells alone, Snow would give the place five stars. Her mouth was watering by the time her friends arrived.

Ignoring Lorelei's comment, Snow said, "Where have you two been? I've been sitting here drooling over this menu for nearly ten minutes."

Carrie sat down at the edge of the seat Lorelei had scooted across, and then she turned to face the table. Only her stomach didn't fit.

"I'm sorry," Snow said, pulling the table her way.

Carrie slid in with a grateful sigh. "Oh, man."

"What?" Lorelei said, suddenly on high alert. "Is she coming? Do we need to call an ambulance?"

The expectant mother turned to scoot back out of the booth. "Get a grip, Lorelei. She isn't due for another month. I have to pee."

Snow camouflaged her laughter by taking a sip of her water. "If you keep this up, Carrie's going to snap and sit on you," she said. "And I hope I'm around to see it."

"I can't help it," Lorelei said, sticking her nose in her menu. "Having a baby is dangerous. Anything could happen."

"Right. Because women haven't been spitting out babies since the dawn of time."

Slapping the menu shut, Lorelei said, "This is different." Glancing in the direction Carrie had disappeared, she added, "Carrie lost a baby before."

This was news to Snow. "What? When? Did Patch—"

"Not Patch," Lorelei said. "The baby was Spencer's. He was born with the umbilical cord around his neck and the doctors couldn't save him."

Snow's heart dropped. "Oh, honey, that's horrible. I had no idea."

"Spencer doesn't talk about it much, but I know he still thinks about the baby. They named him Jeremy." Lorelei leaned forward. "I know this is a weird situation, but Spencer still cares a lot about Carrie, and I've come to like her, too. She's like the little sister I never had."

"Who married your husband while you were away being an actress."

"Technically, I was being a waitress. And like I said—weird. But based on what I know of that woman's life, this baby has the potential to be the best thing that ever happened to her. Carrie deserves some happiness."

Warmth filled Snow's chest at the knowledge that Lorelei was so determined to protect a woman she could have easily deemed an enemy. Whatever had brought Snow to this little corner of the world, she was grateful for the gift. Ardent Springs had good people.

"Carrie got lucky when her path crossed with yours," Snow said, remembering how Lorelei had witnessed Carrie's former husband smacking her around during the summer and charged to her rescue. The fact that Carrie was Spencer's ex-wife hadn't seemed to matter. Within days of that rescue, Patch Farmer had gotten himself killed in a bar fight, leaving Carrie with a baby on the way and nothing else. "Sometimes things happen for a reason."

"You mean like when two people fly off to Vegas and find themselves unexpectedly hitched?" Lorelei asked, turning the conversation away from herself.

Snow huffed and went back to studying her menu, even though she knew what she planned to order. "You're like a dog with a bone, woman." To appease her friend, and hoping to kill the topic completely, she added, "Yes, we are having sex. Yes, the sex is incredible. And yes, I am disgustingly happy right now."

With one manicured finger, Lorelei lowered Snow's menu and caught her eye. "Just right now?"

"Yes," Snow answered, her voice firm. "We've decided to focus on the present and not think about anything beyond that." Which was a lie, since all Snow could think about was everything beyond that. She'd even had a dream the night before in which a little boy with dark curls and startling blue eyes raced up to her, Caleb close on his heels. Their smiles were so alike, Snow had jolted awake with a suffocating yearning in her chest.

Releasing the menu, her friend said, "You're not fooling anyone. You've got 'til death do us part written all over you."

"We've been together less than two weeks."

"You married the man nearly two years ago," Lorelei argued.

Before Snow could form a rebuttal, Carrie returned to the table, doing the same side maneuver she'd used before. "What did I miss?"

"Snow's in denial," Lorelei said.

"Lorelei's being a pain in the ass," Snow said.

Carrie's eyes shifted between the two for several seconds before saying, "So I didn't miss anything. Good. We need to order. I'm starving."

The air had turned chilly by Friday, when Spencer had agreed to show Caleb around the Ruby during the lunch hour. Leaning against his Jeep, Caleb contemplated the bright red marquee of the theater looming in front of him as he waited for his tour guide to arrive, but his mind remained on his wife.

His beautiful, happy wife.

Snow had recommended he give the new Mexican restaurant a call about advertising, which had resulted in landing his first new client and finding the best Mexican food he'd tasted since a trip to Galveston a couple of years before. While greedily devouring his taco, Caleb considered all the ways he would thank his wife for her suggestion, most of which involved her naked and moaning his name.

"Are you eating that food, or making mad, passionate love to it?" Spencer asked as he stepped out of his truck.

After finishing his current bite, Caleb said, "Have you tried Mamacita's yet? This is amazing."

The man in the cowboy hat shook his head. "Not yet, but Lorelei is demanding I take her there tonight, so it must be good."

"Worth every penny," he assured Spencer. Caleb wrapped up the rest of his lunch and wiped his hands on a napkin. "Thanks for doing this on your lunch hour."

"Not a problem." Spencer pulled his jacket tighter as he led Caleb to the theater entrance. "As you heard at the meeting, we used the money raised in October to repair the roof, so at least we won't go through another winter with Mother Nature wreaking more havoc on the interior."

"That was all raised with a festival?"

Spencer slid a key into the lock. "You bet. Lorelei put the whole thing together, and we got lucky when Wes Tillman signed on as entertainment. He provided a lot of equipment for free and gave a sizable donation that helped us hit the goal."

"Wes Tillman? The guy who's won nearly every award Nashville gives out?"

"The one and only." Spencer opened the door and stepped back to let Caleb enter first. "There's no electricity," he said, drawing a small flashlight from his back pocket. "But this is enough for you to see what we're up against."

"Does Tillman live here?" Caleb asked as he took in the busted concession counter in the center of the lobby. "I thought he was from Texas."

"Wes lives outside of town. He's married to a local disc jockey and holds little jam sessions over at the Second Chance Saloon." Dust danced in the beam from the flashlight. "If you're a fan, I think he's got a show coming up on Wednesday."

Snow said she didn't sing anymore, but the train that had derailed her dream was their marriage. If they were going to work, he didn't want her hating him in ten years for taking that away from her. A star like Wes Tillman would have connections. Connections that could put Snow's singing dreams back on track. And if he heard Snow's voice, Caleb had no doubt Wes would be a willing benefactor.

Making a mental note to put in some calls, Caleb said, "Thanks. I'll look into it."

As the tour continued, Caleb grew to understand the magnitude of this project. The screen, seats, and scarlet curtains draped along the walls were all a total loss.

"How does the balcony look?" he asked, tucking a piece of foam back inside a ripped seat.

"Better than this, actually. But you can see now the extent of the project." Spencer pointed the flashlight at the ceiling. "You still want to get involved?"

Following the beam of light, Caleb nodded. "Yeah. I do."

Spencer must not have been expecting that answer. "Really?"

"Really," he said, meeting his friend's eye. "Did you think I'd see this and walk away?"

"I didn't know what to expect, to be honest," Spencer replied. "I don't mean to butt into your business, but are you planning to stick around here in Ardent Springs? I got the impression from Snow when you first showed up that your visit was temporary. This project isn't going to be done in a couple of months."

Was Caleb's stay temporary? Or would he be living in Ardent Springs come this time next year? The questions kept coming up, and the more he ruminated on the subject, the more he landed on the same answer.

There would be no leaving Snow, that was a given, but the original plan had always been to move his wife back to Louisiana with him.

At some point in the last couple of weeks, without Caleb realizing, his plans had changed.

"I can't give any guarantees, but as of right now, I don't see us leaving anytime soon."

A friendly grin split Spencer's face. "Our little burb is growing on you, huh?"

Caleb shared a smile of his own. "I admit, the place has a certain charm about it."

"We do our best," Spencer said, heading back toward the lobby.

"By the way, where did you guys have this big festival?" Recalling his conversation with Cooper about space in town, Caleb added, "The fairgrounds?"

"Nope," Spencer answered, stepping into the November chill. "Right here in the parking lot."

Glancing left and right as he stepped through the door, Caleb saw nothing but Margin Street, lined with brick buildings and no parking lots. "There's a parking lot?"

Spencer nodded to his left. "Around the side and behind the building. Come on, I'll show you."

With hunched shoulders, the men rounded the corner and Caleb was shocked to see a wide alley that led down the length of the building and into a sizable parking lot. An idea instantly came to mind.

"This is perfect," he said aloud.

Spencer shrugged. "It's okay. As far as parking lots go."

"No," Caleb said. "It's exactly what we need."

Snow spent her Friday morning searching the Internet for ideas on what to get Caleb for his birthday coming up at the end of the month. The present carried more weight as possibly the last thing she would ever give him.

Other than a divorce. They'd made progress in the happiness department, but Vivien's threat was never far from Snow's thoughts.

Her husband wasn't the new gadget type, didn't care about clothes, and it wasn't as if they had much room in the apartment for something like a big-screen TV or an extra dresser.

Not that she'd buy him a dresser. That would be weird. Still, she almost wished they had a bigger place so Caleb could stop living out of the box his mother had shipped his clothes in. The thought brought her up short. When had she forgotten that Caleb would be leaving in little over two weeks? Their one-month trial period would end, and she'd send him packing. Or would she?

Imagining her life the way it had been before Caleb found her, Snow tried to find relief in a return to normal. In the thought of getting her life back. But seeing herself alone again only made her feel empty.

"Whatcha doin'?" Lorelei asked as she placed a plastic container on the counter. Without answering, Snow pointed to the bowl with a questioning look. "Granny made dumplings last night," her friend answered, setting a fork and napkin next to the bowl. "This is my way of apologizing for Wednesday. Your love life is your business, and I need to butt out." Crossing her arms, she added, "I'm sorry."

By the time they'd left dinner at Mamacita's, Snow had gotten over her snit with Lorelei. They'd spent the entire meal talking about Carrie and the baby and how to decorate the nursery in the expectant mother's new home. The one good thing to come out of the death of Carrie's husband, other than an end to a violent marriage, had been the life insurance policy provided by Patch Farmer's employer. It turned out all employees at the factory received policies equal to their annual salary, paid for by the company.

Carrie certainly wasn't rolling in dough, but thanks to that policy, she'd been able to buy herself a nice little single-wide trailer not far from town. It had been used, but came with a yard, had been well-maintained, and best of all, provided a safe and comfortable home for the new little family.

"Lorelei, there's nothing to apologize for."

"Look," her friend said, "I'm not good at the girlfriend thing. I'm abrupt and bossy and any filter I might have had disappeared by the time I was ten. But I'm working on that, and a big thing is admitting when I've crossed a line."

Snow couldn't argue with Lorelei's assessment of herself, but the woman also had a big heart, was funny as hell, and regardless of her tactics, always meant well.

However, Rosie Pratchett's chicken and dumplings were really good.

"Well then," she said, pulling the bowl her way, "if me eating these chicken and dumplings will make you feel better, that's a sacrifice I'm willing to make."

Lorelei rolled her eyes. "Maybe you're the one who should move to Hollywood and give acting a try."

"No thank you," Snow said with a laugh. "I'm good where I am." As she lifted the lid, a heavenly scent tickled her nose and made her mouth water. "This is going to be much better than my PB&J sandwich."

But before Snow could dig in, the store phone rang. Having learned her lesson, she checked the ID to see the name of the appraiser who'd given her an estimate on the William Norton painting.

"Hello, Ms. Bolliver. How can I help you?"

"Good afternoon, Ms. Cameron. Is there any way you could have that William Norton painting down here in Nashville by nine tomorrow morning?"

Snow's mind raced to find an answer. She'd need someone to run the store. And they'd need to take Caleb's Jeep since the painting was too large and delicate to shove in her backseat.

"I'm not sure," she answered honestly. "Why?"

"Premier is conducting a special auction that includes three other valuable artworks. That means the buyers will be there, and this is the perfect situation to maximize your profits while putting that piece into the hands of a dedicated collector." Her passion for her trade coming through, the appraiser added, "A piece like that deserves to be in a collection where it will be admired and cared for."

As Snow recalled, Virginia Bolliver had been appalled upon learning the previous location of the painting, and further astonished that no one involved with the Brambleton estate had a clue of the treasure in their midst.

"Doesn't an auction like that require some sort of application and review process?" The Premier Auction House had a reputation for selling only the best items with authentication and full documentation of provenance.

"In most situations, yes," Ms. Bolliver agreed, "but I've convinced them to bypass standard protocol for your piece. You have a rare find, Ms. Cameron. I highly recommend you take whatever measures necessary to be here in the morning."

Well, when she put it that way . . .

"I'll have to find someone to run the store," Snow said, catching Lorelei's eye. "Saturday is a busy day here."

Lorelei caught the hint and raised her hand. "I can do it."

"But I'm sure I can work that out," Snow said into the phone. "Could you e-mail the address and other details?"

"Consider it done." The appraiser sounded pleased. "I'll see you in the morning, Ms. Cameron. Be prepared for an exciting day. If I'm right, and I usually am, your painting will be the star of the show."

Without waiting for a reply, Ms. Bolliver hung up, and a second later Snow's phone chimed, indicating she'd received a new e-mail.

"Wow," Lorelei said, "that woman doesn't mess around. Now, who is Ms. Bolliver?"

Snow stared at Lorelei with what she could only guess was a goofy expression. "I believe she just became my fairy godmother."

If the painting sold for anything near the appraisal amount, Snow could make serious upgrades to the store and still have enough to send money home to her parents. And maybe, even if only for a day, Snow would no longer be the poor nobody that Caleb had brought home to Mommy and Daddy Warbucks.

Chapter 19

"Yes," Caleb said, staring at the Ruby parking lot with his hands on his hips. "This is the perfect spot."

Spencer rubbed his chin as he squinted at the empty lot. "Perfect for what?"

"A cruise-in."

"You mean one of those old car things?"

Caleb gave his new friend a dubious look. "They aren't old cars, they're classics, and the people who own them like to show them off. We're going to give them that opportunity."

"Now you sound like Coop," Spencer said. "I can appreciate an old car"—Caleb increased his glare, and Spencer corrected—"a classic car as much as the next fella, but anything that happens in this parking lot needs to go toward the restoration project. That's not my rule, that's according to the owners."

"It'll all go toward the restoration project."

That announcement caught Spencer's attention. "You're talking about a cruise-in to raise money?"

"I am," Caleb said. "We can hold them all summer long. This lot is large enough for three sections." He pointed to the row directly adjacent to the back wall of the theater. "Cruisers over there." Shifting to the middle section, he added, "Muscle cars in the center, and over on the far side will be the sale lot. We'll charge a higher fee for those spots, of course."

"Let me get this straight," Spencer said, stepping forward and surveying the lot as if trying to picture what Caleb described. "People will pay to park their cars here?"

"They will." He could see it clear as day, as if the cars were already filling the space. "Once the first event is a success, word of mouth will spread, and by the third time around, we'll have to turn people away."

Catching Caleb's enthusiasm, Spencer said, "What about vendors? People will need to eat, right?"

Liking the idea, Caleb nodded. "People will definitely need to eat. It's the perfect fundraiser because it's almost no overhead. Provide a couple generators for the vendors, if they don't supply their own, and maybe set a little of the entry fees aside as prize money. Award a 'best in show' or something. The owners love that, and we can let the attendees decide the winners."

"Buford would cough up the generators with no problem," Spencer said, referring to the local hardware store owner and official Ruby Restoration committee chair. "I can't believe we didn't see this before. Especially after utilizing the space for the festival."

"The idea came from Cooper. He told me that the mayor wouldn't let him use the fairgrounds for something like this." With a conspiratorial smile, Caleb added, "I bet if we team up, we can coax our mechanic friend into coordinating the whole thing."

"Are you sure folks will come?" Spencer asked as he looked out over the parking lot. "Not the owners, but other people?"

Recognizing how his position at the paper could benefit the cause, Caleb said, "If we advertise it right."

That elicited a chuckle from Spencer. "We'll need to get an advertising budget approved by the committee, but something tells me you won't have any problem selling them on the idea."

"Me?" Caleb asked. "You're the one they all listen to."

"Oh no," he said, tipping his hat back. "This one is your baby, and you're the salesman. I doubt you'll have any trouble making them listen."

He appreciated the man's faith in him. "Fair enough."

With a check of his watch, Spencer said, "Time to go." The pair hustled back to the front of the building as Spencer explained, "Carrie's appointment is in less than thirty minutes, and I still need to pick her up out at the construction office."

"You're taking Carrie to an appointment?" Caleb asked, confused once again by the connection between Boyd and the expectant mother.

"Sure," Spencer answered, pulling his keys from his pocket to unlock his truck. "She can't fit behind the wheel of Patch's old truck anymore."

Caleb hadn't heard the name before. "Patch?"

"Her good-for-nothing dead husband." Pausing at his open door, Spencer said, "We'll wait until we talk to Coop before presenting this idea to the board. You good with putting something together for next Friday?"

"Not a problem," Caleb answered.

As the gray Dodge drove off down the street, Caleb wondered if Lorelei knew how her fiancé felt about Carrie Farmer's former husband. Or more importantly, how he felt about the tiny brunette about to be a single mother.

Snow moaned for the third time as she gripped her headboard tighter. "Oh, yes. Right there," she said, her voice breathy and desperate.

"Right here?" Caleb asked, his voice syrupy as he circled the same delicate spot over and over.

"Uh-huh." Snow's entire body melted in pure pleasure. "How did I go without this for so long?" she asked.

Caleb dropped a kiss on her big toe. "I don't know, darling. How did you?"

She opened one eye and shot her husband a warning look. "Don't get smug down there, Mr. McGraw. But it's nice to know that if your job at the paper ever falls through, you have a lucrative career in foot massage to fall back on."

Increasing the pressure on her arch, Caleb ignored her comment. "What do you know about Spencer Boyd and Carrie Farmer?" he asked.

Snow's eyes popped open. What was that question about?

"I know Carrie is Spencer's ex-wife," she said. "And that they're good friends."

The foot massage stopped. "She was his wife?"

"Hey," Snow said, shaking her foot. "Are we talking or massaging?"

"Relax," he said, returning to his task. "I can do both. So Lorelei knows about them?"

Snuggling deeper into her pillow, Snow answered, "Sure, she knows."

"Huh," Caleb said. "And she's fine with her fiancé being in love with someone else?"

Snow jerked her foot out of Caleb's grasp as she sat up. "Her fiancé what?"

"I can't be the only one who sees it," Caleb said. "He hovers over her. Drives her to her appointments. If Lorelei is fine with it, then good for them, but I couldn't handle that."

Though she appreciated knowing her husband was against either of them falling in love with someone else, she needed to disabuse Caleb of his highly erroneous assumption.

"Spencer Boyd is not in love with his ex-wife. He loves Lorelei, and he always has."

"But you said he was married to Carrie."

"He was," she explained, "but that was while Lorelei was in LA trying to be an actress and he thought she wasn't coming back."

Caleb's head tilted. "So he married Carrie, even though he loved Lorelei?"

Why did she have to land the only man on the planet who possessed a feminine view on love?

"Of course he didn't." Snow struggled for a way to explain her friends' situation. Though to be honest, she never totally understood the whole story herself. "After Lorelei broke his heart, Spencer moved on with his life. He married Carrie, whom he loved and thought he'd spend the rest of his life with, but life happens, you know? Their marriage ended, she married someone else, and eventually Lorelei came back to him. Happy endings all around."

"Except for Carrie," Caleb pointed out. "Her husband died, remember?"

"Yes," Snow agreed. "But her husband was a wife beater who got himself killed at a bar. So, really, she's better off without him." She slid her foot back under his nose and wiggled her toes. "Now, please tell me you haven't shared your cockamamie theory with anyone else."

Massaging the back of her heel, Caleb asked, "Who says *cockamamie* anymore?"

"Tell me you haven't spread some rumor about Spencer cheating on Lorelei."

"Of course not," he said, sounding offended. "I'm not an idiot. But are you sure I'm wrong?"

Snow nodded, closing her eyes and letting the tension leave her shoulders. How Caleb found the exact right spots she did not know. But oh, was she thankful he did.

"I'm positive. The other night, Lorelei referred to Carrie as the little sister she never had. I admit, it appears to be a weird situation from the outside, which Lorelei readily admits, but there's nothing salacious going on."

"That's good," Caleb said, sliding his hands up her calf. "Because I like Spencer, and I'd hate to lose respect for him."

She opened her eyes to watch him drop a kiss on her knee. The zing nearly shot out her ears as Snow's body started to melt. "You really don't like infidelity, do you?" Snow asked.

Caleb looked up after kissing the inside of her thigh. "No, I don't. I've seen up close what it can do to people."

"What does that mean?" she asked, struggling to concentrate as he worked his way up her body. With every touch, the need pitched higher.

Shaking his head, Caleb dropped a soft kiss on her lips. "Not tonight," he said. "It's time for a different kind of massage."

She didn't want to let the question go, especially when she saw the demons the subject let loose in his eyes. Her always lighthearted husband was hiding a wound she knew nothing about. But before she could push the issue, Caleb slid the straps of her tank top off her shoulders and took one pink nipple between his teeth. Her gasp of pleasure echoed around them as her questions drowned in a pool of desire.

Caleb had never seen Snow this nervous. After weeks of watching her step on stages in Nashville, he'd expect selling a painting at auction to be the less daunting task. But his wife had become a frantic ball of energy in the passenger seat. He'd asked her twice if she needed him to stop for a potty break, and the second time she nearly ripped his head off and told him to drive and keep quiet.

Being the rational man that he was, Caleb followed the directive and clamped his piehole shut.

"This is it," Snow informed him, as he pulled the Jeep into the auction house parking lot. He didn't bother to tell her he knew where they were going, seeing as he was the one who had mapped the place out. Today was not the day to correct his better half.

"There aren't a lot of cars here. That's a bad sign, isn't it?"

"Not when the show doesn't start for ninety minutes." The e-mail she'd showed him said to arrive by nine, but Snow had demanded they leave the house at seven. He'd talked her into leaving at seven thirty, and that still put them here a half hour early. With only two cars in the lot, Caleb wondered if they were the first to arrive.

Snow reached his side of the Jeep before his feet hit the pavement. "Be careful with the painting," she said, for the tenth time that morning. "Don't hurt it."

"I'm not going to hurt it, darling," he said, looking forward to this sale being over so he could have his mild-mannered wife back. "You've wrapped it well enough to survive the *Titanic*."

"I wanted to make sure it didn't get damaged on the way down here," Snow defended, hovering around him as he drew the delicate cargo from the backseat. "Don't put it on the ground," she ordered, seconds before the painting touched the pavement.

"Honey, it's wrapped in four layers of brown paper. A little asphalt isn't going to hurt it."

"Still," she said, taking her new obsession out of his hands. The thing was nearly as big as she was, making her look like a giant brown rectangle with feet. "I'll feel better once we're inside."

I'll feel better once this is over, he thought. Not that he'd say as much aloud. Caleb had learned a lot about being a husband in the last couple of weeks. Determination to keep a woman happy and his own hide out of a sling made a man a fast learner.

"I'll carry it," he said as she started hobbling toward the large building with the Premier Auctions sign over the door. "You're going to break your neck and the painting—now give it here."

For the first time all day, Snow didn't argue. She let Caleb take the painting without a fuss and didn't even remind him to be careful. Maybe she was starting to relax. And then they reached the entrance.

"Be careful," she murmured, holding the door open for him.

Caleb rolled his eyes, but only because she couldn't see his face. To his relief, an auction coordinator met them at the small counter not far from the entrance. She introduced herself with a welcoming smile, thanked them for bringing the painting on such short notice, and then explained that she would hand it over to the staff to tag and place with the other items up for bid.

As the treasure passed hands, Snow said, "Be careful," to the friendly woman, who nodded and maintained her smile. Caleb assumed the employee was used to overprotective owners, but Snow was acting as if she'd given birth to the thing.

"The auction room is the second door on the right," the woman informed them, nodding toward the back of the room. "Coffee and tea, as well as water, are available on a side table." To Snow she said, "Don't worry about a thing. This is the star of our show. We'll take good care of it."

As if those simple words were all she needed to hear, Snow visibly relaxed and managed a genuine smile in return. "Thank you. I'm not usually this crazy."

"No, she isn't," Caleb said to back her up, but the woman had disappeared through a doorway behind the counter. "Let's go sit down," he said to Snow, dropping a hand to the small of her back.

"She thinks I'm nuts, doesn't she?"

Caleb shook his head. "I doubt you're the first person who cared about something of value."

"But I'm practically twitching, and she gave me that look most people reserve for small children or misbehaving dogs."

Pressing a kiss against her temple, he said, "You're more adorable than either of those things."

She slid her hand through his arm and said, "I'm going to take that as a compliment."

"As it was intended." Together they stepped into the auction room, and both stopped in their tracks. "Holy moly," he muttered.

"That's one way to put it," Snow replied.

Chapter 20

As if Snow wasn't nervous enough already. The auction room—*room* being the understatement of the year—could easily house a college basketball game, including ample bleacher space on each side. A towering set of double doors bookended the long center-stage. The podium on the left was presumably for the auctioneer, and the entire floor was covered with row upon row of folding chairs. Other than two young men working on the stage, she and Caleb were the only people in the room.

"Where do we sit?" she whispered, having no idea why she felt the need to keep her voice down. It wasn't as if they'd walked into a church. Though she'd never seen a church this big before.

"By the looks of things," he said, "anywhere we want."

Feeling small and out of place, she wrung her hands and said, "I need tea. Tea would be good."

"Over here." Caleb led her to a long table covered with a bright white tablecloth and loaded with several coffee dispensers, as well as two marked "Hot Water."

Barely a minute later she was sipping a sweet cup of Earl Grey and feeling less jumpy. "That star of the show thing," Snow said. "Do you think she meant that, or was she patronizing the crazy painting lady?"

"I told you, William Norton paintings don't come up for auction often. Especially not in that size." Caleb sipped his coffee as they strolled down the middle aisle heading for the stage. "I still can't believe you got it for such a cheap price. Whoever runs that estate auction business in Ardent Springs needs to find another field."

"That's our fine mayor you're talking about," Snow said, turning into a row of chairs about ten back from the front. "Jebediah Winkle bought the whole setup not a month before you got here. The Presley family handled all the estate auctions three counties wide for at least fifteen years, but when the elder Presley passed away, his children weren't interested in continuing. I think Jebediah bought it to earn himself some credibility with the local merchants. He got himself elected with the promise of improving the economy, and so far, he hasn't done squat."

"Considering nearly everyone I've met doesn't like the man, I'm wondering how he got elected at all. Anyone can make a promise to turn things around, but if he's a known jerk, why check his name on the ballot?"

"Don't look at me," Snow said. "I wasn't around for the election. And anyway, I doubt he'll get a second term."

She almost mentioned how busy advertising at the paper would be the following year, with the election coming up, but she kept the thought to herself. Talk of the future would lead to talk of their future, and Snow was still avoiding that emotional quagmire. Though she couldn't help but note that Caleb hadn't mentioned returning to Louisiana since the weekend he'd arrived.

"Gerald says election time gets crazy at the paper. I could as much as double my regular commissions in the three months or so before voting day."

Snow sat very still, unsure of how to reply. Did that mean he planned to be living in Ardent Springs a year from now? Presumably still married to her? This wasn't good. He needed to start spouting bossy orders about living in Baton Rouge and taking his wife with him. How else was she supposed to send him packing if he no longer intended to leave?

"Darling?" Caleb said, sliding an arm around her shoulders. "You look like you've seen a ghost. Are you okay?"

She gave a vigorous nod in the affirmative, but couldn't speak. Fear and dread were strangling her vocal cords while simultaneously tying knots in her colon.

"There's nothing to worry about," Caleb said. "The painting is going to be a hit."

"Right," she said, sipping her tea and reining in her monkey brain. "I just want this over with." And she didn't mean the auction.

Getting a hefty sum for the painting lost its luster when all she could think about was the possibility of a real happily ever after with Caleb. They could have that happy ending in Ardent Springs, away from the toxic influence of his parents. Why couldn't she win for once? He'd picked her. He wanted her. And she wanted him.

So Vivien lurked in the wings, waiting to spill Snow's secret and possibly break her son's heart. Caleb had said there was nothing that could make him change his mind. Nothing short of cheating, and that was one sin her mother-in-law couldn't throw in Snow's face.

Caleb would stay with his wife, no matter what. That's what he'd said. Snow clung to the hope that he meant those words.

Caleb had never wanted to see something sell so badly in his life. He almost wished he'd set up an anonymous bid of his own to make sure the number kept going up. Or he could have let his father know the painting was available. Jackson McGraw had been looking for another Norton for years. But knowing how he felt about Snow, Caleb would burn the painting before letting his father have it.

They'd watched Ming vases, silver flatware from the eighteen hundreds, and a turn-of-the-century pocket watch go for well over their top estimates. The moment the Norton was brought on stage, Snow grabbed his hand and squeezed hard enough to cut off circulation. To save his digits, he extricated his hand and put his arm around her, pulling her tight against his side. At some point, her nervousness had infiltrated his system.

He sent out high-dollar thoughts to the crowd around them, who had filled in more than half of the seats by the time the first item was rolled out.

The low estimate on the painting had been set at ten thousand, and the bidding started at five. When the action slowed around eight thousand, Caleb cursed himself for not grabbing a paddle. What the hell was wrong with these people? Didn't they know fine art when they saw it?

But then a phone bidder joined the party, and the number went up. Two gentlemen in the audience remained determined, and soon a casual Saturday morning auction turned into a bidding war. When the auctioneer yelled, "Do I hear twelve five?" Snow squealed and nearly climbed into his lap. The war continued and crested at fourteen thousand before both sides started to back down.

And then the bidder on the phone came in at an even fifteen thousand, two thousand over the high estimate, and the room fell silent. The auctioneer tried to goad the attending bidders into going higher, but no one was willing to top the fifteen mark.

"Sold to bidder thirty-four ten on the phone!"

Snow danced in her chair as Caleb silently thanked the powers that be for giving his wife the good day that she'd hoped for. "What are you going to do with all that money?" he whispered in her ear.

She flashed him a smile that took his breath away. "I'm putting in a coffee shop," she said, taking him completely by surprise.

Lorelei was going to be so surprised. Snow had intended to add the little coffee and baked goods nook in the back of the store come spring, though that would only be possible if the store hit record sales during the holiday season. But now, the project could start right after the new year no matter what happened over the next six weeks.

Another bonus of her big day was that she'd be able to buy Caleb the present she really wanted to get him.

"How long has this coffee shop idea been brewing in that little head of yours?" Caleb asked as they traveled north up I-65.

"Since the festival," she answered, still a little shocked to be holding a check for fifteen thousand dollars in her lap. "As I'm sure you know, the specialty coffee business is booming. Pairing that with Lorelei's amazing baked goods is a no-brainer."

Or so she hoped. Ardent Springs wasn't the hippest town on the planet, but they loved Lorelei's desserts, and she had faith they'd be willing to pay for tasty coffees to go with their cookies.

"Is Lorelei going to share the start-up costs, since you're willing to put her name on it?"

She hadn't thought of that. "You mean, like a partnership?"

"Sure." Caleb passed a BMW, adding, "If it's going to be called Lulu's Café, then Lulu should put up some money."

The café wasn't Lorelei's idea, but they had talked about her running it. She'd only been selling the baked goods for six months, and though she never complained, Snow knew that Lorelei was only making enough to cover her ingredients and keep herself mobile and fed. Not that she needed a lot of money, living with Spencer over her grandmother's garage and all.

"I don't know," Snow said, uncomfortable with the idea of mixing friendship and business. "I'll have to think about it."

"Do you have a coffee supplier in mind?" he asked. What was up with all the questions?

"No, Caleb, I don't. I don't have all the answers. I don't know if I want Lorelei to put up money, and I don't know where we'll get the coffee." She tightened her jaw and stared out the window at the passing landscape. "Forget I said anything."

Caleb squeezed her knee. "I'm sorry," he said. "I got carried away. This is your thing, and I'll stay out of it."

"I don't want you to stay out of it," she replied. "I want just to enjoy the fact that a painting I bought for three hundred dollars just sold for fifty times that. Can we focus on the victory for right now and think about all the minute details later?"

"Yes, ma'am." A goofy grin split his face. "You have my support and my advice whenever you want it," Caleb said, pride clear in his voice. "But as part of this team, I should have a hand in taste-testing the new menu, right? Whenever that comes around," he hastened to add.

Ignoring the warning bells ringing in her mind, Snow kept her eyes on the highway ahead and said, "That probably won't come up until after the first of the year. You plan to still be around then?"

Taking her chin between two fingers, Caleb turned her face until their eyes met. With a serious expression, he said, "The only way I wouldn't be around is if you decide we should move. You thinking about moving?"

The relief was so strong that tears threatened at the back of her eyes. Happy tears.

"What about your parents and Baton Rouge?"

He returned his focus to the road. "There's always phone calls and holiday visits."

Christmas with the McGraws sounded as pleasant as having her appendix removed through her big toe. Snow would much rather see her own family during the holidays, and if her mother-in-law followed through on her threat, that's exactly where Snow would be. Headed to Birmingham by herself.

At some point in the last two weeks, hope had taken root in Snow's heart. Could there be a chance that Caleb learning the truth might not mean the end of them? Could he forgive her?

More importantly, was Snow willing to risk it?

"You're awfully quiet over there," Caleb said.

Snow took his hand, choosing to stay in the moment. "Just happy," she said.

And tried to believe it.

⚬

Caleb spent the rest of the drive home thinking about this new development. Though Ardent Springs had been growing on him, he hadn't actually made the decision that this was where he wanted to live. Not that he had any intention of leaving Snow, but he'd never pictured himself living in a small town either.

He had no family here. No history. They didn't even have a real home. The apartment behind Hattie's house was cozy enough, but not anywhere he'd want to live long term. Caleb was living like an interloper in Snow's frilly little cottage as it was.

But living arrangements were easy enough to change. If he insisted they move back to Baton Rouge, everything they'd accomplished in the last two weeks would be for naught. And Caleb had to admit, being this far from his parents wasn't such a bad thing. Other than his mother's constant phone calls, which he'd been ignoring more and more, there was a certain freedom in being completely on his own.

Even when he'd lived in Nashville, trips home had been frequent. His ego fought against the admission, but Caleb had to face the truth. He'd never truly cut the cord that tied him to his overbearing and demanding parents. This was his opportunity to do that. To be his own man, not Jackson and Vivien McGraw's trophy offspring.

In Ardent Springs, he could simply be Caleb—salesman, husband, and contributing member of a community that valued his input. To the residents of this small town, he was no different from and no better than they were. A new experience he found oddly refreshing and rewarding.

So the only real problem was the little apartment, and that could be fixed with the right agent. Luckily, one of Caleb's soon-to-be-inherited clients was the best realtor in Ardent Springs. And that would be his first call come Monday morning.

He had to admit, all the pieces of creating his and Snow's happily ever after were falling amazingly into place. As if all they had had to do was land in this little town and start all over again. He'd have preferred *not* to have endured the eighteen-month hiatus to get to this point, but Caleb wasn't one to complain about a good thing.

However they reached this point, he was just happy they'd gotten there.

Chapter 21

"I think the counter color should be blue," Carrie said, "to match the logo."

Carrie was referring to the Lulu's Home Bakery logo that Snow had created back in the summer. The word *Lulu's* stood out in bold blue letters on a brown oval background.

"The whole thing can't be blue," Lorelei commented. "It would be too masculine and stand out like a turd in the punch bowl around all the girlie stuff in the store."

"Isn't standing out the idea?" Carrie rubbed her protruding belly while tilting her head to the side and sizing up the corner where the café would be. "Are you sure this is the right corner?"

Snow and Lorelei gave the pregnant woman a collective stare of disbelief. "Where else would we put it?" Snow asked. They'd sized up every corner in the place and determined that this particular area, visible from the entrance and the front desk, was the perfect spot.

"Maybe it should be up front." She leaned forward and nearly fell off her stool.

At three weeks from her due date, Carrie was under strict orders to sit as much as possible. She was also supposed to have her feet up, but refused to follow that particular directive, claiming she had too much to do to lounge around with her feet in the air. Because her boss, Lorelei's father, Mike, was afraid she'd go into labor while in the office alone, he'd insisted she cut back to half days, which was why she ended up hanging around Snow's Curiosity Shop on a Wednesday afternoon.

"Are you trying to give us a heart attack?" Lorelei asked, righting her friend. "The idea is to get customers to check out the whole store and not just come in for a treat and leave. That's why we all agreed the café should be in the back."

"Oh yeah," Carrie said. "I forgot that part."

"You're forgetting a lot of things these days."

In her defense, Carrie said, "You carry a human being around for nine months and see how well your memory does."

Lorelei looked at Snow. "Did she just curse me?"

Snow rolled her eyes. "Can we focus here? I think blue might be a good idea, but a pretty blue and only on the bottom along the front of the display case and counter. The wall behind should be white, and we'll put the logo really big in the center, with the coffee menu on one side and the dessert menu on the other."

"Yes," Lorelei said. "I can see that working."

Snow smiled as the plans fell into place. Sharing the good news with Lorelei on Saturday afternoon had been the highlight of her year. Though reuniting with her husband stood to take the lead in that race, provided the two of them could overcome the speed bump that was Vivien McGraw.

"Are we ready to break ground on this café or what?" Caleb asked, sneaking up on Snow and wrapping his arms around her.

Speak of the devil. Snow leaned into her husband, letting the rush of having him close fill her senses. "We've decided on the location and color scheme so far."

"You mean you don't have blueprints and a construction crew lined up yet?" he asked, squeezing her tight.

Snow wiggled out of his grasp. "We have a rough drawing and a good start on the menu."

He slid his hands into the pockets of his khakis. "I still get to be taste-tester, right?"

As his exit date was still in question, Snow said, "We'll see. Now, what are you doing here in the middle of the afternoon?"

"Can't I stop by to see my pretty fiancée?"

"You can, but I know you're up to something, so spill."

This time he couldn't distract her with sex. She should have confronted him in public before now.

"You got me," he said, taking her hand and twirling her around the floor. "I'm here to say hurry home this evening because you have a hot date."

They didn't make a habit of going out on weeknights. "On a Wednesday? I've got this café to plan and holiday displays and sales to figure out."

"Business can wait. Tonight we celebrate your auction triumph." Addressing the other two women, Caleb added, "Lorelei, you and Spencer will be joining us. And Carrie, if you're up to it, Cooper has agreed to bring you."

"I don't think twirling around Brubaker's is for me," Carrie answered.

"Nope," Caleb said. "Not Brubaker's. The men know where we're going, and you ladies will find out when we get there."

"Look at the boys getting all take-charge-y," Lorelei mumbled. "And what time should we obedient women be ready?"

"Seven thirty should do it."

Carrie arched her back and said, "I hope Cooper has taken his vitamins because I can barely stay awake past nine these days. He's going to be carrying me to the car before the night is over."

Caleb grew serious. "This night is for Snow, and I promise, you ladies are going to want to be there."

Lorelei and Carrie exchanged a look while Snow's heart skipped a beat.

"You've reeled us in, hot stuff," Lorelei said. "We'll be there."

He shouldn't have given Snow such a hard time about being anxious the day of the auction, because tonight was Caleb's turn to be a sweating mass of nerves. He'd set this up with the certainty that Snow would love it, but the closer they got to the Second Chance Saloon, the more he questioned his decision. She'd told him she didn't sing anymore, but Snow had loved being on stage back when they were dating. The joy on her face translated to anyone watching. He wanted her to know that their marriage didn't mean she had to give up on her dream.

"What are we doing here?" Snow asked as Caleb parked the Jeep in front of the country bar. The Second Chance was smaller than Brubaker's, and it looked at least twenty years older.

"I told you," he said, "you'll find out soon enough."

"If you wanted to dance, we could have gone to Brubaker's. There was no reason to come to the edge of the county."

Caleb took her face in his hands. "We're not here to dance, Snow. You're here to sing."

Amber eyes went wide. "What?"

"I've set it up. Wes Tillman is playing tonight, and he's agreed to let you sing with him."

"Sing with Wes Tillman?" Snow shoved his hands away. "Are you crazy? What makes you think I'd want to do that? I told you, I don't sing anymore."

"Singing was your passion back in Nashville. Why would you give that up?"

She clung to her seat belt and stared out the windshield. "Take me home, Caleb."

"I can't do that." He didn't know why, but something told him to push her on this. "We're going inside."

"You might be going inside," she argued, "but I'm staying right here."

"Snow—"

"Better yet, I'll walk home." She was out of the Jeep before he could react.

Caleb unhooked his seat belt and bolted out after her. "Why won't you do this?" he asked, his voice demanding an answer.

"I don't want to."

"That's not an answer."

"Well it's the only answer you're going to get."

"Snow," he said, spinning her by her shoulders. "I've seen you light up on stage. I know that you love it. Now tell me what's really going on."

A Dodge truck pulled into the lot and stopped next to them. "Is everything good out here?" Spencer asked through his open window.

Without taking his eyes off Snow, who was staring at the gravel, Caleb said, "We need a minute."

"You got it," Spencer said, driving across the lot to park closer to the entrance.

"I can't believe you did this," Snow said, her voice low. "I thought you'd changed. I thought you were listening to me, but nothing has changed."

On the verge of panic, Caleb stepped close, but kept his hands to himself. "Darling, I heard you when you said you don't sing anymore. I swear I did. But I was there. I saw what this meant to you in Nashville. The only thing that stopped you was us getting married, and I don't want you to give up your dream because of me. I don't want you to look back ten years from now and resent me because you gave this up."

Snow met his eyes with fierce determination in her own. "I didn't give up singing for you, Caleb. I never wanted to sing in the first place, okay? I just used my talent to get away from my hometown. To break away from the boring life available to me back there. But I never really intended to become famous or really do it for a living. That's not me at all."

As if the wind had been knocked out of him, Caleb backed up to lean on the back of the Jeep.

"I don't need to chase that dream, Caleb," she said, closing the distance between them. "All I need is you."

He pulled her close, leaning his forehead against hers. "You have me, Snow. But this isn't a major Nashville audition." Caleb lifted his head. "This is you getting to spend a little time back in the spotlight doing something you love to do. That's all. Let me give this to you."

Placing a kiss on his lips, she said, "I'm sorry you thought you killed my dream."

"I want you to be happy," he said. And he'd never meant anything so much in his life.

Snow sighed. "I'm happy, I promise."

Relieved to hear the words, he asked, "Are we going inside?"

She nodded. "We are." Slipping her hand into his, she turned and stepped toward the bar. "Am I really about to sing with Wes Tillman?" she asked, a trace of awe in her voice.

"You are." He gave her hand a squeeze for encouragement. "And you're going to blow him away."

"I don't know. I'm a bit rusty."

"Darling, even on your worst day, you're still the best singer I've ever heard."

She tucked in close against his side. "That's complete BS, but I love you for saying it."

"It's the truth," he said. "And I love you, too."

They stopped and stared at each other, both realizing what the other had said. Caleb looked as if she'd smacked him with a two-by-four, and Snow felt the same.

"Did you just . . ." he started.

Snow's chin bobbed up and down. "And you did, too."

Lifting his wife off the ground, Caleb kissed her until she was dizzy and gasping for air.

"Are y'all done with your lovers' spat?" Cooper asked from the front of the building. "We gots us a pregnant woman in need of the little girls' room out here."

"By all means," Caleb yelled, dropping Snow back to her feet, "let the woman pee!"

❧

Several minutes after entering the bar, Snow was still reeling. She'd said she loved him, and Caleb said it back. Without hesitation. And then he'd kissed her with unmitigated joy as if she'd given him the best present ever.

As Lorelei would say, shit just got real.

"I can't believe how empty this place is," Lorelei said. "Wes Tillman might not be ruling on the radio much anymore, but I'd expect a bigger crowd for a guy who's won pretty much every award out there."

Wes Tillman was a superstar. And Snow was about to sing with him.

During her time in Nashville, she'd met a few big names. It was impossible not to when living in Music City. She'd also dealt with her fair share of wannabe stars, or worse, people who fancied themselves star-makers. Those were the worst.

Usually older men with an eye for the new young thing in town and the hope that she was naive enough to fall for the well-worn "I'll scratch your back if you scratch mine." Snow's coloring and look stood in sharp contrast to the Southern debutantes with their wavy blonde hair and blue eyes. One exceptionally greasy character had referred to her as "exotic."

Snow *hated* being called exotic.

So though she loved being onstage, doing so for a living never really held any appeal. In fact, the thrill had gone long before she'd met Caleb, but Snow had been too scared to admit as much at the time. Who wouldn't want to be rich and famous with the world at her fingertips?

Snow didn't, that was who.

"Do you see Wes anywhere?" Lorelei asked. The guys had gone to find a table while Snow and Lorelei waited for Carrie to reappear from the ladies' room.

Scanning the bar, Snow said, "That's him over there, isn't it?" Wes had played the Ruby festival in October. Lorelei had dealt with him directly as the organizer of the event, but Snow hadn't gotten a personal introduction.

"Whoa," Lorelei said. "Is that guy he's talking to his bodyguard or something? I've never seen a guy that big." The man had to be six foot seven at least.

Before Snow could say she didn't know who the guy was, Caleb approached the two men at the bar and exchanged greetings. Neither Wes nor his buddy looked put out by the intrusion, which was good, since she'd hate to see her husband stomped into a speck of dirt by the potential bodyguard.

When Caleb motioned for Snow to join them, she grabbed Lorelei's hand. "You're coming with me."

Lorelei stumbled behind her saying, "I guess I am."

"Mr. Tillman," Caleb said as the pair approached, "this is the woman I've been telling you about."

Snow took the older man's hand and tried not to look like a swooning moron. Wes was even better looking in person. Tall and lean with broad shoulders and the baby blues that donned every album cover he'd ever had. A bit of gray showed along his temples, and was likely more prevalent beneath the black Stetson. He smelled like a masculine waterfall, if that was possible, and most of all, the man looked genuinely happy.

"It's nice to meet the little lady I'll be singing with tonight."

Lorelei took that opportunity to smack Snow on the arm. "Are you shittin' me? You sing?"

Why was she friends with this woman again? Snow held on to as much dignity as possible as she said, "It's a pleasure to meet you, Mr. Tillman. This is my friend Lorelei. I believe you know each other."

"Hi," Lorelei said, looking like a twelve-year-old meeting her favorite boy band. "We worked together on the Ruby festival."

"Yes, I remember you," Wes said. "How's the theater project going?"

"We're off and running, thanks to you and your generosity."

"My pleasure."

"Snow, this is Judd Farley," Caleb said, motioning toward the larger man. "He owns the Second Chance Saloon."

So much for the bodyguard theory. "Hello, Mr. Farley," she said, taking in the scarred-up bar, neon beer signs, and deer heads mounted on the walls. "Nice place you have here."

"I doubt *nice* is the word most would use, but it has character." A friendly grin peeked out from the wiry red beard that covered the bottom half of Farley's face. "Caleb here says you've done some time in Nashville."

"I did," she answered. "But I'm not cut out for that business."

Wes said, "Even the ones at the top aren't always cut out for the business."

"You did pretty well," she said with a smile, liking the man's down-to-earth nature. Though Snow didn't like that Caleb had gone behind her back to arrange this, she knew his intentions had been in the right place.

"That was a whole lot of luck and a hefty dose of too stupid to give up."

"It paid off, and as one of your fans, I can say we're glad you stuck with it." Snow fought back the nerves as she asked, "What are we going to sing tonight?" She did a mental flip through the song Rolodex in her head, hoping he'd suggest something she remembered. Well-intentioned or not, Caleb had put her in an uncomfortable position.

"Do you know 'You're the Reason God Made Oklahoma'?" Wes asked.

"I do," she answered, relieved he didn't suggest a more modern tune, as she wasn't a fan of the pop swing the genre had taken in recent years. "And there's always the Johnny and June version of 'Jackson.'"

Wes took Snow by the hand. "She's the perfect woman, Caleb. I'm going to have to steal her from you."

"My cousin might have something to say about that," Farley chimed in. "You know, your wife?"

"Oh, yeah." Tillman gave Snow a look of regret. "I'm afraid we'll have to limit our relationship to the stage only."

"That's okay," she said, flashing a smile Caleb's way. "I already have a man."

She did for now, anyway. A man who wanted to make her dreams come true. If only Caleb could build her a time machine. Maybe then she wouldn't have to tell him good-bye.

Chapter 22

What the hell?

Late for a meeting with Spencer, Caleb had been climbing into his Jeep when a VW Bug pulled past him in the driveway and disappeared into the garage. He stood on the gravel blinking, wondering if he'd imagined the whole thing. What he thought he saw couldn't be right. Who painted a car two different colors?

Stepping closer, he watched Hattie exit the moving art piece with several bags in her hands. Caleb couldn't stop staring at the car. The front end was sky blue and covered with white puffy clouds, while the back end faded into a deep purple sprinkled with tiny stars.

"What did you do to that car?" he asked, spotting the circle on the roof that was half sun and half moon.

"I painted it," Hattie said, reaching into the car for more bags.

The colors blended perfectly in the middle. "You had it painted like this?"

Withdrawing from the vehicle, she answered, "No. *I* painted it. Now are you going to help me carry this crap or not?"

Caleb hopped to attention, realizing she'd set several bags at his feet. "Yes, ma'am," he said, collecting the groceries off the garage floor. The older woman stayed busier than a beaver during dam season, so while he had her here, Caleb took the opportunity to pay her the balance on Snow's ring. "I have the rest of the ring money for you."

"I thought we were doing that in installments," she said, charging toward the side of the house. A dark ball cap teetered on her gray curls, and the usual giant sunglasses shaded her eyes. "I've heard you're doing well at the paper, but that doesn't mean you have to give me all your earnings at once."

"Actually," he said when they reached the porch, "I had the money before I got the job."

Hattie stopped in her tracks, spun his way, and narrowed her eyes. "You had five thousand dollars sitting around while you were in between jobs?"

If he and Snow would be making a home in Ardent Springs, Caleb thought it time to let people know the truth about who he was. At least the folks who deserved to know. "You ever heard of McGraw Media?"

"Of course I have." Her words were clipped with offense, as if he'd insulted her intelligence.

Caleb raised his brows in answer and waited for the revelation to sink in. Once understanding lit her face, he said, "I didn't mean to mislead you. Guess I wanted to make my way without throwing around my family's name."

The older woman gaped at him long enough for Caleb to grow uncomfortable. And then she laughed. Full-out, bent-over laughter. What was so funny, he didn't know.

"Are you okay?" he asked, when the laughing faded into wheezing. Hattie waved her hands in some communication Caleb didn't understand. Was she begging for help? Did she need a doctor? He prayed she wouldn't need mouth-to-mouth.

"This is hysterical," she said as she straightened. "I offered a McGraw a job at a newspaper." Removing the sunglasses to wipe tears from her eyes, Hattie added, "We must be the dinkiest operation you've ever seen."

"The *Advocate is* small." Caleb couldn't argue that. "But I wouldn't call it dinky. You run a solid operation with a lot of history. That paper offers an irreplaceable service to this town. Not all papers can say that."

Her laughter diminished to a chuckle as she propped the sunglasses on the bill of her cap. "Are you defending my own paper to me?" she asked. Then before he could answer, she said, "You really like it over there, don't you?"

"Yes, ma'am." He liked his job, but he liked being part of the community more. And Caleb really liked that whatever respect he'd earned had been on his terms, and a result of his hard work. Not because of who he was, who his father was, or how much his family was worth.

A broad smile stretched the wrinkles along Hattie's pale skin. "I'm glad to know my instincts are still as sharp as ever." She drew the screen door wide and shoved the interior door open. "I had a feeling about you from the moment I caught you nosing around my garage. Though I guess my money sniffer is on the fritz. I didn't see that coming at all."

Caleb followed her inside. "To be fair, my dad has all the money. I mean," he corrected, "I have some of my own, but he runs the company. He's the man behind McGraw Media, not me."

"If what Wally tells me is true," Hattie said as she set her two bags at the bottom of the stairs, "you could take over the family business tomorrow and not miss a beat."

He appreciated the compliment, but Caleb had no desire to be handed a conglomerate anytime soon. "If it's all the same to you, I'd rather keep doing what I'm doing."

"And we'd like you to keep doing it, too. I was worried there for a bit, as we got closer to Gerald's retirement." An unpleasant expression crossed her face. "Don't know what that man is thinking. He's going to be bored out of his mind inside of a week."

Caleb added his bags to the ones Hattie had set on the floor. "I don't know about that. His wife has already booked them on a Caribbean cruise for January, and then she's dragging him to Europe for two weeks at the end of March."

"Dolly has been wanting to travel for as long as I can remember. Back in high school she was always talking about the places she'd go after graduation."

"You went to school with Mrs. Nichols?"

"Yep." Hattie plopped down on a step and rummaged through one of the bags. "We're all Ardent Springs class of '49." Looking up, she added, "We were a mighty foursome."

Gerald had mentioned that he and Dolly were high school sweethearts, but the two of them plus Hattie equaled three. "Did you say foursome?" he asked.

Hattie grew serious, a rush of loss filling her eyes. "Jack was my beau," she said. "We lost him in Korea."

With those simple words, the pieces fell into place. Miss Hattie had never been a Mrs. because she never got the chance.

"I'm sorry for your loss," Caleb said, out of his depth on how to console the elderly woman.

She took in a deep breath and let it out, shaking her arms as she did so. "Ancient history. So you want to pay off the ring?"

"Yes." He pulled his wallet from his back pocket and handed over the check he'd written earlier in the week. "I had the ring appraised to make sure I paid you what it's worth."

Lifting the reading glasses from their ever-present chain, Hattie squinted at the slip of paper. "But this is two thousand over my asking price."

"Like I said, I want to pay you what it's worth." In truth, the ring had appraised at only five hundred over the original price, but the sentimental connection was worth more than that. She looked ready to argue, so Caleb cut her off. "I need to head out," he said. "Spencer is going to think I got lost."

As he turned to leave, Hattie said, "Tell that boy to call me. I want to add new cupboards to my craft room, and I want the same ones we put in the kitchen this past summer." Caleb looked back to see her waving the check in the air. "I'm finally going to get the craft room I've always wanted."

Delighted to see the childish joy in her eyes, Caleb said, "Yes, ma'am. Oh, and you should probably know that later today, I'm going to see a man about a house."

With bushy gray brows floating high on her forehead, she said, "You're full of surprises today, Mr. McGraw." Then she narrowed her eyes. "Who are you using?"

"Ronnie Ottwell," he answered.

She nodded approval. "Good choice. When you're ready, see Myrna over at First Federal. Tell her I sent you."

Caleb hadn't planned on taking out a mortgage, but he kept the fact to himself. "I'll do that, thanks."

He'd taken two steps toward the door when Hattie asked, "Does that mean we'll be having a wedding soon?"

Preferring to keep any wedding talk between him and Snow, he said, "You never know," and made his exit before the older woman could push for a better answer.

Snow hummed a Beatles tune while she worked, pulling items that had been in the inventory long enough to earn a steep discount for the holiday season. Business had already picked up, forcing her to officially add

Lorelei to the sales staff. The baker was proving to be an asset, holding down the entire store while Snow went back and forth between the sales floor and the stockroom.

"There you are," said a familiar voice as Snow was gathering a collection of Christmas-themed dishes. "Let me see your finger." Hattie looked as excited as a child about to open her favorite toy, but Snow had no idea what the woman was talking about.

"It's nice to see you, Miss Hattie. You have something for me to try on?" Her landlady maintained a booth in the store with small antiques for sale, but she'd never offered a piece of jewelry before.

"Don't be silly." Propping her reading glasses on the end of her nose, she said, "Come on. Let me see it."

There was definitely a miscommunication here. "Let you see what?" Snow asked, holding out her hands to show her bare fingers.

"But . . ." Hattie took Snow's left hand, turning it over as if whatever she expected to be there might appear with a flip and a shake. "Why aren't you wearing it?"

"Wearing what?" Had Miss Hattie's age caught up to her? Was the woman suddenly imagining conversations that never happened?

Dropping Snow's hand, Miss Hattie barked, "I don't understand. Why did he—"

"Is there a problem?" Lorelei asked as she joined them.

"This little lady's supposed to have a ring on her finger."

"We haven't gotten around to that yet," Snow said, feeling as if she were somehow disappointing the older woman. Maybe she should see if there was a ring in the store that would suffice until she and Caleb could pick out something new. While she was distracted, trying to remember what she had available in the jewelry display, Lorelei whispered something in Miss Hattie's ear that Snow couldn't make out.

The older woman's eyes went wide at the same moment her mouth clamped shut.

"You think?" Hattie said.

With lips pressed tight, Lorelei nodded that she did indeed think. "Think what?" Snow asked.

"I've got to go," Hattie said, backing away. "Don't mind me, my dear. I'm old." She made the universal sign for crazy next to her ear.

"Okay," she said as the older woman beat a hasty retreat. *What exactly just happened?* "Lorelei," she said, turning her attention to the person who seemed to know something Snow didn't. "What was that about?"

"Like she said. She's old." Waving to an invisible customer, Lorelei added, "I'd better get back to work," and bid a farewell of her own.

Snow wasn't an idiot. Miss Hattie had expected her to be wearing a ring, which was fair enough, since Caleb had told the older woman that they were engaged back when he first arrived. But what had Lorelei whispered in the woman's ear that would make her take off like that? It wasn't as if her *fiancé* needed to spring a proposal on her. They'd crossed that bridge nearly two years ago.

Something fishy was going on, and Snow intended to find out exactly what it was.

The day had been a success. Cooper agreed, with less arm twisting than Caleb had expected, to become the cruise-in guru on the Ruby Restoration Committee. They set a goal kickoff date of late March and locked down enough details for Spencer to present the idea at the next committee meeting, which wouldn't be for two weeks due to the Thanksgiving holiday. By the time Caleb had driven off for his next appointment, Cooper had created a contact list of every old car enthusiast he knew. Without a doubt, this would give the cause massive publicity while creating a steady income stream.

All they had to do was sell the rest of the committee on the idea, and among the three of them, that would not be a problem. He hoped. There was always Jebediah Winkle and his cronies, who attempted to stifle any idea they didn't come up with on their own. Not that they'd offered a single suggestion that Caleb knew of.

His afternoon meeting was the real victory of the day. Not that anything was decided until Snow had her say, but he'd liked the house and hoped she would, too. Buying a home in Ardent Springs was the perfect solution to keep Caleb's parents' negative attitudes out of his marriage.

"You've been cooking again," Snow said as she stepped into the house. "I could smell it before I reached the porch."

"I didn't soak those beans overnight for nothing." Caleb gave the sausage and beans a stir. "This is authentic Louisiana red beans and rice. Prepare to lose your mind."

He scooped a piece of andouille sausage onto the wooden spoon and offered her a bite. The moment it hit her tongue, amber eyes closed with sheer pleasure.

"That is delicious," she said around the food. "How long have you been working on this?"

"All afternoon." Caleb checked his rice. "And in less than fifteen minutes, we'll be chowing down on the best food ever invented."

Snow leaned over the pan of sausage and breathed deep. "What about gumbo?" she asked.

He'd forgotten about gumbo. How did a Cajun forget about gumbo? "You're right. We'll be chowing down on the second-best food ever invented. So how was your day?"

"Funny you should ask," Snow said, sliding past him to pull a glass off the shelf. "Miss Hattie came into the store today."

Caleb's hand hesitated in stirring the rice. He hadn't expected Hattie to see Snow before he did, which meant he hadn't asked her to keep the house thing a secret.

"She did, huh?" he asked, keeping his attention on the stove.

Filling her glass from the faucet, she said, "Yes. And she seemed to know something that I don't."

So much for his big surprise. "I was going to wait until after dinner."

"Wait until after dinner for what?" Snow set her glass on the counter and then wrapped her arms around his middle, laying her cheek against his back. "You aren't really going to make me wait, are you?"

"All right." Caleb extricated himself from her arms and wiped his hands on his apron. "Since the surprise is ruined." He disappeared into the bedroom and returned seconds later with his hand behind his back. "If you don't like it, we can look at something else. And I want you to be honest. Don't say you like it to make me happy."

"I'm sure I'll love it," she said, her eyes glowing.

"Okay," he said, taking a deep breath. "Here we go." Caleb pulled a flier from behind his back and held it under her nose. "What do you think?"

"I . . ." Snow's eyes dimmed and clouded with confusion. "I don't know what to say." She tried to cover her disappointment while shoving the curls off her forehead. "What is it, exactly?"

Caleb glanced over the top of the slip of paper. "What does it look like?"

"It's a real estate ad," she answered. "For some house over on Green Street."

"Three bedrooms, two baths, fenced yard, and still under construction so we can decide on the finishings we want." Caleb tapped a picture in the bottom corner. "Two-car garage in the back, and we'll have to do some landscaping, but that's easy enough."

"Hold up." Snow took several steps away. "You bought us a house?"

"No," he assured her, kicking himself for doing this all wrong. "I looked at it to make sure it was worth you taking time away from the store to check it out." Caleb had expected Snow to be happy that he really wanted to settle down here. That they could have their own place. A real home. "We can look at something else. It doesn't have to be this one."

"You went to see this?" she asked, nodding toward the flier. "Today?"

"I did," he said, feeling like an idiot. Of course he should have included her from the beginning. "We can forget it for now." Caleb returned to the stove, removing pans from burners and pulling plates from the bottom shelf.

As he loaded the first scoop of rice onto a plate, Snow said, "I don't know what to say."

Trying not to sound disappointed, Caleb said, "You don't have to say anything."

"Of course I do," she said. "You want us to buy a house in Ardent Springs. That's a big step. That deserves a response."

He'd hoped her response would be a little more than "I don't know what to say."

"We don't have to buy anything," he said, turning to face her. "If you're not ready—"

Snow set the flier on the counter as if it were on fire. "*We're* not ready."

Caleb ran a hand through his hair. "Will you at least look at it? For me?"

If she'd only walk through the front door, she'd see the life they could have. A married couple needed a place they could make their own. That was the rational next step. Caleb just had to convince her.

Snow looked as if he'd asked her to drink vinegar, but she said, "I'll go, but I'm not making any promises."

Chapter 23

By Thanksgiving morning, Snow had picked out paint colors, a new couch, and marked off where all the flower beds would be. She'd also earmarked several pieces from the store that would decorate her and Caleb's first home.

Not that she'd agreed to buy the house. But she *really* wanted to buy the house. Damn the man for convincing her to look at it.

Though she regretted not spending the holiday with her family, knowing she'd be with them at Christmas made the day easier to get through. She'd called them first thing this morning and spoken to several relatives. Mama must have put them all on their best behavior, since no one gave Snow a hard time about her extended absence.

"Does this pie look burnt to you?" Caleb asked. He'd been fussing all morning, stressed about getting the pecan and apple pies just right. Apparently, knowing his would be measured against Lorelei's grandmother's concoctions turned her carefree husband into a frazzled mess.

Of course, he couldn't be happy with an old-fashioned apple pie. Caleb's pie had to include caramel. Her husband had a sweet tooth the length of Main Street, and he loved being in the kitchen almost as much as being elbow-deep under the hood of an old car.

Snow leaned over the warm pie and breathed deeply. "Lorelei is going to insist you give her the recipe for that," she said. "And I'm tempted to cut the thing right now."

"Don't even think about it." He covered the confection with aluminum foil before she could reach for a knife. "Grab a couple bath towels so we can get these over there without burning your lap along the way."

"My lap?" Snow asked. Why couldn't his precious pies ride in the backseat?

Caleb ripped another piece of foil. "I'm not taking the chance of these things flying around in the Jeep. One quick stop and they'll be nothing but a pile of mush on the floor."

He had a point. Snow retrieved two towels from the tiny linen closet in the bathroom.

"You know," he said, helping her settle both pies across her lap, "next year, we could be the ones holding this dinner."

Their eyes met, and Snow winced at the joy in Caleb's eyes. "Like a real married couple," she said, cutting her eyes away.

Dropping a kiss on her palm, he said, "I'm thankful I found you."

"I am, too," she said, her voice catching on the emotion. "Though I wish I'd never left in the first place."

"But you got us here." Caleb gave the pies one last check to ensure they wouldn't move. "So none of that matters now."

She wished none of it mattered, but there was still the issue of his mother, who had left Snow a less than friendly message the day before, reminding her that she expected her son to return home by Christmas. Alone.

Snow didn't want to give her husband up to please the hateful woman, but she also had no idea how or when to make a full confession.

What she did know was that she would not ruin Caleb's Thanksgiving by clearing her conscience today.

"You ready?" he asked.

Coming back to the present, Snow held tight to each pie pan. "Ready and already getting warm thighs. Let's get moving."

∽

Dinner was incredible. Rosie Pratchett, Lorelei's grandmother, along with her friend Pearl Jessup and Lorelei, offered a feast like nothing Caleb had ever seen. He'd grown up with all the typical Thanksgiving staples, but his mother had never touched a ladle let alone prepared the home-cooked versions of what had been on the table today. Eight people had gathered at the Pratchett house to celebrate together, including Carrie, who could barely reach the table for her protruding belly, and Mike Lowry.

"I'm thinking I should have worn sweatpants to dinner," Spencer said, leaning back in his chair with hands flat on his gut. "These women are trying to kill us."

"As if I held a gun to your head and made you eat that third helping of dressing," Lorelei teased, giving Spencer's stomach a conciliatory rub.

Rosie Pratchett sure knew how to cook a turkey. Caleb had taken it easier than Spencer on the dressing. Though he'd snatched all the white meat he could without hogging it all.

"It wasn't only females who did the cooking today," Snow said. "Caleb did make two pies."

Spencer groaned while Mike said, "I've been dying to try that apple pie since my first whiff. I'll help you cut, Rosie."

Once the sweets were dished up and passed around, Caleb brought up the suggestion that had come to him a few days before. "Has anyone around here considered setting up a preservation society?"

The table occupants exchanged glances before Spencer said, "Like a historical thing?"

"Yeah," Caleb said. "I attended an auction out at the Brambleton place with Snow, and it seems a shame that all those antiques were scattered far and wide. And then there's Silvester House. Not that Hattie is going anywhere anytime soon, but I'd hate to see the same happen there. Add the Ruby to the list, and Ardent Springs has a solid collection of historic structures."

"Some of downtown would qualify, too," Pearl said. "But what would forming a preservation society require?"

Between his family's association with restoration projects and his own research, Caleb had a ready answer. "First would be to talk to folks around town. Civic organizations. Chamber of Commerce. Merchants. See what kind of interest and response we get on the subject. Eventually, if we really wanted to form a nonprofit, we'd bring a key group in for organizational meetings, draw up bylaws, and file some papers." Accepting the slice of pie Rosie offered, he added, "The Ruby committee has proven that enough locals are willing to step up with their time and energy. My guess is a full-out preservation society would be a welcome option."

The crowd grew quiet enough that Caleb thought maybe he'd crossed a line he didn't know about. After all, *he* wasn't a local, and probably shouldn't be suggesting how these people should or shouldn't run their town. But then Spencer broke the silence.

"We were so focused on the Ruby, we missed the bigger picture."

"When you say 'file some papers,' what do you mean?" Lorelei asked.

"Establishing the group as a nonprofit would require filing with both the IRS and the state of Tennessee. That way anyone who donates to the society would be able to write it off on their taxes."

"And the society wouldn't have to pay taxes on the money raised," Lowry added. "But how would this tie in or conflict with the Ruby committee? A group looking to preserve the history would have a lot to say about what restorations should and shouldn't be done."

This was true. Caleb had been involved in a restoration project in the French Quarter that turned into a nightmare when the New Orleans preservation group insisted on approval of the building's exterior colors. In the end, the building had been painted three times, at an exorbitant expense, only to have the original colors approved in the end.

"That's a hiccup I didn't consider, but in this case, the committees would probably share several members, meaning the new society is less likely to become an obstacle. And from what I've seen at the meetings, preserving historical details are already a major consideration in the plans for the Ruby."

"You know where you'd get pushback," Lorelei said, looking at Spencer.

"We can handle Winkle," he said.

Caleb hesitated with his fork halfway through his pie. "I thought Winkle was the one who wanted things to stay the same. Why would he be against a preservation society?"

"The auction business, remember?" Snow said, speaking up for the first time. "If these old houses stay intact, he has nothing to auction off."

"So he'd cut up local history to turn a profit?" Caleb put his fork down. "How did this man get elected again?" With all the stories he'd heard, this was the one mystery he couldn't solve.

"Same as every other politician with no business being in office," Spencer said. "Tell 'em what they want to hear, turn up the fear, and make promises you can't keep."

"You going to run against him next year?" Caleb asked. Boyd might have been young for politics, but he was a born leader.

Lorelei choked on her pie while Rosie said, "I wish to heck he would."

Pearl added her support, saying, "I'd vote for him."

"I'm not running," Spencer said. "Maybe someday, but not next year."

His words put Lorelei at ease. "Thank God."

"You don't think Spencer would make a great mayor?" Pearl asked.

"He would," Lorelei answered. "But you know as well as I do that once anybody gets into that office, they stay for years. Well, anyone other than Jebediah. And then the town acts like he belongs to them." She took Spencer's hand. "Call me selfish, but I want him to belong only to me for a while, before the town takes him."

"I'll always belong to you, Lor," Spencer said, leaning in to give her a kiss.

"And I thought this pie was giving me a sugar high," Pearl said, but the remark was accompanied by a wide smile.

Caleb gave Snow's hand a gentle squeeze beneath the table. He'd floated the idea of the preservation society with positive results. Now if his second mission of the day went as well, this would be a Thanksgiving that neither of them would forget.

❧

"I can't believe he looks that good *and* he cooks. You are one lucky woman," Lorelei said, as they watched Spencer and Mike do the dishes with Caleb as supervisor. Since the females had cooked, as Spencer had pointed out, the males got to clean. And Caleb's pies had earned him a reprieve from getting his hands wet.

"Considering that sickeningly romantic display you and your fiancé put on during dessert, you have nothing to complain about." Snow slid a finger along the rim of her wine glass, enjoying the view of Caleb putting away plates as Mike dried them. This wasn't the country club set, and yet her husband fit right in. Much better than she would ever fit into his world.

"What are we talking about?" Carrie asked, returning from her fourth trip to the bathroom. Or was it five? The poor woman had reached the waddling stage.

"Nothing," Lorelei said. "How is little Molly today? Did she like the meal?"

"She's kicking up a storm, so she either hated it or wants more. I'm not sure which." Carrie sank into the chair next to the sofa. She took several seconds to connect with the cushion. When Lorelei offered assistance, she said, "I can do it. Getting back up is when I'll need a hand."

"I hear you guys looked at a house," Lorelei said to Snow. "Spencer and I have talked about buying, but neither of us want to leave Granny alone. And, of course, we can't really afford it right now, with my business still small and his school stuff."

Spencer was going to school online. Snow didn't know what something like that cost, but it couldn't be cheap.

"We looked," Snow said. "But I don't think we're ready for that yet." When everything blew up in her face—though Snow preferred to say *if*—she couldn't afford to buy the house on her own. That meant no home buying until the Vivien issue was dealt with.

"It is a big commitment," Lorelei said. "I don't blame you for waiting until you guys are better off financially."

Snow couldn't help but laugh at the comment. As if money was the obstacle.

"What's so funny?" Carrie asked.

Surprised by the question, Snow realized she'd never shared much about Caleb's background with her friends. "Well . . ." she hedged. "Caleb is kind of . . . rich."

Lorelei and Carrie looked at each other, then back at Snow. "How rich?" Lorelei asked.

"Like 'trust fund baby in line to inherit a giant media conglomerate' rich? But he doesn't really want the business. I don't think." She knew that Caleb wanted to make his own way in the world, but would he really turn down running the company? Or would staying with him mean she'd someday be thrust into high society whether she liked it or not?

"Shut. Up." Lorelei stared with wide eyes and mouth agape. "You tried to walk away from that?"

The question rang in Snow's ears. Yes. She'd tried to walk away from that. Was still trying. She never wanted to leave Caleb. His money, upbringing, and impending inheritance were what scared her into running. Regardless of where they lived, he was still heir to the fortune. He still lived with enormous expectations, and if they stayed together, so would she.

Before Snow formed an answer for Lorelei, the men joined them.

"What's that look about?" Spencer asked Lorelei as he sat down beside her with a beer in his hand. "You look like someone said Neiman Marcus is moving in downtown."

"Close," Lorelei said, her eyes shifting from Snow to Caleb and back.

Snow wanted to change the subject, to defuse the situation, but her mind was racing like a rat caught in a maze. She loved Caleb. They could buy a house and start their life together. Embrace a second chance and get it right this time.

But someday, everything would change. Her life would be turned upside down. She would be Mrs. McGraw, obligated to host dinner parties for executives and their wives. Attend charity functions and don the fake smiles that Vivien had perfected long ago.

No. Snow would *never* be Vivien. She'd never be a petty, materialistic manipulator who endured her bitter existence with the aid of vodka and tonic.

"Did I miss something?" Caleb asked.

"No," Snow said, rising to her feet and sliding her arm through his. "I was telling the girls a little about your background." She loved Caleb and would not be embarrassed or intimidated by who and what he was. Not anymore. "I mentioned you'll someday run your father's company."

As if talking about the weather, Caleb said, "I might own it someday, but that doesn't mean I'll have to run it. I'm sure Jackson McGraw will groom someone else for that job, since I've refused to do it."

"What kind of company are we talking about?" Spencer asked.

"McGraw Media," Caleb said. "Newspapers, TV stations, and a few radio stations around the Southeast."

"Your family owns all that," Carrie asked, "and you're selling ads for the *Advocate*?"

"My father owns it," Caleb corrected. "And yeah, I'm selling ads for the local paper. There's something rewarding about making a living that has nothing to do with who my parents are."

Relief washed over Snow as she watched their friends process Caleb's explanation. She wouldn't be throwing dinner parties for elites wearing suits that cost more than her car, but now she had a new fear. Would these people see Caleb as the same person? As the man who'd joined their community and instantly gave back? If the truth of his background changed that vision, they could always start their life over somewhere else.

The thought took Snow by surprise. In order for Caleb to be happy, she would give up everything she'd built in Ardent Springs. Sell the store, withdraw the offer on the house, and return to Baton Rouge if that's what it took. Something she should have been willing to do before now.

"I get that," Spencer said, snapping the line of tension that tightened Snow's shoulders. "So when our preservation society goes looking for donations, we come to you first?" His brown eyes showed total acceptance, and Snow audibly exhaled.

"I'll have to ask my wife," Caleb said, "but if she agrees, then sure."

"Did you say wife?" Rosie Pratchett asked as she stepped up behind the couch. "Did you two run off and get married without telling the rest of us?"

Lorelei stared at Snow, her blue eyes wide and questioning. Caleb hadn't said anything to Snow about revealing their state of matrimony. It was one thing to tell the others that he had money, since he'd already shared as much with Miss Hattie, but he should have talked to her first before letting everyone know that they'd been lying to them for weeks.

Before anyone said another word, Snow's reality shifted into slow motion.

Ignoring Rosie's question, Caleb dropped to one knee.

"Jumpin' Jehoshaphat," Carrie said.

Snow's left hand shook in Caleb's warm grasp. He pulled something from his back pocket, never breaking eye contact.

"Snow Cameron," he said, love clear in his eyes, "will you make me the luckiest man in the world and be my wife?"

She didn't know how to respond. Though they were already married, Snow had never been proposed to before, especially not in front of an audience. Did she remind him that they were already hitched? Did she say yes and keep up the act? Did it really matter if everyone knew the truth?

No. No it didn't.

"Yes," Snow said, the tears falling freely. "Yes-yes-yes!"

Chapter 24

Black Friday wasn't limited to big cities. No sales calls could be conducted the day after Thanksgiving with most businesses opening early, keeping their doors open late, and dealing with three times their usual volume, freeing Caleb up to help out at Snow's shop. Which was good, since this was an all-hands-on-deck situation.

"Excuse me, young man," said a frail voice from his left. "Could you come get something down for me?"

"Of course," Caleb said. He'd been helping little old ladies all day. On several occasions, the women could have reached whatever bit or bauble they wanted to see, but he never called them on it. Lorelei found this endlessly entertaining, claiming they all wanted to talk to the pretty man.

Caleb had ignored her until a particularly feisty customer waited until his arm was above his head to pinch his ass.

This new one looked tame enough, with her cane and grandmotherly smile. She led him to a display near the back and pointed to a blue vase he was sure had been a shelf lower the last time he saw it. "Here you go," Caleb said, keeping a grip on the heavy piece so the woman could examine it.

"That's nice," she said, touching his arm instead of the merchandise. "You're such a sweet boy to help me with this."

If she wanted the vase, she gave no indication.

"Should I set it behind the counter while you look around?" he asked, following Snow's instructions to encourage as much browsing as possible.

"Nah," she said, waving the suggestion away with one gnarled hand. "But maybe you should stay with me in case I see something else."

"Happy to," he said, searching for Snow in the crowd. At least all the older ladies were short, meaning he could pretty much see over everyone. But before he could spot her, Snow came up behind him.

"Hello, Mrs. Leibowitz. How are you today?" she asked the customer.

"I was having this nice young man help me do some shopping," the older woman said, holding tight to Caleb's wrist. "My grandson is in here somewhere, but that boy is useless."

Caleb gave Snow a pleading look, but she'd already planned to rescue him. "Yes, my fiancé is very nice," she said, putting emphasis on the *fiancé* part. "But I'm afraid I need his assistance with something else right now." She waved to someone to their right, saying, "And here's Jacob now." A guy who looked slightly younger than Caleb joined them.

"I've been looking all over for you," Jacob said. Noticing the vase in Caleb's hand, he added, "You looked at that vase a little while ago and had me put it back on the top shelf. Why didn't you tell me you wanted it then?"

If Lorelei learned about this one, Caleb would never hear the end of it.

"I'm old," Mrs. Leibowitz said. "I'm entitled to change my mind."

"You certainly are," Snow said, her voice never losing its helpful tone. "You and Jacob keep looking around until you find something you absolutely love. And don't forget, nearly every item in the store is on sale for fifty percent off, with everything along the back wall discounted even more."

The older woman walked away with a grumble, leaving her grandson to trail behind.

"Why do I feel like I should have a price tag on my forehead?" Caleb asked.

Snow laughed. "You might as well put it a little lower, since that's where you're getting the most attention." He tugged on a curl in retaliation, and she added, "I really do need you. Mrs. Handleman bought the dresser-turned-vanity for her B&B, and her husband needs your help to get it in his truck."

"I can do that." In truth, Caleb was happy to finally be useful. "Is he taking it out the front door?"

"I've asked him to pull around to the alley so we can load it out the back. Less shuffling of customers that way."

After planting a hard kiss on her mouth, Caleb said, "I'm on it," and charged off toward the back room, taking care not to cross Mrs. Leibowitz's path.

Snow watched her husband squeeze past a shabby chic display and cut around a Pfaltzgraff china collection on his way to the back room. She couldn't blame the little old ladies for wanting the hunky guy with the nice butt to give them some attention. So long as the *young* ladies didn't get the same idea. Looking down at the beautiful ring on her left hand, she knew she was wearing a silly grin, but Snow didn't care.

"Where is my son?" came a voice from behind her. A voice that could cut glass. Or Snow's heart out.

Spinning, Snow stood face-to-face with Vivien McGraw, who was looking as brittle and cold as ever.

"What are *you* doing here?" she asked. Not in her wildest night-mares did Snow expect her mother-in-law to set foot in Ardent Springs, let alone her store.

"My son didn't even call me yesterday, and I know that's your doing." Holding her Kate Spade purse tight against her side as if some small-town mugger might steal it at any moment, she said, "I told you not to do anything stupid. Now where's my son?"

Determined not to let this woman make a scene and ruin her biggest selling day of the year, Snow kept her voice low. "It's not as if I kidnapped him. Your son is here of his own free will."

Vivien raised a brow. "Does he know?"

Three words that hit like a punch to the chest. "No," Snow answered.

"Get him here," she demanded. "Now."

She was *not* going to do this. Not before Snow had a chance to explain.

"I'm running a business here," Snow said, bolting for the front of the store. "You can see Caleb this evening."

"You will not walk away from me, missy," Vivien said, following Snow and grabbing her by the arm.

"Don't ever touch me," she said, anger bubbling to the surface. "This is my store, and you are in *my* territory now. You have no say here. I told you, this is not a good time and you can see Caleb tonight."

With a look of derision, the older woman all but snarled, "If you think claiming some kind of home field advantage puts you in charge, you're sadly mistaken. Now I didn't come all the way up here to wait around. Where is Caleb?"

"He isn't here," Snow said between clenched teeth.

But before Vivien could make another demand, they were interrupted.

"Mother?" Caleb said. "What are you doing here?"

"I'm here to put an end to this," his mother said, with the same voice she'd used when he was ten and she'd caught him making cookies with the new cook. Whom she proceeded to fire immediately.

"Have you lost your mind?" he asked. A question to which the answer seemed blatantly obvious. "And keep your voice down before you cause a scene."

"This piece of trash has manipulated you long enough," Vivien said.

"I'm the manipulator here?" Snow said.

Caleb stepped close enough to his mother to see the red lines in the whites of her eyes. In a deadly voice, he said, "Snow is my wife, and if you ever call her a piece of trash again, you can forget you have a son."

Eyes a shade lighter than his own flared wide. "Your wife used me and made a fool out of you at the same time. When are you going to wake up and see the truth?"

"That's enough," Snow said. "If you're going to insist on having this out right now, we'll do it in the back room." She motioned for Caleb to lead the way, with his mother between them. As soon as they were out of sight of the customers, Snow took his hands. "Caleb, I promise, I can explain everything."

"Give it up," Vivien said, pulling her expensive coat tight across her chest. "You can't lie your way out of the mess you've made anymore." Turning to Caleb, she said, "I've known where your *wife* was the entire time she's been gone. She made me swear not to tell you and threatened to drag us through an endless divorce."

"That's not true!" Snow said. "You kept the secret because you wanted to."

Caleb didn't know whom to respond to first. His mother had known?

"I would never lie to my son about something so important," his mother defended. "You used your threats to get what you wanted. You made me pass those messages to your mother to save *her* from having to lie, but you had no hesitation in making me betray my son."

"You can't believe her, Caleb. It wasn't like that."

He wanted to believe Snow, but how could he not believe his own mother? "Did she send messages to your parents?"

A cry escaped Snow's lips. "Yes, she did. But not because I threatened or forced her."

Staring at the floor, Caleb struggled to process what was happening. His mother had known where his wife was. All the phone calls home with updates on where he'd looked. Leads he'd gotten. All the times she'd encouraged him to file for divorce on the grounds of abandonment, and she'd known.

"How could you do it?" he asked the woman who'd given him life. "How could you lie to me all that time?"

"I didn't have a choice," she answered. "She threatened to take everything."

No threat would have frightened Vivien McGraw. "As you've said yourself. We keep the best lawyers on retainer to handle these kinds of situations. She never would have gotten a penny, and you know it." Stepping closer, he demanded, "So why did you lie?"

His mother stuttered. "I . . . I was protecting you."

"From what?" he asked. "From finding the woman that *you* didn't want me to marry? From being happy?"

"From being hurt," she said. "From finding out that there was another man."

∽

"How dare you?" Snow wanted to lash out at this hateful woman who would do anything to get her way. "That's a lie and you know it."

"I saw him," she said, cutting her eyes to Snow. The loathing in their blue depths made the younger woman step back. "He was waiting outside that night."

"You're out of your mind." That had to be the answer. What kind of a person would tear her own son apart like this? "There was no one outside that night. Tell him you're lying."

She had yet to learn the source of Caleb's strong feelings about cheating, but Snow understood what Vivien's accusation meant. Infidelity was the one thing that could take Caleb away from her. The one thing Snow never feared because she knew she had never and would never cheat on her husband.

With a steady gaze, Vivien continued to lie. "Someone must have dropped him off. She ran to him the moment she was out of the house, and then they drove off together in her car."

Caleb's eyes were on her face, but it was as if he were looking through her. "You have to listen to me," Snow pleaded. "There was no one else. There's never been anyone else."

"I can't do this," he said, pulling away from her.

Vivien went in for the kill. "I saw him with my own two eyes. She left you for another man and forced me to betray you. She tried to turn your own mother against you, and now she's taking you away from your family. Staying here means falling for her endless manipulations. What's going to happen when she finds another man? Do you really think she won't leave you again?"

Snow ignored her mother-in-law, keeping her focus on Caleb. The more he backed away, the more she followed. When he reached the wall, she took his face in her hands and made him look at her. "I love you, Caleb. I always loved you. There's no one else and there never was. You know I'm telling the truth. Look in my eyes. You have to see that I'm telling the truth."

He wanted to believe her. She could feel it in his grip on her arms. See it in his eyes. But Vivien had planted doubts. She was making him choose between them, and knew she had the upper hand. As if determined to fire the final shot, his mother played her last card.

"You've watched me be made a fool of, Caleb. Don't let her do to you what your father has done to me. Come home and we'll put an end to this entire episode."

Episode. As if Snow was nothing more than a bad plot twist in Caleb's life.

"Please," Snow begged. "Don't let her destroy what we have. This is real, Caleb. I love you."

Seconds passed, and Snow clung to hope. The hope that he would see his mother for the liar that she was. But then he pushed her away.

"I need to think," Caleb said, and disappeared out the back door.

❧

Once the shock of Caleb leaving wore off, Snow turned on Vivien. "How could you do that to him? He's your son!"

"And that's why I have to protect him from women like you," she said, looking for all the world as if she'd just purchased a toaster and not destroyed her own offspring.

"Caleb is out there hurting, trying to decide which of the women in his life is lying to him," Snow said.

Vivien didn't look the least bit concerned. "I'm his mother. He's never going to doubt me."

"Wake up, Vivien. This isn't your stupid country club." As her mother-in-law turned to leave the storeroom, Snow cut her off. "This is the real world, where money doesn't always win. You think you're so damn important because you can buy whatever you want, but you can't buy yourself a soul. Or a heart. Or your son once he figures out that I'm the one telling the truth."

With a tilt of her head, Vivien said, "It's cute that you think my son will choose you over me, but that's never going to happen."

"He'll choose a bitter, cold woman with nothing to cling to but her fancy purse and a bottle of gin? Not likely. This world will continue to spin whether you're here or not. And Caleb and I will be happy long after you're gone." Snow stepped aside to clear the path. "What you did was guarantee that your son will never speak to you again. And though I'm sure you'll blame me for that, rest assured, we both know that was all you. Now get the hell out of my store."

Though the armor was still up, Snow had landed a shot hard enough to make the woman waver on her feet. Her mouth pinched into a tight knot, Vivien McGraw kept her head up as she marched through Snow's Curiosity Shop. If she had any heart at all, she might regret what she'd done. She might even find Caleb and confess her lies.

But the McGraw matriarch was nothing but an empty shell of a woman, and Snow knew full well she would never do the right thing.

The urge to scream boiled in Snow's chest. As confident as she'd been in her speech to Vivien, the fear that Caleb would never believe her was suffocating. The thought put her feet into motion. Snow flew out the back door and ran down the alley in time to see Caleb's Jeep drive down Main Street. She patted her pockets for her cell phone, forgetting she'd left it in her purse.

Plowing through the front door of the store, she nearly knocked three customers down in her haste to reach the counter.

"Where's the fire?" Lorelei asked, stepping out of the way before Snow could barrel her over. "And where did you go? I've been running the entire floor out here by myself."

Snow ignored the questions as she grabbed her phone. She called Caleb's cell, but after one ring the line went to voice mail. She tried again with the same result.

"Dammit." This couldn't be happening. Every second he drove might as well have been a hundred miles.

"What happened?" Lorelei asked, her normal smart-aleck nature gone. "Take a breath and tell me what's going on."

"He's gone," she said, holding her phone in both hands as if it were her only connection to Caleb. "My husband is gone and I don't know if he's coming back."

Chapter 25

Caleb drove with no destination in mind, running on autopilot while his mind was back at the store, standing in Snow's storage room as his heart was being ripped from his chest and volleyed back and forth between the two women who claimed to love him. If there had been another man, where was he now? Was it over? Was he the reason Snow ended up in Ardent Springs? She never did explain how she got here. No one wanders into a speck of a town that they've never heard of before.

She'd been adamant that she hadn't left him for another man, but if Snow was telling the truth, then his mother was lying. Why would his own mother lie to him? Then again, she'd lied to him for a year and a half. Months of anger, panic, and flat-out worry about his wife and she'd known all along. How could she watch him go through that?

But then how could his wife ask his own mother to lie for her? She was so concerned about her own parents not being burdened with her secret, but she never gave a second thought to how he'd feel when he learned how much he'd been betrayed.

By both of them.

One gave him life, and the other gave his life meaning. But they'd both lied. Last time Caleb checked, you didn't lie to someone you loved.

Surfacing from his thoughts, Caleb realized he was headed for the interstate. Coming up on Cooper's garage, he veered in and parked at a pump. If he was going to keep driving, he'd need a full tank.

Turning off his brain, he followed his instincts and pumped the gas.

"Hey there," Cooper said, coming up behind him. "You out battling the crazy shoppers today?"

"No," Caleb said, locking the pump handle to run on its own. "Just taking a drive."

Cooper learned against the pump. "You don't look good, man. What's going on?"

With a shake of his head, Caleb said, "I wouldn't know where to start." Then a question popped out of his mouth. "Do you remember when Snow came to town?"

"Sure," the mechanic said. "I'm the one who towed her in."

"Towed?"

"Her car broke down on I-65, and she managed to get it up the exit ramp. Brody over at the PD found her and called me." He crossed his arms. "Poor thing needed a new transmission, and I was backed up for days. Miss Hattie happened to be here getting her oil changed, and she gave Snow a place to stay. By the time I got her up and running, she'd decided to stay."

"Was she alone?" Caleb asked, not sure he wanted to hear the answer, but unable to hold his tongue.

"She was when I found her. I wondered why she never put herself on the market around here, but I guess since y'all were doing the long-distance thing, that explains it."

"Yeah," Caleb said, sliding the nozzle back into the pump. "That explains it."

So she'd been alone when she landed in Ardent Springs. That didn't mean she'd been alone the night she left him.

And she *had* left him.

As he stared east toward I-65, anger and hurt churned in his gut like something rotten brewing in the late-day sun. Maybe it was time Snow learned how it felt to be the one left behind. Only this time, there would be no happy reunion.

"Thanks for everything, Cooper," Caleb said, climbing into his driver's seat.

"Anytime," the mechanic answered, giving a brief wave.

With anger pushing him on, Caleb headed for the interstate and never looked back.

"I need to fix this," Snow said for the fifth time in the last half hour. She leaned forward with her elbows on her knees, her hands clutched at her scalp. Lorelei had forced her into this position when she'd cried herself into hyperventilating. "I need to make him listen to me."

"Maybe you should give him some time," Lorelei said as she rubbed Snow's back. "Let him cool off and he'll come around. He can ask any one of us if you ever cheated on him and we'll all tell him no."

She squeezed wads of hair in her hands. "You weren't there the night I left. She planted that seed in his mind, and now there's no way for me to prove she's lying. It's her word against mine. Either I'm lying, or his mother is lying, and who do you think he's more likely to believe?" Sitting up, Snow took a deep breath. "Was Spencer sure that Caleb wasn't at the apartment?"

"He checked twice." The pity in Lorelei's blue eyes made Snow want to cry again. "No luck at the newspaper office either."

Snow lurched from her chair to pace her back room. Thankfully, Lorelei's grandmother, Rosie, and her friend Pearl had been milling about and were watching the store while Lorelei stayed with Snow in the back. Once Caleb had left, she couldn't have cared less about the store and her big sales day. All she wanted was to go find him.

"There's no place else he could be," Snow said. "He must have left town. He left just like I did. This is exactly what I deserve."

"Bullshit," Lorelei said, her voice stern. "So you screwed up. Fine. But you owned up to it, explained your reasons, and he said he understood, right?"

"He did, but—"

"No buts, Snow. Bailing is not the same as lying. If anything, it's the most honest thing you can do. It's a hell of a lot better than staying married for however long his parents have been and playing the martyr the whole damn time. If he pulls a disappearing act now, over what he knows deep down are nothing but lies, then he doesn't deserve you."

Everything Lorelei said was true, but she didn't understand. Caleb had drawn one very clear line in the sand, and according to his mother, Snow had crossed it. And even though she knew the truth, he didn't. That doubt would always be there.

"Do you remember how to close and open the store?" Snow asked, determination straightening her spine.

Lorelei blinked. "Sure, but what are you going to do? You can't head for the interstate and chase him down. You don't even know which way he went."

"I know he isn't going back to Louisiana, at least not yet, because his mother has already called twice looking for him. When I left Baton Rouge, I essentially headed back to the scene of the crime."

"Las Vegas?" Lorelei asked.

"Okay, not the scene of the crime, but the place where we met." Snow snagged her jacket from a hook on the wall. "I went back to Nashville, and that's as good a place to start as any. My keys are up at the register with my purse. I'll leave the store keys for you."

Following her into the showroom, Lorelei had to use long strides to keep up. "How long are you going to be gone?"

"I haven't thought that far ahead," Snow said, hustling behind the counter. "If I find him today, then we'll be back tonight. If not, I'll keep looking."

"Snow, this is crazy." Lorelei caught the tiny hoop of keys Snow hurled her way. "This is the biggest shopping weekend of the year. You're going to walk away from everything to go find your runaway husband?"

"That's exactly what he did for me. Now it's my turn." When the look of confusion remained on her friend's face, Snow said, "If Spencer took off, would you go after him?"

Lorelei took a step back. "I'm here to run the store as long as you need me. But keep me posted, okay?"

There was a reason they were friends. "Thank you," Snow said.

As she stepped through the doorway, Lorelei yelled, "Good luck!"

Snow didn't need luck, she needed a miracle. And if Caleb loved her as much as she believed he did, she might get one.

Without conscious thought, Caleb landed at a small bar off Division in Nashville, not far from his old Vanderbilt stomping grounds. The bar where it all started one cold New Year's Eve night that felt like decades ago. In some ways, that was the first night of his life—when he spotted a tiny woman with big hair and sparkling eyes shuffling to stay warm on the other side of the crowd. There was a band playing on the outside stage, but once Caleb had spotted Snow, he'd lost interest in the entertainment.

Drawn to her instantly, he asked her to dance and was rewarded with the prettiest smile he'd ever seen. Innocent and yet promising at the same time. She hadn't gone willingly, claiming her inability to put two steps together would be the death of them both, but he'd pulled her into a slow dance, and something clicked into place. As if everything he'd always wanted was right there in her fragile frame and golden eyes.

Not two years had passed, yet Caleb couldn't remember his life without Snow. Every day since meeting her had been a balancing act between happiness and madness. When she was with him, he couldn't get enough. When she wasn't, he couldn't breathe.

Once he stepped inside the bar, Caleb gave his eyes a second to adjust to the dim lighting. Losers didn't put much stock in illumination. The bar was sparse, as expected on a Friday afternoon when the whole world was out hunting for the bargain of the century. He took a seat two stools down from one with an Army jacket thrown over it and waved for the bartender.

"What'll it be?" the slender man behind the bar asked.

"Bud, please."

A pinup in a hula skirt flexed as the bartender popped the top. "Three fifty."

Caleb pulled a ten from his wallet and said, "That's for the first two."

"A man with a plan. Got it." He pushed a couple of buttons on the register, made change, and slid three dollars next to the bottle. "My name's Watts. Let me know when you're ready."

After a quick nod of acknowledgment, Caleb took a long swig as he spun on the stool. The place looked the same. The tiny indoor stage by the front door. Poker machine at the end of the bar. Christmas lights strung along the top of the walls. Not the most glamorous spot in town, but the beer was cold, the music was good, and the service friendly. When Caleb was a single guy looking for a good time, Losers had served his purpose. It didn't hurt that the place had been walking distance from his apartment.

"No freaking way," said a voice from his left. "Caleb McGraw? Is that you?"

Tucker Holcomb, one of his regular running buddies back when he'd met Snow, stood outside the bathroom door staring as if Caleb were the second coming.

"Hey, Tuck. How you doing?" He wasn't in the mood for reminiscing, but Caleb should have expected to run into someone he knew.

"I'm good, man." The two shook hands and did the bro hug greeting, bumping shoulders accompanied by two pats on the back. "Haven't seen you in forever. Not since you swiped Snow out from under us."

Caleb stalled by taking a drink of his beer.

"Sorry that didn't work out, buddy. I thought you two were going to make it."

He came close to spewing Budweiser across his friend's Slipknot shirt. "You know?" Caleb asked.

Tucker picked up the green jacket and settled onto the stool. "I saw Snow a couple months after y'all left for Vegas. She was staying over at Deb's place."

Deb had been Snow's roommate when they'd met, and the first person Caleb had checked with in Nashville after she disappeared. The lanky brunette had claimed not to know where Snow was.

"And Snow told you what happened between us?" he asked, struggling to keep his voice conversational.

"No details," Tucker said, holding out his hands. "She was pretty bummed. Deb and I tried to get her to come out for a drink, but she wouldn't do it."

Tapping the side of his bottle, Caleb stared at the red label. "Was she alone or did someone come back to town with her?"

Rubbing his blond goatee, Tucker looked to be searching his memory banks. "No one that I know of, man. You're the only guy she ever gave the time of day. We all took a turn trying to catch that honey, but she turned the rest of us down." He tapped Caleb on the knee. "That's why I thought you guys were really gonna do it. Get that happy ending everybody's always talking about."

"Yeah, I thought so, too," Caleb said.

So she'd been alone when she stayed at Deb's. But was Snow bummed, as Tuck had put it, because she'd left her husband, or because whatever guy she ran off with had left her?

"You in town for a while?" Tucker asked. "Me and the boys are playing outside tonight. It's gonna be cold as hell, but a party to be sure."

Caleb hadn't considered anything beyond the present since watching his wife and mother battle to see who could hurt him more.

"I'm just passing through," he said. Even if he stayed the night at a local hotel, a late night at Losers held no appeal.

"Damn." Tucker pulled cash from his pocket. "Next time, then. You need to come around more often, bro. You were our ringer for drawing the hotties. You gotta help your boys out."

There was only one hottie that Caleb wanted, and she wouldn't be found at Losers. Not this time.

"Good luck with the show tonight," he said, making his way toward the exit.

"Hey," the bartender called. "You never had that second beer."

"I'll pay for Tuck's," Caleb answered and stepped into the sunshine.

Chapter 26

Snow had looked everywhere she could think of, but Caleb was either a step ahead of her, or he'd driven through Nashville without stopping. By the time she'd reached the city, the sun had set and the shoppers all seemed to be on the roads at once. Thinking that he might have maintained some kind of home base while looking for her, she drove by Caleb's old apartment. The eight mum-filled hanging baskets decorating the entry made it unlikely that Caleb still held the lease.

She drove the streets around Vanderbilt, certain that if he planned to blow off steam, that's where he'd go. Checking the smaller venues first, she'd inquired inside but no one remembered seeing a man who fit Caleb's description. Though one female bartender said if she found a guy like that, she'd be keeping him for herself. Not what Snow needed to hear.

Fighting off the memories, she drove by Losers, but the crowd was too thick and the music too loud to ask questions. Caleb's Jeep wasn't in the parking lot, and though he could have left it parked at a hotel and called a friend for a ride, she doubted that would be the case. The man had a thing about being in the driver's seat, something that had bothered her before, but tonight she'd gladly scoot over if she could find him.

Thanks to changing phones when she'd arrived in Ardent Springs, Snow's phone didn't have most of her old friends' numbers. Not that she knew who was still around and who wasn't. The one person she did contact was Deb, her old roommate. Unfortunately, Deb didn't answer, forcing Snow to leave a message. How was she supposed to tell the person who'd helped her hide out when she ditched her husband that said husband had now ditched *her*?

If by some miracle Snow managed to find Caleb and make this right, they'd have to make up a story about the beginning of their marriage so their kids didn't know how bad they were at this.

On the chance that he'd ventured downtown, Snow cruised Broadway trying to keep her car on the road while checking out every male pedestrian over six feet tall. When a glimpse to her right revealed a white Jeep pulling into a parking space at the Union Station Hotel off Tenth Avenue, she nearly took out an elderly lady in the crosswalk trying to make the turn. But when she reached the Jeep, the man who climbed out was not Caleb.

Adrenaline had sent her heart racing, and the letdown was like someone pulling a plug. She rested her forehead on her steering wheel until a car honked behind her and she was forced to drive on. By ten that night, defeat had settled in, but Snow wasn't ready to give up. Traveling a short distance north of downtown, she found an Econo Lodge off the interstate and settled in for the night. When three more calls to Deb got her nowhere, she turned off the light, but left the TV on for company.

And then cried herself to sleep.

Standing at the window of his hotel room in the downtown Omni, Caleb watched the dawning sun glisten off the skyscraper that locals liked to call the Batman building, contemplating his next move. When he'd booked the room, his intention had been to get an early start for Baton Rouge. But a night's sleep, not that he'd slept much, along with some distance allowed him to process things more rationally.

His instincts told him Snow wasn't lying. That there'd never been another man. But if he accepted her word, then his mother was lying. Vivien McGraw could be overbearing and opinionated, but to fabricate a story like this? To claim she'd seen the other man with her own eyes? She wouldn't go that far.

Caleb's phone vibrated on the nightstand, but he ignored it. Snow had been calling every couple of hours. He hadn't brought himself to listen to the messages. Or read the texts. Now she knew what he'd gone through. How he'd worried and panicked, desperate to find her and clueless where to look. Only in his case, Caleb had a good reason for leaving.

As he reached for the bag holding the change of clothes he'd bought the night before, his phone went off again. He was close enough to see the screen, and he was surprised to find his father was the caller.

"Hello?" he said, curiosity getting the better of him. Jackson McGraw *never* called his son.

"Where the hell are you?" his father clipped. No *hello*. No *how are you.*

He should have known his mother would bring in reinforcements. She'd also called several times. And been ignored.

"Nashville," Caleb answered with annoyance. As if he needed to report in with his whereabouts like a kid out after curfew.

"Is your mother with you?" his father asked, taking Caleb by surprise.

"Why? Did you lose her?" Caleb wouldn't expect his mother to pull this cluster of an intervention without telling her husband she was leaving.

Sounding more tired than Caleb remembered, Jackson said, "I came home from work late last night to find out from the maid that she'd flown up there to see you. But Rosa didn't know when she was coming back."

Caleb doubted that whatever kept his father out late the night before had anything to do with work.

"She showed up without warning yesterday." Curious if his father had also been keeping Snow's secret all this time, he asked, "Mother claims that Snow left with another man on the night she disappeared. You know anything about that?"

"I didn't see anybody out there."

So both of his parents were holding out on him. Freaking amazing.

"She didn't meet some guy at the end of the driveway?"

"Not that I saw."

"You saw Snow take off in the middle of the night and didn't go after her?" Could his father not have mentioned this fact sooner? Like the next day when Caleb had been frantic.

"If you recall, not long before she left, you told me the only reason you had to stay married to her was to save her from taking half of everything." Pausing to speak to someone in the room with him, Jackson returned to the conversation, saying, "For all I knew, you'd come to your senses and sent her packing."

"Did you talk to her before she left?"

"Why would I talk to her?" Frustration and impatience laced his father's words. "I watched her go from the window in my study. And why does any of this matter? Your mother said you found her so we could serve the papers and get this over with."

His mother *had* lied. She'd pushed the one button she knew would get her what she wanted. Snow out of her son's life.

"I need to go."

"When are you coming home?" the older man asked.

"Never," Caleb said, ending the call and grabbing his keys.

Just like the previous day, Snow spent Saturday driving around Nashville, visiting every spot to which Caleb had ever taken her. She even checked the locations he'd merely mentioned as places they should go. Asking at every hotel was impossible, but she checked several parking lots for his Jeep. She finally reached Deb, who'd pulled a double shift the night before and had no idea if Caleb was in town. Her former roommate had been surprised by the switch in roles, from hunted to hunter, but Snow was beyond thinking about her pride, nor was she up for explanations.

She just wanted to find her husband.

Around sundown, Snow was forced to admit the likelihood that Caleb was well on his way to Baton Rouge, if he hadn't reached that destination already. She attempted to call Lorelei to let her know she was coming home, but her phone had died while she'd been trolling the Nashville streets. Thanks to a blown fuse that she'd meant to replace, she had no way to charge the phone without pulling over and finding an outlet.

All Snow wanted at that moment was to curl up in her bed and cry. Caleb's scent lingering on her sheets would rip her chest open even more than it already was, but at least she would have some tiny piece of him to hold on to.

Squaring her shoulders, she drove north on I-65, assuring herself that this wasn't over. What was twenty-four hours compared to eighteen months? If she had to fly down to Louisiana and beg at his doorstep, Snow would do it. She'd take a lie detector test, sell the store and move to be close to him. Whatever it took, giving up was not an option.

She didn't blame Caleb for believing his mother. The woman possessed ninja-like manipulation skills, and her son had been on the receiving end of them his entire life. There was no way for Snow to prove that she'd never cheated. As much as her heart wanted to scream that she shouldn't have to prove anything, that if he loved her he'd believe her, Snow was realistic enough to know that life didn't work that way.

If put in the same position, she couldn't say how she'd react. Except that everything she knew of Caleb said he'd never cheat.

The tears remained in check until she reached the Ardent Springs exit. The store would have closed an hour before, which gave Snow the excuse she needed to go straight home. By the time she turned off Main Street, her cheeks were soaked and she'd used every napkin in her glove box to wipe her nose. Though she'd taken a quick shower before leaving her hotel that morning, she'd been wearing the same clothes since yesterday morning, with the one concession of a new package of underwear.

If she'd been thinking straight on Friday afternoon, Snow would have packed a bag, but she'd driven out of town on panic and instinct, the practical incidentals not entering her mind. Tomorrow, she would come up with a plan. Maybe if Spencer or Lorelei called him, Caleb would answer. Or even Cooper.

Miss Hattie's porch light glowed in the distance as Snow swiped a hand across her cheek. A hot bath, a cup of tea, and her pillow would get her through the night ahead.

And then she pulled into the driveway and her heart fell out of her chest.

Caleb managed to keep his ass on the porch, but barely. Watching Snow walk his way, looking fragile enough to split into pieces any second, set his lungs on fire. But they had to deal with the mess between them before he could hold her again. No more secrets. No more doubts. The next time they touched, there would be nothing in the way.

And there would be no going back.

"Hi," she said, wiping her eyes on her sleeve as she sniffled. "How long have you been here?"

"A few hours," Caleb answered, gripping the porch step to keep his hands off her. "I tried to call."

Snow lifted the phone in her hand. "It died," she said. Two words that could apply to more than a phone in this situation.

His jaw tight, Caleb said, "I need to know something."

"I swear, Caleb. There was no one else."

"I know that," he said, watching her jerk back in surprise. He reached up to brush her cheek, but held back. "Are you still willing to marry me?"

With little more than a whimper, she nodded her head yes.

"No more running," he said. "For either of us."

"I'll never run again," she said, "unless we run together. I'll sell the store. I'll move to Louisiana. Whatever it takes."

Caleb felt as if he could breathe again. Pulling her tight against his chest, he said, "We're not moving anywhere but to that house on Green Street." Leaning back to look her in the eye, he brushed a tear away with his thumb. "This is it, Snow. Now and forever. You and me."

Her face crumpled as she said, "I thought I'd lost you."

"Of course not," he said, giving her a smile. "You can't lose me, darling. No matter what."

"I love you, Caleb McGraw," she declared, squeezing his neck. "And I'm never letting you go."

Chapter 27

The tension filled the room in an almost tangible miasma. Caleb hovered next to Snow on Miss Hattie's bright orange settee, his jaw tight and his eyes on the cat painting on the opposite wall. Snow considered sharing her knowledge of the three furry subjects, but discussing how the home owner liked to immortalize her felines was a topic for another day.

After a night spent making love as if it were their first time together, Snow woke to find a determined Caleb standing in their kitchen fully dressed and making waffles. Without having to ask, she knew that today was the day they would deal with his mother. The woman had spent the night at a hotel in Nashville, certain that she and Caleb would be flying out together by Monday.

When Caleb made the call, he'd kept the details to a minimum. Snow had listened to the conversation, knowing the exact moments he'd dodged a direct question. Would Snow be present? Was he finally seeing the light?

Though she knew that Vivien would not leave the meeting happy, Snow didn't know for sure what Caleb intended to say. As much as they were a team, this was a battle he needed to handle for himself. She would be by his side for support, but she'd remain as silent as possible.

"A long black sedan just pulled up," Miss Hattie said, then disappeared from the room entrance. Ever since Caleb had paid her a visit that morning, the older woman had been a live wire. Snow assumed Caleb had simply asked her to provide some neutral ground where he could meet his mother, but Hattie acted as if she'd been granted a role in a Scorsese film.

Caleb's grip tightened on Snow's knee. "You good?" he asked.

She rubbed his arm. "I'm good. How about you?"

"I feel like I'm about to fight a dragon."

Snow couldn't help but chuckle. "The good news is that this one doesn't really breathe fire. She tries, but it's all for show."

They heard the front door open, and Caleb shot to his feet. Snow considered doing the same, but this wasn't some royal call. She remained on the settee, ready to tag in if necessary.

"They're right in here." Hattie's voice carried from the entry hall, as did Vivien's.

"They? So *she's* with him?"

To her credit, Hattie maintained her sociable smile as she escorted the elder Mrs. McGraw into the room, ignoring the question and the tone with which it was posed.

"Thank you for coming, Mother," Caleb said. "Have a seat."

She held her ground near the doorway as if waiting for her son to come to her. "Aren't you going to come hug your mother?"

"Please," he said, gesturing toward a wing-back chair opposite the settee. "Sit down."

A bit of the hoity went out of her toity at the brush-off. Snow held her grin in check. Barely.

"I'd hoped we could have this visit alone," Vivien said, glancing from Snow to Hattie, who stayed in the room, but kept a safe distance near the exit. "Surely you've had time to come to grips with the situation and what must be done."

"Yes, I have." Caleb waited until Vivien settled in the chair before sitting. "I want you to know this will be the last time we see each other."

Cutting her eyes his way, she said, "Surely that line is intended for your wife."

Snow looked to Hattie for a reaction and caught a wink. Caleb must have confessed the truth during his earlier visit.

As if she hadn't spoken, Caleb continued. "You've done everything possible to destroy my marriage, including lie about Snow leaving with another man."

"But I saw—"

"I spoke to Father yesterday," Caleb interrupted. "He happened to be in his study the night that Snow left." He hadn't told her that part. Snow was clearly the worst sneaker-outer ever. "He watched her get into her car and leave. Alone."

Vivien didn't have an answer for that one. She was searching for one, if the suffocating fish impersonation was any indication, but no defense came.

Leaning back and dropping his arm around Snow's shoulders, Caleb said, "Snow is my wife, and she's going to remain so until death do us part. Soon, we'll renew our vows here in Ardent Springs, with our new friends in attendance. You are not invited."

Her mother-in-law's blue eyes reflected confusion that quickly turned to rage. Shifting her gaze to Snow, she said, "This is your doing."

"None of this had to happen," Caleb said. "You made me choose, and I have. Now you get to live with it." Rising to his feet, Caleb said, "Don't expect a Christmas card."

"But . . ." Vivien stayed in her chair, her usual haughty glare replaced with panic and desperation. "Your father won't allow this."

"My father has no say in what I do with my life."

Caleb's face remained calm. Implacable. But Snow knew this was killing him. No matter what Vivien had done, she was still his mother. Snow supported Caleb in his decision, but she didn't envy him having to make it.

"He'll cut you off," Vivien said. "You'll never get another penny. How do you like that, missy?" Vivien pointed a finger at Snow. "You won't get your hands on our money."

"Enough," Caleb said. "I haven't taken a penny from Dad since I left college, and I don't need his money now."

"He'll . . . You . . . You won't get the company."

"Caleb will have a company," Hattie said, drawing everyone's attention her way. "Don't you worry about that."

Was Hattie going to give Caleb the newspaper? When did that happen? Snow wanted Vivien to leave so she could find out exactly what these two schemers had agreed on.

"Who are you?" his mother asked.

"I'm the woman who owns this house and half of this town. I've been dealing with your kind longer than you've been alive, my dear, so don't turn that condescending look on me." Waving one arm toward the front hall, Hattie added, "Now get your bony ass out of my house."

The dying fish act returned as Vivien looked to Caleb for support. He held his ground, arms crossed and face stern.

Caleb, Snow, and Hattie followed Vivien out as she attempted to leave with the last bits of her dignity, ignoring them all until she reached the front door and said, "I don't know who you are, but you are *not* my son. She's changed you, and if you're willing to be her fool, then you deserve each other."

Vivien stormed out without waiting for a response, leaving nothing but a cloud of perfume in her wake.

Caleb took Snow's hand and said, "She's changed me all right. For the better."

⌒

"Well," Hattie said, "I thought you might be exaggerating, but that woman is exactly how you described her."

Caleb wished his mother would have proved him wrong. Hoped that when faced with the real possibility of losing her son, she might admit her lies, apologize, and show some remorse. But no. Not Vivien McGraw. That wasn't her style.

"I'm really sorry, Caleb," Snow said. "I never wanted things to go this far."

He dropped a kiss on the top of her head. "None of this was your fault, darling. She made her bed."

"You really think this is the end of it?" Hattie asked. "She doesn't seem like the type to give up this easy."

"Doesn't matter." Caleb had made up his mind. Cutting the cord was something he should have done long ago. "It's over for me." Ignoring the pain in his chest, he said, "Now we can get on with our lives."

"Speaking of that," Snow said, following Hattie back into the sitting room. "What did all that 'He'll have a company' stuff mean?"

That morning, Hattie had expressed an interest in eventually handing the paper over to Caleb. He'd been flattered, but hesitant. Interning with his father and selling ads for a few weeks at the *Advocate* didn't exactly qualify him to run the entire ship. If, at a later date, he felt qualified, Caleb would consider it.

"It's only an idea for now," Hattie said. "Your husband is being stubborn, but I'll wear him down."

Snow returned to her seat on the colorful couch and said, "I'm sorry we lied to you about being married."

Hattie brushed off the apology. "You had your reasons. I'm just glad you kids worked it out, especially considering what you were up against."

Taking his hand and pulling Caleb down beside her, Snow said, "My husband gets the credit for that. When I think of what I almost lost, I want to kick myself."

"You *were* a bit annoying in the beginning," he said, giving her a heartfelt smile. "It's a good thing I don't give up easy."

"I'd like to think I was worth the trouble." Her amber eyes revealed she already knew the answer. "Wait," she said, sitting up straight. "Your birthday is Monday. I almost forgot."

"I don't blame you," he said. "We've never technically been together on my birthday."

"Then I suggest you make this a good one, my dear." Hattie leaned back in the chair Vivien had vacated. "It's been a long time since this house hosted a party. You're welcome to change that."

Twisting her lips, Snow looked to be considering the idea. Then she gave him a look that said this birthday was going to be a good one.

"Thank you, Miss Hattie, but this year, I think we'll keep it a quiet night for two."

With a knowing chuckle, the older woman said, "Smart woman."

∽

By the time they'd finished eating Caleb's birthday dinner of Granny's fried chicken, which Snow proudly made all by herself, she had nearly talked herself out of giving Caleb his gift. When she'd come up with the idea and Spencer had generously agreed to help her out, Snow had been excited to see his face. Now she wasn't so sure. What if he hated it? What if he expected something else?

"What are you fretting about over there?" Caleb asked, tapping his fork on Snow's plate to get her attention.

"I'm fine," she said a little too quickly. "No fretting at all."

"You really are a terrible liar," he said.

Giving her husband a narrow-eyed glare, she said, "Fine." Snow reached under the end table on her side of the couch and pulled out a long box. "This is for you." Before he could take the gift, she pulled it back. "But if you hate it, you have to tell me."

Caleb reached for the box. "I'm not going to hate it."

"I mean it." She struggled for a few seconds before surrendering the present. "I won't be mad if you don't like it."

"Let me have my present, woman," he said, ripping into the balloon-covered paper like a little boy on Christmas morning. Once he'd loaded her lap with shredded balloons, Caleb opened the end of the box and peered inside. "What is it?"

"Take it out and you'll see," she said, anxiety making her words sharper than necessary.

Turning his attention her way, he said, "Is that any way to talk to the birthday boy?"

"You're killing me." Snow pulled her legs beneath her, sending the paper onto the floor. "Let's forget it. I'll get you something else."

"Now I'm really curious." Caleb tilted the box until the triangular block of mahogany slid into his hand. Turning it over, he stared at the metal plate across the front that read his name. "It's a nameplate."

"For your desk," she said, as if this wasn't obvious. He continued to stare as if waiting for the sliver of wood to do a trick. "You don't like it."

Rubbing his finger over the engraving, he said, "I love it."

"Really?" she asked, doubting his sincerity. "Because you don't have to lie."

Setting the gift on the coffee table, he sat back and looked at it. "It's perfect." Without warning, he leaned to his left and pulled her on top of him. "Thank you. I couldn't have asked for a better gift."

"Spencer made it," she blurted, reluctant to take full credit. "It was my idea, but he did all the work."

"It's the idea that counts," Caleb said, placing hot kisses along her jawline. "Allow me to show my true gratitude." He took her mouth in a searing kiss that communicated much more than a simple thank you.

"There's a second part to the present," she murmured, struggling to remember her plan.

The kisses stopped long enough for Caleb to say, "Oh, really? What could be better than a custom-made nameplate?"

Tapping his chin with one finger, she said, "There's a little red number in my dresser that I thought I might put on."

"You know, Mrs. McGraw, this is shaping up to be my best birthday ever."

She wiggled her hips against his. "Then hold on, Mr. McGraw, because we're just getting started."

Chapter 28

Though they'd chosen not to take Hattie up on her birthday party offer, Snow and Caleb did throw another event inside the spacious Victorian—their New Year's Eve wedding.

Technically, the ceremony was a vow renewal, but only three people in the room, other than the bride and groom, knew that fact. For all intents and purposes, this was the joining of two young people who were madly in love and ready to spend their lives together. A fact that kept a radiant smile on Snow's face the entire day.

The ceremony was small, with only a handful in attendance. Snow's parents and a few aunts, uncles, and cousins made the trip up from Alabama. Hattie had insisted they all stay in the big house, and the visit started two days before Christmas, which made this the best holiday in Snow's recent memory.

Her new friends, who felt more like family every day, were also scattered about the room. Spencer and Lorelei served as maid of honor and best man, and they would clearly be the next to host a similar celebration. Cooper sat next to Carrie, who held two-week-old Molly in her arms. Simply looking into the little cherub's face made Snow feel at peace.

As for the mechanic, Snow almost didn't recognize him. Free of grease, flannel, and backward ball cap, the good old boy cleaned up well.

Rosie Pratchett dabbed her eyes, as did Pearl Jessup sitting beside her. Miss Hattie Silvester beamed at the couple she'd adopted as her unofficial grandchildren. If anyone wondered why the groom had no family in attendance, no one asked. The evening ceremony was filled with nothing but love and happy tears. Most of which were shed by the bride, with the groom spilling a few of his own.

Finding a wedding dress on such short notice hadn't been easy, but Lorelei, along with Carrie on the phone since she'd been in no condition to take a trip to Nashville, stuck with Snow until she'd found the perfect choice. The champagne-colored silk chiffon complemented Snow's skin tone, while the illusion neckline and simple silhouette fit her style as well as that of the wedding. Caleb wore a tailored black suit, and the sight of him at the front of the room threatened to steal his bride's breath away.

How had she gotten so lucky as to not only marry this man once, but twice?

"Are you happy?" Caleb asked as the couple watched their friends devour the cake that Lorelei had made. She'd been reluctant to accept the task, but once agreed, she spent weeks perfecting her decorating skills. The finished product was white and elegant and the best thing Snow had ever tasted.

"I have never been happier in my life," she answered, meaning every word. "Thank you for not giving up on me."

Caleb hugged her tight against his side. "Never," he said. "We're together 'til death do us part, remember?"

"Once upon a time, I almost forgot." She kissed his cheek. "That won't happen again."

Their conversation was interrupted by the tinkling of silverware on glasses. "Kiss!" Lorelei yelled.

The happy couple appeased the crowd with a passionate kiss that garnered another request.

"Get a room," Spencer said, earning him boos from the rest of the attendees.

Laughing too hard to continue, Snow pulled back and used her thumb to rub lipstick from her husband's mouth. "I like this get a room idea," she said. "Do we have to wait until midnight to ring in the new year with everyone else?"

"Lucky for us," he said, "this is a wedding, not a New Year's Eve party. That means we can leave whenever we want."

"Then I suggest you take me home, my husband. Right now."

"Anything for my wife," Caleb said, pulling her toward the foyer.

The bride and groom ignored the protesting crowd behind them as they strolled hand-in-hand toward the exit. They had a wedding night to begin, and they'd waited long enough already.

Acknowledgments

There were times I was certain this book would do me in. Goodness knows I whined about the fear and panic often enough. Which is why my steadfast writing buddies, Fran, Maureen, Marnee, Jessica, and Kim, have my undying gratitude. Your restraint from telling me to shut up and deal, as well as your cheerleading and unwavering support, is a gift I do not take lightly.

Special thanks to the smalltownmarketing.com website for providing clear, detailed, and easy to understand tips and tricks regarding marketing and advertising with small-town newspapers. Though Ardent Springs is described as north of Nashville, the town is actually based on Franklin, Tennessee (south of the capital), and while writing this book, I was fortunate enough to spend a week in the area. My fictional little town was brought fully to life thanks to Margie Thessin from Franklin on Foot. She provided a fabulous and thorough walking tour, sharing her abundant knowledge of the people and history of the area.

And to my hostess for the week, Kim Law, thank you for opening your home and going out of your way to make sure I had a great visit. When you're ready for a week at the beach, the door is open.

As always, I wouldn't be on this crazy ride without my amazing agent, Nalini Akolekar. Thank you for your support, guidance, and occasional moments of tough love. Gratitude and good wishes to my editor, JoVon Sotak. May the next phase in your journey be an epic adventure. And last but not least, Krista Stroever worked so hard to help make this book the best that it could be. Thank you for letting me keep my groaners, making me sound smarter than I am, and, most of all, for caring about this book as much as I do.

About the Author

Photo © 2012 Crystal Huffman

Although born in the Ohio Valley, Terri Osburn found her true home between the covers of her favorite books. Classics such as *The Wizard of Oz* and *Little Women* filled her childhood, and the genre of romance beckoned during her teen years. In 2007, she put pen to paper to write her own. Just five years later, she was named a 2012 finalist for the Romance Writers of America® Golden Heart® Award, and her debut novel was released a year later. You can learn more about this international bestselling author by visiting her website at www.terriosburn.com.